THE ABSURD LIFE OF BARRY WHITE

ROB HARRIS

www.bloodhoundbooks.com

Print ISBN: 978-1-917214-15-5

To Dad, thanks for everything.

ONE
LOVING LIFE IN THE SLOW LANE

BARRY WHITE, content creator for the LesCargo Express Logistics Company – not the chunky 1970s sex god with the voice like chocolate fudge cake – sat in bed with his laptop perched on his knees. His office was his bedroom, the same childhood bedroom he'd slept in all his life. A simple room in his ma's home, an ordinary two-up and two-down in a land that time had forgot. Wales. Or more specifically, a tiny dot of a village in South Wales called Caeau Anghofiedig, right near the English border with the Forest of Dean.

What a scary place that could be – the Forest of Dean. A land betwixt two rivers, the Severn and the Wye. A land betwixt two parallel universes, more like. It seemed to Barry that the thing that distinguished Foresters from the rest of the population was their complete disregard for either self or pain – rumour had it, most of them did their own dentistry using string, doors and putty just to save a few quid. Barry had also noticed how the menfolk liked to brag about how many cardiac arrests they'd survived, or how they got smashed off their faces just a couple of hours after undergoing open heart surgery. Barry's best pal, Romeo, reckoned he'd heard a story about some older Foresters who, back in the day, had killed a few dancing bears because they had looked at them in 'a funny way'. But you daren't mention that over the border. Foresters had long memories and they did love a scuffle. The women especially.

Barry rarely ventured over the border without a good reason. And why would he need to go straying into foreign, unpredictable English territory? Caeau Anghofiedig – which translated literally meant Forgotten Fields – was more than enough world for him. It had everything a simple man with simple needs could ever wish for: a pub, a chippy, a church, a brass band hut, a rugby club and John John's Mart, which sold everything from *Racing Posts* to verruca cream.

There was also the massive logistics company depot that employed most, if not all, of the village. Why any major logistics company worth its salt would choose to plonk its HQ in a rural backwater with unskilled workers, intermittent wifi and terrible roads was anyone's guess, but most assumed it was down to a raft of generous grants (local government back-handers) around the time the last Anghofiedig pit shut in 1985. The year Barry White started primary school. Two years before his old man, Barry Senior, got killed driving a LesCargo Express juggernaut the wrong way down the M4. The poor fool had worked down the pits scavenging for coal all his life. He was too old and too set in his ways to suddenly branch out and learn new tricks in broad daylight. Swapping the confines of dark seams for open roads and ten-ton lorries was never going to end well. LesCargo swallowed up those dusty old codgers with their chronic lung conditions, bad eyesight and knackered backs and ate them alive.

Locals reckoned Barry Junior got what brains he had from his ma's side not his dad's, hence his fancy job title. Reality was though, he hadn't created a scrap of LesCargo content for days, mostly on account of his current fetish for watching gorillas eat fruit on YouTube and TikTok.

Gorillas had always fascinated him: the way they moved and skulked around, walking like middle-aged humans on all fours. He was currently obsessed with one particular silverback called Chico, and he'd watched a video of him devouring a pineapple over fifty times today alone. It was a hard one to explain or justify, but he just found it soothing. Therapeutic. 'What time is it?' the Chinese host would bellow at the start of every video. 'It's Chico time!'

Often, the all-powerful algorithms would direct random videos of other celebrity gorillas doing all kinds of things to Barry's screen. Just this morning, Ma got the shock of her life when she caught sight of his laptop out of the corner of her eye, whilst dropping off a cup of tea and a bacon butty around eleven in order to keep her son's strength up until lunchtime.

'Ooh look at that dirty little fellow rubbing his pink lipstick like there's no tomorrow. I'll give him Chico time,' was all she'd said, before putting down Barry's elevenses and making her exit. No questions asked, as if watching herbivorous great apes rub themselves was all part of her son's daily workload, set for him by those reputable and hard-working in-the-know bosses of LesCargo Express Logistics.

Such was the life of Barry White, flitting from his bed, with a Welsh dragon duvet cover, to the desk in the corner, underneath the poster of the 1990 Welsh rugby team, featuring heroes of his youth such as Arthur Jones, Gary Jones, Mark Jones and Robert Jones. He used his desk for work meetings, otherwise he propped himself up on his bed all day, surrounded by seven or eight pillows, eating food brought to him by Ma every couple of hours, watching his precious gorillas or horse racing or any other sport on his work laptop, gambling senselessly online – on anything, anywhere – or talking nonsense on Teams to Romeo, a maladaptive daydreamer and fellow middle-aged waster, who was also part of the ever-spiralling LesCargo content creation team.

In times BC, Before Covid, Barry used to go out to work in the smart red and gold LesCargo offices, 8.30am until 5pm with an hour for lunch, Monday to Friday – sitting opposite Romeo – surrounded by an army of his communication and media peers, all chained to their phones and computers, working in silent misery or pretending to work in a more visible misery. Bosses with nothing much to do walked around the place on their daily rounds, acting like they understood everything in the universe, from the meaning of life to what people were working on, and nursing clipboards to make themselves appear important.

Covid was a blessing in disguise to Barry and his kind because it saved them from the hell of this daily grind. It made them realise there was a smarter way to live and use their time – namely, lying in their underpants, eating bacon butties and watching gorillas pick their noses, analyse it, then eat it.

At 4.15pm Barry noticed a new message on Teams chat so he clicked on it to see who could possibly still be working.

What you doing now? came the prompt from Romeo Davies.

Watching Chico peel a banana. How about you? was Barry's measured response.

Me? I'm drinking San Miguel and watching a repeat of The Sweeney *on ITV4. Bit bored to be honest, it's the one where Carter's missus gets run over. Waiting for the racing from Dubai to come back on. Got any tips?*

Yeah, don't drink Spanish beer.

Fancy a trip to the Forest tonight?

Okay, typed Barry. *But not going mental or watching you fight – got rugby tomorrow. I'm in the starting XV cos Graham Price has an injured left bollock. He still wants to play with it strapped up, daft beggar, but it's the size of an Emu egg apparently, though I've not seen it myself, and Doc Humphreys says he needs to rest it, whatever that means. He won't get any more sick notes off him if he plays. And the doc never misses a home game.*

Pricer don't need anyone thinking his nut is the rugby ball, typed Romeo.

Thumbs-up emoji of agreement, added Barry.

TWO
OLD SCHOOL FRIENDS REUNITED

BARRY HAD a love-hate relationship with rugby. He had grown up surrounded by the game and, of course, the Caeau Anghofiedig club, the shining beacon of the community in which his dad remained a local legend. At school, having the White name – the White credentials – had opened plenty of doors and saved him from a fair few beatings.

As he warmed up for the match against the Wye Ziders with a bit of gentle toe-touching by the corner flag, whilst the rest of his teammates ran laps, he thought back to some of the run-ins he'd had with Psycho Daniels, a classmate from the Bonk Hill Estate, all those years ago.

'Hang on there just a handsome minute, Psycho Daniels, before you shove my head down that filthy pan and use it as a bog brush, can I just inform you that my name is Barry White Junior. That's right. And yes, he was. Barry White Senior – menacing tight-head prop of the Anghofiedig First XV, formerly of Cardiff Blues – was indeed my father. Use one hair of my little head as your shit-stick and my uncle Derek will most certainly come looking for you down a dark alley. You're a rugby fan, Psycho, you've seen what he's like on the field, haven't you? Absolute

mentalist? Correct, I'll give you that one. I prefer fearless. He's a puppy dog around me, do anything I ask him to. He's a bit extra protective, on account of my dad being dead and all that. Still, it's in the genes, know what I mean? You've got to understand what you're taking on here.

'Ah, right again, Psycho, my old man did once snap the neck of a former New Zealand All Black international in a scrum. It was an accident, he would never have done such a thing intentionally, well, not on a rugby field. Well, not anywhere, unless provoked in the extreme. You know what I'm saying here, don't you, my dear Pyscho? Have you ever heard the sound of a neck snapping? Not pleasant.'

Photos of gnarly old Barry White, God rest his soul – handlebar moustache and stubble all over his head, face and neck – adorned the Anghofiedig clubhouse walls and kept his rugby playing achievements alive. Captain every season from 1975 until his premature demise in 87, player of the year for six of those consecutively, South Wales Player of the Year in 1977, Barbarian in 1978, leader of the club's finest team in its history – the 78/79 crew, who went the whole season almost unbeaten, save for a 25–23 defeat at the hands of a star-studded Llanelli team at Stradey Park in the Challenge Cup. Oh yes, those were the days, my friend, and we thought they'd never end.

In their 1970s heyday, Caeau Anghofiedig regularly put out six teams every Saturday across three pitches and would still have players left over, not getting a game. Now, the club was scratching around every week just to get fifteen bodies on the field to fill one team. Yesteryear's unpicked, unwanted players would have trounced today's lot by fifty points. It was a source of constant pain and frustration to Barry's Uncle Derek, who used to scrum down alongside his brother in that famous side of the 70s but now served as first XV coach (or rather, only team coach since the seconds folded).

Embarrassingly, when faced with having only thirteen players for the short hop to Monmouth two weeks ago, Derek came out of retirement and put his trusty old Patrick boots – with illegal sharpened metal studs – back on to play hooker at the age of seventy-three. He was Anghofiedig's player of the match, despite barely being able to run. Next day, he couldn't move at all and Barry's Aunty Ruth called him a 'pathetic old dipstick' in front of everyone down The Dragon – after it had taken him most of the morning to get his socks on. Poor old Uncle Derek didn't deserve to have half the village taking the rise out of him in the pub, not after his heroics the day before in the fiery red colours of the village. His roast beef carvery should have tasted extra special that Sunday, but it didn't.

Barry White nearly wasn't Barry White at all. His dad, Barry Senior, wanted to call him Graham – after Graham Price, the famous tight-head front-row forward from Pontypool, not the modern-day Anghofiedig painter and decorator, he with the massive sideburns and even larger left testicle. It was Barry's mum – hardly the go-to person when it came to names, seeing as she became Pearl White on marriage – who insisted on Barry. After what subsequently happened to her husband, she was glad she kept the name going for at least one more generation (she'd all but given up hope of her only son carrying the name on). Barry was just relieved not to carry the weighty name of yet another rugby tight-head god. It was hard enough following in the size eleven footsteps of his old man, let alone an international rugby giant who personified human granite.

Thing was, Barry White Junior was a truly terrible rugby player. He was so bad he once overheard his Uncle Derek telling someone in the bar, 'I'm glad our Bazzer isn't around to see him play, to be honest. He'd have nineteen nervous breakdowns every week.'

Barry Junior started out wanting to be a tight-head prop as

an homage to his late father – and his own lumpy roly-poly figure dictated he would have to play in the front row or not at all. He wasn't tall enough or hard enough for the second row, not fit enough or agile enough for the back row. As for playing anywhere across the back line, forget it. He wasn't fast enough or clever enough or opportunistic enough or skilful enough. He couldn't catch a ball or kick one. He didn't have any of the attributes or aptitudes required for rugby at all, apart from the White name and a determination not to let his father or uncle down. What Barry didn't know was that Uncle Derek secretly hoped his nephew would do him and everyone else a favour and just stop turning up on a Saturday, like most of the other men in the village had done. But Barry kept coming back for more. Every Saturday lunchtime, Derek would sit in the Anghofiedig dugout, hoping this would be the day when things finally changed – until over the horizon he'd spy a large, whistling figure, walking lopsided, swinging a kitbag in one hand and munching on a couple of chocolate eclairs grasped loosely in the other. Derek would sigh to himself. And reflect that if international caps were handed out for thick skins, Barry White Junior would be an all-time Welsh icon by now.

Pricer's infected bollock, and the fact that Anghofiedig only had fifteen available bodies for the home match with the Wye Ziders, meant Barry was in the starting team by default. Even Derek couldn't bring himself to drop his nephew from a team that did not have enough players.

First scrum of the game, the front-row forwards, got acquainted with each other and Barry was heartened to discover his opponent was not particularly muscular and roughly his own age. It was only when he got close enough to stare into the eyes of the Wye Ziders loosehead and smell the Rottweiler on him, that his heart swelled up faster than Pricer's left nut.

'Well, looky here, if it ain't Barry No Balls. Long time no

see.' Psycho Daniels spat a dollop of mucus on Barry's right boot.

'Oh bugger. Psycho D. I didn't know you were a Wye Zider.'

'I ain't. Not usually. But I've come here specially to shove your head up your own arse, that's what. Your crazy old uncle won't save you today, arsewipe.'

'That's an awful lot of arse talk, Psycho.' Barry tried to make his words sound calming and grown-up. He further attempted to placate Psycho by placing a gentle cupped hand on his shoulder, but the gesture had no place on a rugby field and just looked weird. 'Listen, we're not kids anymore, we're men. I'm prepared to let bygones be bygones if you are too?'

'Screw you sideways, you spanner,' said Psycho, this time venomously spitting out his s's right in Barry's face like a demented serpent. 'I've been waiting years for this. This is better than Christmas Day. And you're my shiny new bike under the tree. I'm gonna enjoy unwrapping you, from the insides out. Kidneys first.'

'Crouch, bind, set.' The referee gave the instructions for the two packs of forwards to scrum down. Psycho threw his head forward like a wrecking ball, catching Barry squarely on the bridge of his nose to make his eyes water. He then burrowed his head upwards from a low angled position into Barry's neck – twisting it and going right through him as if he was made of wet loo roll.

'Aargh, my neck, get off, you're hurting me,' shouted Barry, frog-like eyes bulging out of their sockets.

One by one, Barry's own teammates disowned him as they felt themselves tumbling backwards like a mob of drunken bank holiday cheese rollers. Somersaulting arse over tit, they denounced him for desertion of duty and shameful cowardice.

'Start pushing back and stop screaming, pussy...'

'Yeah, give over, you weak streak of piss – get shoving.'

'You're an embarrassment to your family.'

'And this club...'

'And the village...'

'And mankind...'

'I can't breathe, stop it, Psycho, you ain't supposed to squeeze me there, it's illegal,' cried Barry in his best mezzo-soprano.

'Wos matter, Whitey – don't like a bit of foreplay?' whispered Psycho menacingly. 'I'm gonna snap your neck today. Just like your old man did to that All Black in them old stories you told me.'

'Ref, he's abusing me, not just physically but emotionally and psychologically too. Have a word. It's got to be a yellow card offence if ever there was one,' shouted Barry for all to hear.

With that, the Anghofiedig scrum landed in a big heap and their opponents whipped the ball out to their backs to launch a promising attack.

'Don't worry, Whitey, only another twenty-five or so scrums to go,' yelled Psycho as he pulled himself off Barry's gasping body, shoving a clump of mud mixed with dogshit down his throat on the way up.

Groggily, Barry got to his feet, looked at his surroundings like a newborn fawn, spat out dogshit, and saw all the other Anghofiedig players scrambling back towards their own line in a desperate attempt to stop a try. Their attempt failed.

Barry looked down the field to where the game was happening, bent over gingerly and felt the top of his leg.

'Uncle Derek,' he bellowed in the general direction of the home side's dugout. 'Think me hamstring's gone again.'

Uncle Derek looked like he was about to smile for the first time that day.

'No problem, son, no point making it worse, eh?'

And with that Barry feigned a limp off the field to utterances of 'thank fuck for that' from all of his own teammates. The game was only seven minutes old.

'You get back out here, White, I ain't finished with you yet,' bellowed Psycho.

'Nighty night, Huw,' said Barry in a loud camp voice, waving at him like he was Queen Camilla. He then made a phone sign with his right hand and shouted, 'Call me. Let's do lunch.'

The home crowd laughed, clapped and whooped.

Psycho fumed and went redder than an Anghofiedig jersey. Thwarted again.

Years ago, people came to Anghofiedig from miles around to watch Barry White Senior in full physical glory do amazing things with his fists and a rugby ball under his arm. Now they travelled from even further away to see, first-hand, the pantomime escapades of his wayward son.

In the surrounding trees, an unsettling wind scattered a trail of musty leaves onto the field in a single angry shaking motion. Make that nervous breakdown number twenty for the restless handlebar-moustached ghost of the home club's favourite son.

THREE
SUNDAY MORNING, STARING AT ANGHARAD

ALTERNATE WEEKS, Barry played the organ in church on a Sunday morning – mostly classics, old faithfuls such as 'The Old Rugged Cross', 'Make Me a Channel of Your Peace', 'How Great Thou Art' and 'Abide with Me'. Other weeks, he sat in the pews with the rank-and-file worshippers to watch and listen to Dotty publicly murder every hymn as if she was Eric Morecambe or Les Dawson from Saturday night telly in the seventies, playing all the right notes, but not necessarily in the right order.

When he wasn't playing the organ, Barry's mind would usually wander to places where he – and God – didn't want it to go. Especially if his childhood crush was there, Angharad Davies. Sister of Romeo. He'd been friends with Romeo since day one of primary school, the day Romeo shat himself in class and Mr Barrowclough refused to help. He sent five-year-old Barry – who could barely wipe his own arse let alone anyone else's – to the toilets to assist and in such moments fledgling friendships either sink or swim. The boys had a whale of time, though it looked like they'd carried out some sort of dirty protest by the time Barrowclough inspected the crime scene an hour or so later. Barrowclough wouldn't survive in education, not even during the anything-goes eighties. He went on to pursue a career on the oil rigs, save for short stints in Wandsworth and the Isle of Wight for embezzlement and ABH respectively.

Angharad was beautiful and only a year or so younger than her brother. When Barry went round to the Davies' house to play, it wasn't always Romeo he wanted to hang out with. Angharad saw something in Barry that others did not. When the Year Sevens and Year Eights combined for country dancing practice, ahead of the annual South Wales Primary Schools' Country Dancing Festival in Newport, she always chose Barry as her partner, even though he moved around the place like he was playing British Bulldogs, wiping couples out with his clumsy travelling steps and shouting 'sorry' in a high-pitched twang. Still, the girl on his arm, in her flowing blue skirt with large white dots all over it, ignored it all and danced on through the tripwire of bodies, encouraging her partner enthusiastically and ignoring every mistake.

Ah, beautiful Angharad, one day I'll make you mine, thought Barry, as Reverend Jacob Hill read something from Ephesians a little too loudly for his liking.

Angharad sat alone in church that morning looking sad. When the service was over and everyone was sharing mundane chatter, tea and home-made cakes in the vestibule, Barry noticed her still on her own, wiping tears from her eyes behind the half-closed door of the kitchen.

'What's wrong?' he said, proffering the same cupped hand to shoulder that he had unsuccessfully loaned to Psycho Daniels just yesterday.

'Greg's left me, for some bimbo called Heather Holland from Barry's Island.' Angharad's tone sounded comical. It was her pronouncement of 'Barry's Island' (just like they used to call it in *Gavin and Stacey*) that made Barry chuckle inwardly. 'I don't know how I'm gonna pay all the bills without him...'

'You've got friends,' said Barry, still wondering what to do with his lingering cupped hand and taking extra care to ensure it didn't slip anywhere near her breasts.

'I mean, she's half his age. Half my age. She's pretty, I'll give her that. No wrinkles.' Angharad was obviously fishing for a compliment but Barry missed the bait and swam right by.

'I did try and warn you about him.'

'I know, and I'm a bloody fool for not listening to you, aren't I?'

Yes, you bloody well are! You thought I was just being jealous but I could always see through his bullshit Prince Charming act. Barry voiced these words to himself, in his head, before cleaning up the transcript to one that was more suitable for public broadcast.

'It was an easy mistake to make,' he said, getting the cupped hand back out and inadvertently swiping her ear after missing the nape of her neck with his first movement. 'Pesky flies.'

'I wish Greg was thoughtful like you.' Angharad's flickering eyelashes were more than enough weapon to keep the flies at bay.

Angharad had been the bright young thing with the golden future and the golden looks, the girl who all the boys chased after in kiss tag, but now she was on her own and scrimping to get by on benefits and handouts. That wasn't the life Barry saw for her at all, and he was certain it wasn't the one she envisaged for herself. Barry always thought she'd marry a wealthy accountant or a financier and live the high life in a big, gated house with a long driveway, spending weekends in the Cotswolds or South Kensington. Her hubby would work all hours and she would raise perfect children, bake lots of biscuits and help out in a women's refuge a couple of mornings per week, giving away Versace dresses that she had only worn for a couple of hours to battered women from council estates like Bonk Hill who were addicted to Valium and making piss-poor life choices.

How did she ever fall for flash Greg and his salesman's patter? Okay, he was good-looking in a 'Merthyr Tydfil Mel Gibson' kind of way, but anyone could see he was one of those guys who would lose his hair and watch his muscles turn to flab once he stopped working out and settled for weeknights on the Stella Artois. *Things could have been so different*, Barry thought. *You could have married me. I might have been different.*

He remembered the night at Davey Fisher's party. 1997. So many great records out at the time, 'Tubthumping' by Chumbawamba, Puff Daddy's 'Missing You', 'Never Ever' by All Saints. Oasis, Blur, The Verve, the Spice Girls.

Barry could recall the details of the party vividly and talked it through in his mind during church, occasionally out loud, to the consternation of the small congregation and the sweating, gesticulating, arm-throwing Reverend Hill.

We sat on the table in the kitchen and sang along to Hanson's 'MmmBop' at the top of our voices. It was late and you asked me to go to bed with you. I never saw that coming at all. I remember you undressing me and taking the lead but I was incapable of doing anything. I didn't really know what I was doing and was a bit surprised you did. Just like our country dancing days, I suppose. We gave up, rolled over and fell asleep with our backs to each other. In the morning you cooked sausages and hash browns and we acted like nothing had happened because, on the face of it, nothing did, apart from a bit of frantic fumbling. Of course, when we saw Davey and the others that morning, I let them think the earth had moved for both of us. You went along with it to spare me more blushes. Everything changed between us that night, didn't it? How could we pretend that nothing happened? What you don't know, because I've never told you, is the real reason why nothing happened. It wasn't because I didn't fancy you, because I did. I still do. It wasn't too much booze on my part, either. Sure, I was inexperienced around girls, but with you that wouldn't have been a problem. The problem was, at the very moment when you asked me to go upstairs with you, I was plucking up the courage to ask you out on a date. You were at least four steps ahead of me. And when we got upstairs, and I found myself lying naked on Davey Fisher's parents' bed, with you sat astride me and a younger version of Davey grinning over my shoulder through a ten-by-eight-inch glass frame, you threw out a casual one-liner that killed everything stone dead for me. I bet you don't even remember it, but you said, 'I'm not expecting you to go out with me, you know. Relax, it's just sex.'

I didn't know how to react to that because I wanted to go out with you. More than anything. And I wanted you to want to go out with me. I still don't know how you would have responded if I'd got to speak first after our shared singalong and asked you out on that date. It would have been for a drink in The Dragon. Maybe the quiz night. Or the cinema by bus, definitely not The Full Monty, *but maybe* Good Will Hunting *or* Titanic, *plus a bag of chips and a fishcake on the way home as we held hands and looked up at the stars. Plotting our futures. Making more movie dates. Discovering and singing more new records together. We could have found The Foo Fighters or Blink 182 or back-tracked to The Small Faces and Boney M together. Would you have said yes? Would you still have asked me to go to bed with you? Would knowing that a date in The Dragon was in the bag have inspired me to perform better in Davey Fisher's parents' sack – knowing I was giving my cherry to someone deserving of it? Would we have enjoyed a lasting relationship – carrying us to very different places from the ones where we find ourselves now? Or would I have just disappointed you later rather than sooner?*

Barry White had thought about this stuff probably every day for over twenty-five years and lived out every possible scenario. His favourite was the one where they were in their sixties, still deeply in love. With children and grandchildren, yet they giggled like the teenagers they once were every time they heard 'MmmBop'. They would burst into unrestrained voice, the song as energetic and fresh with each play as the first time they heard it.

Barry never felt able to tell Angharad she was the secret no one knew about. Hers was the first – and last – bra he ever undid successfully, but he wanted so much more. He thought she should have realised. He thought he made it obvious.

When he got home from church, he pulled down an original 45-inch single of Hanson's 'MmmBop' from a shelf in his bedroom, examined the sleeve and saw the spot where he'd written his and Angharad's names in bold felt tip, connected by a broken love heart with an arrow through it. Cupid's arrow.

He didn't do that drawing in 1997 or even 1998. He did it that morning, just before church.

FOUR

WELCOME TO CONFERENCE WITH SLICK BISH

MONDAY MORNING CONFERENCE, the one time of the week when LesCargo's external and internal communicators would actually get together on Zoom to talk to each other, with their cameras on, to discuss what they were working on. This start of the week catch-up was a large egocentric free-for-all, a giant bumper edition of *Jackanory* storytelling, a Pinocchio-stuffed masquerade of lies, damn lies and statistics, with gross hyperbole and wild exaggeration thrown in for good measure. Typically, it went on for around ninety minutes or so and was a truly British spectacle to behold.

Adrian 'Bish' Bishop, LesCargo Logistics' Supreme Head of Communications ('Why don't they just call him Emperor?' joked Juliet), chaired proceedings, moving around from team leader to team leader and manager to manager with an airy cheerfulness, cracking jokes as he went, bantering with those colleagues he had known the longest in mini performances designed to put the rest of the crowd at ease, all carefully choreographed down the pub and in the canteen. Traditionally corporate, yet appearing mildly irreverent at the same time, in a loosened tie, open-necked shirt, 'call me Stevo' sort of way. The meeting carried the same geniality you'd find at the end of a local radio show when one excessively chirpy presenter would say, 'Bye for now, my lovelies' and hand over the microphone to his esteemed chum, Sally Sunshine, equally chipper, filling time as he went.

Barry detested LesCargo's Monday morning conferences because they pitched him straight into work when he wanted a rest after the weekend. It meant he had to be up, dressed and sat at his desk by 9am (with a tidy room and a neutral background), with all other devices, including the TV, turned off. Ma knew not to enter his room during conference calls, but would slide coffee and hot buttered croissants through a gap in the door to ensure he didn't fall back to sleep at his desk. He did this once, but she saved the day by flicking off his camera – and his audio too, because he was snoring.

This particular Monday morning, Barry's supervisor, Juliet, was on leave, so he would have to speak up for himself and a few of his less-experienced colleagues. He had butterflies in his stomach when he knew his time on the centre of the Zoom screen was coming, so he rehearsed a few deep breaths and ran through his lines like he was Michael Sheen getting into character.

'Right, guys, so now we come to the external teams – Juliet's sunning herself in Costa Del Weston-super-Mare, I believe, so Barry White is going to give us a lowdown on this week's website uploads. Good to see you, Barryo, I half expected you to be off sick today, judging by the way you limped off the pitch holding your hamstring again on Saturday.'

'Thanks, Bish, and morning, everyone. Yes, the hamstring is all good, thankfully, I came off mainly as a precaution. And it was nothing a few sherbets in The Dragon on Saturday night couldn't sort out.'

'And a few more on Sunday morning no doubt, eh, Barry? Under doctor's orders of course.'

Cue polite laughter all around the Zoom squares. And now we hand back to Sally Sunshine for the traffic news.

'So what's on the books this week, Barry?' continued slick Bish.

'Well, the priority is developing a thought leadership piece looking at how LesCargo provides lifecycle management sustainability in traditional warehouse settings, you know, greener solutions – for things going out and things coming in, maximising performance, value and customer satisfaction, not compromising on supply chain dexterity in any way. I'm going to be picking the brains of Douglas McAllister, a supply chain champion at our Inverness branch, to see how they do things up there in bonnie Scotland. They're international pioneers in Inverness when it comes to supply chain dexterity.'

'Sounds interesting,' said Bish, lying through his teeth, but still appearing upbeat and sincere like the pro he was.

No one else on the call had a clue what Barry was talking about – including Barry himself.

'Anything else going down in external comms this week?' said Bish.

'Oh yes, it's a packed schedule, our fabulous team is working flat out, not quite twenty-four-seven but certainly seven-five,' said Barry. 'Romeo is going to be rushed off his Reeboks tweeting extensively about our latest charity deliveries to the homeless in Puerto Banús.'

'Cool beans! Exciting, with potential newsworthy appeal!' said Bish. 'Anyone got any questions for Baz?'

There was an emphatic silence. Just as Barry had hoped for. And on went Bish to the next fall guy, Feargal Hargreaves, LesCargo's public information specialist for rail and freight.

Barry sat back in his seat, temporarily flicked off his camera and muted his audio.

'I am Superman,' he bellowed at the top of his voice before letting out the loudest, longest fart he had produced in months. The kind that sounds like a motorbike engine backfiring.

When he returned to the conference call everyone was properly laughing, so Barry double-checked his audio in a blind panic, hoping he hadn't just broken thunderous, rapturous wind directly down every single superfast line and channel of LesCargo's communications network.

He needn't have worried. The laughter was all for Romeo who, despite not having to do anything on the call except sit there quietly, smile occasionally and listen semi-attentively, had managed to let down the whole of the external team by getting up to open a window.

In doing so, he had revealed a pair of bright-pink buttocks on a body that was completely naked from the waist down. Who knew that Romeo had the faces of Dennis Waterman and John Thaw, AKA Carter and Regan from *The Sweeney*, tattooed on each bum cheek? Certainly not best pal Barry.

FIVE

THE HUNT FOR THE ARTFUL DODGER

BARRY PRINTED off the letter he had been working on for most of the morning, the one formally headed 'To the Supervisor of Toby Donald'. Being something of a stickler for good grammar (it was his job, after all), he read it back carefully to himself to check for any factual inaccuracies or obvious punctuation errors, before popping it into an envelope on his bedside table for Ma to add a stamp to and post later.

It read:

> *Dear Sir or Madam,*
>
> *I wish to make a complaint about one of your delivery guys in the Caeau Anghofiedig area (a shithole village in South Wales/a small country somewhere in the North Atlantic). His name according to the tag on his uniform is Toby Donald, he's forty-ish, sweaty, unkempt and ruder than any awakening I've ever previously experienced.*
>
> *He came to deliver a parcel today to my neighbours at 74 Cerys Matthews Heol. They were out so he tried to leave it with me, even though I told him I did not wish to do his job for him and deliver it at a more suitable hour when*

working people were no longer at work. He got shirty and asked me what I was doing that was so important, that I couldn't 'be a bit neighbourly' and pop the parcel around to the Edwards clan when they came home. Despite my protestations that it was none of his business what I was doing – and not my responsibility to do his job for him – he refused to go quietly.

Eventually, in a desperate effort to get rid of him, I told him I was in the process of writing a series of suicide notes. It was a complete lie, but in the heat of the moment it was the first thing that came into my head, and I thought it might force him to take a more sympathetic and less cocksure tone with me, and get his foot out of my door frame. However, he muttered 'good one' and asked me how many notes I was planning to leave and how long would it take? When I said around forty or fifty and weeks if not months, he almost wet himself laughing. His exact words were 'Mate... if you're going to top yourself just do it. Don't go all War and Peace about it.'

It's incredible to me how many ignorant and uneducated plebs, like your employee Mr Donald, cite Tolstoy's epic tale about France's invasion of Russia and the impact of the Napoleonic era on Tsarist society, when looking for a metaphor for 'going on a bit'. Sadly, I fear, Tolstoy's work is more famous for 'going on a bit' than anything else, which I'm sure was not his intention at all when he sat down to write it. All 1,225 pages.

Mr Donald had no right to doubt the serious intent of someone who said they were suicidal on the basis that they were writing quite a few goodbye letters. He gave me his personal telephone number and told me to text him when I planned to carry out my suicide because, in his own words again, 'I'd like to see it with my own eyes rather than take your pissing word for it.'

I do not know what company rules, if any, Mr Donald has contravened here or if chronic insensitivity/stupidity is a crime in your organisation, but if nothing else he left number 74's parcel against a wall in my hallway against my will and without my permission. I don't particularly like the Edwards clan, so I opened up their parcel and, to my great joy, discovered a good number of bottles in many fabulous colours from a gin mail-order club.

I have already consumed most of them because I cannot be completely trusted around booze. A bit like Mr Donald and people. Or Russian literature, even?

Bottoms up!

Lechyd Da!

PS: Please relay to Mr Donald that War and Peace is 561,304 words long, considerably shorter than Vikram Seth's much acclaimed A Suitable Boy, which weighs in at 591,554 words. I would also like to point him in the direction of Marcel Proust's In Search of Lost Time books (1,267,069 words) and Ayn Rand's Atlas Shrugged (561,996 words). I have not, I confess, read any of these tomes, nor am I ever likely to – unless I am unfortunate enough to find myself marooned in one of your obscenely large warehouses for any length of time with the aforementioned Mr Donald.

———

Romeo called unannounced via Teams around three in the afternoon, all of a tizz.

'Baz, I'm a bloody idiot,' he blurted out, without any prior greeting. He was red-faced and more dishevelled than usual. Bizarrely, his bed was made and he wasn't in it.

'What's the problem? You gotta compose a tweet on greener packaging solutions in less than two hours?' said Barry.

'Worse,' said Romeo. 'I took my neighbour's dog, Foxy, for a walk lunchtime cos she's away for a couple of days and I'm looking after it.'

'And?'

'Well, now he's puking and shitting everywhere like he's Krakatoa and the vet tells me he's lactose intolerant and might need his colony irrigating,' said Romeo, frantically flicking through the text messages on his phone, leaving Barry with just the top of a ruffled head to look at.

'Did you give him chocolate or something?'

'Not exactly.'

'What d'you mean "not exactly"?'

'I mean I didn't give him anything. He just took it. When my back was turned.'

'Took what?'

'Not hundred per cent sure but Jack Jones reckons he probably had half a tub of mint choc ice cream, a fair few Fabs and Feasts, including the sticks, some raspberry ripple and maybe a dozen or so crumbly Flakes.'

Jack Jones, just out of school, had recently started work in Lazarus Taylor's ice-cream van. Lazarus liked to park up in Lincoln Park most afternoons and leave Jack in charge, whilst he killed both time and takings in Albie Grindle's independent betting shop. When trade was quiet (which was often), Jack would leave the van unattended to hit golf balls into the swings and slides with his best pal, Freddie Truman. Romeo found the casual invitation of smacking a few golf balls into an empty playground hard to resist and forgot all about Foxy, who made the most of being off the leash to climb into the back of the ice-cream van and fill himself senseless with all the cold creamy goodies he could get his paws on.

'I phoned Betty – me neighbour – to tell her Foxy's poorly and she's doing her nut,' said the lumbering voice no longer attached to a computer screen, though in the background Barry could just about make out the shadow of a man pacing up and down the room like a marching ninja.

'Foxy's her baby, she fusses him something terrible – feeds him steaks from Ieuan's Butchers for dinner – but he's off his tucker good and proper, wouldn't even look at a prime ribeye. She's cancelling her hols and coming home from Billy Butlins – the Maidenhead one – pronto. She's a scary lady, Bazzer, a genuine Hammer house of horror. What am I going to do?'

There was still no one sitting at the laptop on the other end of the call for Barry to respond to or eyeball for body language clues.

'You need to calm down,' said Barry, to nothing and no one, scanning his screen for any sign of human life.

Half a head popped into the right-hand corner of Barry's laptop, upside down, at a frustrated 45-degree angle.

'I even had to give a statement to Sergeant Sargent,' shouted Romeo, forcing Barry to save himself from falling off the chair he had been rocking back on, upon two legs. 'Police are now looking for a thin posh boy aged about ten with blond curly hair and his mate, a little older, darker and chubbier, bit more streetwise, with a puckered nose and a minor speech impediment.'

'I'm confused.com,' said Barry.

'Think Mark Lester and Jack Wild, from *Oliver the Musical*. I watched it yesterday with Angharad at her house. They were the first people to come into my mind when the sarge started grilling me. I panicked.' Romeo looked at the ceiling and scrunched up his face. 'I told Lazarus that I was walking Foxy in the park when two kids with guns jumped out of a bush and raided his ice-cream van. It was a stupid thing to say, I know, but Jack Jones asked me to lie for him cos he didn't want to lose his job and it was the first thing that popped into my head. I said me and Jack chased after them and they dropped all their lollies. Foxy grabbed the bag and ran off into the trees. When he came back, he was sick as a dog. Lazarus called the sarge, which I didn't expect. The sarge said strange kids don't jump out of bushes and do armed robberies on stationary ice-cream vans.'

'What did you say to that?' said Barry.

'I said, "they do in Caeau Anghofiedig".'

'Did he buy it?'

'Don't think so.'

Barry started to laugh loudly. Uncontrollably.

'What do you think you're bloody well doing? This is serious!' said Romeo, with his face now pressed directly against his computer screen so that all Barry could see were flickering angry tonsils, shaking their tiny fists at the world from the back of his throat. 'The vet says Foxy will need intestinal rehabilitation, whatever that is. All I know is it's going to cost a pretty packet. What do you think I should do? Betty says I gotta pay. She might actually murder me for real. It's like an Agatha Christie all this. She's a violent woman, Bazzer. Not right in the head. She's not a pretty sight enraged. She's not a pretty sight when she's not enraged. You know what I'm saying, don't you?'

Romeo was now headbutting his keyboard like a lazy woodpecker, firing Russian-looking messages full of random consonants down Barry's chat line.

'Listen up, Foxy's not dead, he'll be chasing postmen again before the month's out. Betty isn't going to kill you, she's all bark. Like her dog. The vet will get his money somehow. The sarge is going to ignore all your cock and bull nonsense cos he knows you and what you're like and he doesn't like hassle. Or paperwork. Lazarus isn't going to tell the world, or more to the point, his missus, that he left Jack in his van on his own while he handed all his hard-earned choc-ice profits over to Albie Grindle. It's all going to go away. This time next week you'll be laughing about all this, just like me.'

When Barry had finished talking, Romeo slowly lifted his forehead out of his keyboard and rubbed the bits that hurt.

'I knew you'd make me feel better,' he said, smiling for the first time that afternoon.

Barry feigned the response of an efficient but soulless call centre operative. 'Thank you for calling The Barry White Helpline. We appreciate your business. Have a wonderful day.'

'I'm a bellend, aren't I?' said Romeo.

'Affirmative,' replied Barry, flashing a farewell-bidding hand across his screen like a fast setting sun, to leave Romeo stewing on his afternoon of madness in solitary laptop darkness.

SIX

WE NEED YOU TO LOOK AFTER THE
JELLY BABIES

ROMEO CALLED Barry to tell him Foxy's colony wouldn't need irrigating and he wasn't going to die of his ice-cream overdose.

'Good news,' said Barry, not looking up from his *Racing Post*.

'He looked so pitiful, so sorry for himself, I couldn't stare him square in the eye,' said Romeo, restlessly. 'He's holding a grudge. I know him.'

Foxy had stopped spraying the vet's premises every shade of brown but he still needed to stay under their watch for another day or two. He was severely dehydrated and bloated. Stomach cramps were making him cry so he needed regular pain relief. He barely got out of his basket.

Betty had virtually knocked down Romeo's door to get to him after he refused to return her calls. She found him hiding inside an old freezer in his ma's cellar and threatened to turn it on and leave him there if he didn't start talking and making sense. He told her the truth about what had happened. Eventually, she calmed down a bit, but only after she'd made

Romeo promise that he would foot all of Foxy's vet bills, which were likely to come in at around £1,500.

Sergeant Sargent had also gone round to Romeo's earlier in the day and found him hiding in the same freezer. The sarge didn't believe a word of Romeo's story but said he wouldn't be taking the matter any further.

'At least you won't get done for wasting police time, making them search all over South Wales for Oliver and the Artful Dodger,' said Barry, sympathetically.

'The sarge gave me a verbal warning but it's Betty I'm scared of.' Romeo grabbed a lump of hair in each hand and started tugging outwardly from the sides of his head, as if trying to give himself elephant ears. He did this whilst gurning, the same gurn Lazarus Taylor had expressed when Romeo told him a couple of kids with guns had run off with his rum and raisin. 'What am I going to do? I mean, I haven't got £100 let alone £1,500. Say, I don't suppose you could lend me the money, Baz?'

'Sorry, mate, I would if I could but I already owe Uncle Derek £500.'

'Just a bad week all round, ain't it? I've had HR on my case today as well.' Romeo stopped playing with his hair and shoved his hands down the front of his pants instead.

'Trousergate?' asked Barry.

'Yeah,' said Romeo. 'I got a verbal warning off them too. Roger Meredith told me I had to be fully clothed at all times while representing LesCargo on official business.'

'What did you say to that?'

'Not much. I sucked it all up and told him it was a genuine mistake. That I honestly forgot I wasn't wearing anything below.'

'Juliet's going to have another go at you about it all when she gets back next week, you know that?' Barry watched as Romeo continued to scratch himself vigorously downstairs. He wanted to tell him to stop because it was both unpleasant and off-putting but decided against it. His friend was having a rough enough time as it was.

'Had any stick off the comms lot?' said Barry.

'Yeah, quite a few memes and a lot of *Sweeney* theme-tune related stuff on Facebook and WhatsApp.'

'How long you had Regan and Carter on your backside anyhow?'

'About eighteen months. Got it done post lockdown to cheer meself up. I really got into them old *Sweeneys* big time when we were furloughed, watched them every day on ITV, along with *Minder* and *The Professionals*. They kept me going. I love all them old-school hard-nut cop shows as you know. I would have liked to have lived back in those times, when men were men. Know what I mean?'

Barry looked at the black-and-white photograph of his dad and Uncle Derek as young pit men, covered in coal dust but smiling from ear to ear, on his wall. 'I do,' he said.

Barry's call with Romeo and the fact that it was a Wednesday left him sinking into a midweek dip. He'd not felt full of pep for quite a while, truth be told, and he was struggling to motivate himself to do anything. Ma seemed a bit more subdued lately as well. It wasn't anything Barry could put his finger on, she still fetched and carried for him and waited on his every whim, but she seemed more distant, less in the moment. As if she had other things on her mind. Maybe it was her age finally catching up with her? Or perhaps she had her own problems? Barry was worried that she might have found out he'd borrowed money from Uncle Derek. But how? Derek wouldn't tell her, no way, he was old-school, a man's man. Plus, Derek wouldn't have told Aunty Ruth that he'd lent money to his nephew for fear of reprisals. Their marriage was successful because information was largely shared on a need-to-know basis. Like the SAS.

Barry was watching Chico videos when he heard a firm knock at the front door. Chico had managed to lift his spirits a little, firstly by feeding grapes to a dappled horse, then by scrolling through his own mobile phone, looking at pictures of himself, smiling and beating his chest defiantly. Watching Chico munch his way through a whole broccoli brought a proper grin to Barry's face, like Heinz tomato soup on a cold day. He could identify with the way Chico so obviously enjoyed eating. He could identify with so many of Chico's traits and mannerisms, so much so that he wondered if they might be related in some long-lost distant cousin way. Was that even possible? Perhaps he was part of an evolutionary process no one yet knew about? The in-between by-product of a transformation in process?

He heard another knock at the door, which told him Ma must be out. He pushed through his pillows, forced himself off his bed and plodded downstairs in Ma's old red fluffy slippers, with the toes cut out, expecting to be greeted by some Amazon delivery guy saying, 'Take a picture?'

'Hello, Barry boy, got a few minutes?' said Uncle Derek, wringing his hands behind his back.

'Sure.' Barry ushered Derek into the lounge and they sat down at either end of the sofa.

'Training cancelled tonight?'

'No, it's on.'

'What's up then?'

Derek shuffled up the sofa to get closer to Barry and leant forward to inspect his right leg. 'How's the hamstring?'

Barry ran his hand down the back of his leg as if stroking a cat. 'Oh it's fine. Cured itself completely.'

'Good, good...' muttered Derek, looking awkward and

uncomfortable. 'Look, Barry, there's no easy way of saying this, but what happened on Saturday was embarrassing. It was embarrassing to me, to you and to the club. The other players, they've been talking amongst themselves. A couple of them came to see me last night, at my house, telling me that I need to do something, else they're threatening to quit. The club would probably fold if that happened. No rugby in Anghofiedig. All that history down the pan. Your pop's legacy. Unthinkable. You don't want that to happen do you, Barry boy?'

'Course not, Uncle Derek.'

'I mean you're forty-four now, aren't you? You've had a better innings than most. I know the game's never come natural to you but you have got a whole load worse recently. You used to be less chunky, you got around the park a bit more. Not great, but better. Bad, without being terrible. It's the scrummaging that really bothers me most. We can't carry you like we used to. We used to have fabulous forwards who were happy to do your job for you, give you an armchair ride, and I wish we still had them. But we don't. You're much more exposed now. You stand out. We can't hide you. You've become a target for the oppos too. Seeing an Anghofiedig tight-head prop – a red number three – mocked and ridiculed by crappy village teams who used to fear us on the rugby paddock, well, it's a hard pill for me to swallow, I'll not lie. For the team too. We're proud men. Proud Welshmen. Rugby runs through us like the letters in a stick of rock. That's all. You understand don't you, Barry?'

'Sorry, Uncle, no. Not a word of it.' Barry cocked his head sideways like Chico often did when he was puzzled.

'You're my nephew and I love you and I'll do anything for you because you're the last living link to my brother who was my ultimate hero. I'm trying to protect you in all this.'

'All what?'

'I want you to retire. To quit rugby. With immediate effect, no swansongs. No fuss or fanfares. For the good of the team. And for the good of Anghofiedig. It's what the other players want. It's what I want. It's what your ma wants. It's what your old man would have wanted.'

Barry sunk back deep into the sofa's absorbing cushions and said nothing. He felt a few tears welling up inside of him.

'Look, you don't have to walk away from rugby completely, I've got a proposition for you. How about you become my assistant? My number two?' said Derek.

'What, a coach?' said Barry.

'No, not exactly,' said Derek, backpedalling faster than Barry Junior in a scrum. 'More of an administrator. A matchday manager. In charge of tackle bags and water bottles and beer kitties and kicking tees and the pre-match jelly babies. You could be another set of eyes for me. My eyesight's not what it was, I miss things nowadays. And I know you understand rugby, even if you struggle to play it. You've got the theory side of things cornered, you're just no good at the practical.'

There was a lengthy silence before Derek got up and headed towards the door with the familiar heavy, mechanical sloping strides of an old sportsman.

'Just think on it, will yer?'

'Okay. What about training tonight?'

'Give that hamstring a night off, eh.'

'Yeah.'

Uncle Derek opened the front door to let himself out and headed for his car.

'Uncle Derek,' shouted Barry, after him. 'This job as your assistant, is it paid?'

'Could be,' said Derek, thinking on the spot. 'How much would you want?'

'What about another £300? Up front in advance, cash in hand, preferably.'

SEVEN

TALKING GOBLEDEGOOK WITH DOUGLAS MCALLISTER

AT 9.10AM ON a chilly Thursday Barry was lying on his bed, laptop on knees, checking a few Google alerts, looking over Romeo's only Instagram post of the past two days, considering what the LesCargo working day had in store for him. He jotted at the top of his daily to-do list the words 'find a winner at Newbury' with four exclamation marks after it. Just beneath, he scribbled 'pop into village and get haircut'. The next thing he knew it was 11.57am and Ma was standing over him with a mug of coffee, a copy of *The Racing Post*, a double round of sausage sandwiches plastered in brown sauce, plus a couple of cherry bakewells.

'Barry, I think you nodded off. I didn't want to wake you but I was worried you'd get in trouble.'

Typically, a two-hour nap in the heart of the working day was nothing to stress over. However, today he had a midday appointment on Teams with Douglas McAllister, boss of LesCargo's flagship Inverness branch, to discuss all things 'supply chain dexterity'. Not much in his working regime ever mattered, but this did. Get it right and Juliet would be off his case until 2025.

He knew the story was deemed important by his superiors because Juliet had prewarned him that his article would need to be signed off and approved by a dozen people at least, including some very lofty senior figures who he only knew by name and had never met in more than twenty years at the company. By the time a dozen pairs of hands were through with taking their metaphorical red pens to both his and each other's work, the finished article would probably possess no actual meaning, save from the banal platitudes and oft-repeated quotes and slogans that were already plastered all over the company website and anything else that bore their red, gold and green (coincidentally, also the colours Boy George sung about in 'Karma Chameleon') logo.

What frustrated Barry most was that all these sets of hands were attached to bodies, minds, heads and imaginations that couldn't write, spell or string a cohesive written sentence together for toffee, let alone tell a complete story about anything from start to finish. Most of those involved in the sign-off process didn't even work in communications; they were the people who had climbed the greasy company ladder by generally being good at doing the same things every day, managing depots with dull, reliable, repeatable, tried and tested processes. Their priority – whenever someone flashed a Word doc into their inbox marked 'urgent' or 'for external use' – was to panic then sanitise it, strip away all risk, make it anodyne, make it sterile, apply HR and health and safety policies all over it, apply best practice, and ensure no edge, be that real or imaginary, could ever be handed to any competitor, once again, real or imaginary. Not a single LesCargo comms worker liked or agreed with the way their work was handled but they lumped it. For an easier life. And decent pay.

Barry's meeting today with Douglas McAllister was just the start of a long and tiresome road that would ultimately cost the company thousands of pounds and countless senior management man-hours, incorporating umpteen internal meetings and discussions, some of which would be solely focused on the use and applications of not just single phrases, but single words. Ultimately, once this self-congratulating, pat-on-the-back exercise was over, the company would gain little, save from a hundred or so web hits, mostly from those involved or close to the content creation process itself. Even pioneering Inverness was not able to change this world.

Today, it was Barry's job to avoid using jargon such as 'big data', 'deep dive', 'holistic', 'KPI', 'strategic and blue sky thinking' – in order to get his piece approved by the likes of Juliet and Bish – before everyone else, out in the logistics field and in the boardrooms, on much bigger salaries and with much more personal and professional clout than him, slid all these words and phrases right back in again. Barry would strive to write a story that a few people – and maybe even a local paper or two – might want to use and promote. His bosses and superiors would then make darn sure that this would never happen.

'Hello there, can you hear and see me okay? I'm Barry White, content creator down in deepest, wettest Anghofiedig.'

'Hi there, Barry, great to meet you. I'm Douglas. Douglas McAllister, in charge of operations up here in sunny Inverness.'

Douglas was an amiable if one-dimensional chap, obviously fiercely proud of both his Scottish heritage and his depot. Bizarrely, he was wearing a tartan kilt and Barry wondered if this was regular everyday workwear in the 'we do things a bit differently up here' Inverness branch, or whether he'd dressed up specially for the Teams call. Barry thought about the trouble Romeo had got himself into recently, inadvertently revealing his tattooed pink arse in the workplace, and he hoped and prayed that Douglas wouldn't drop anything important and feel the need to pick it up.

The interview rolled along easily enough with Barry not having to do too much work as he was recording it. Occasionally though, Douglas would chuck him a big curveball.

'Personally, I see supply chain dexterity as the ability and the capacity to build in key components such as agility, digital enhancement and data literacy,' said Douglas. 'Barry, tell me, because I'm always interested in gauging the views of others, especially a fellow Celt like yourself, what do you consider the nuts and bolts of supply chain dexterity to be?'

Barry froze on the spot and momentarily considered pretending that his screen had done the same.

He'd worked at LesCargo for decades – written all kinds of long and short leaders for them and about them – but, when push came to shove, he wasn't entirely sure he knew what the term logistics actually meant, let alone anything else. He'd discovered that talking logistics with people who worked in logistics was a bit like discussing philosophy or sociology. There were no right or wrong answers. You just had to put an argument together, sound convincing and follow through to the end, come what may. If you tossed in a few things that you'd heard other people say over the years – and had managed to remember – you were home and dry.

'Supply chain dexterity to me, Douglas, is essentially interconnection and facilitation,' said Barry. 'It's all about pivotal optimisation. Resilience. Flexibility and above all, sector awareness and diversification with a capital D.'

'Yes, yes, you're absolutely right,' said Douglas, getting all excited about the nonsense Barry was making up on the spot just to stop his cover being blown.

After forty minutes or so, Barry knew he had gathered enough clichés to garble together some kind of draft for Juliet to have first pop at rewriting next week.

'Fabulous talking to you, Barry, do stay in touch,' said

Douglas. 'And if you ever fancy coming to visit us, to see what we do up close and personal, just let me know. I can make it happen. And we'd love to have you.'

'Thanks, Douglas, much appreciated. And may I just say, what you're doing in Inverness is truly remarkable in my humble opinion. I felt this morning that you were giving me a peek under the covers into the logistical future for all of us.'

Douglas beamed a broad, satisfied Scottish grin. Barry beamed inside too. He knew he could talk bollocks with the best of them.

Exhausted, and now behind schedule for the day, Barry opened up his *Racing Post* and quickly began assessing the form for the first of the televised races from Newbury.

'Ma,' he shouted at the top of his voice. 'Are you in?'

'Yes, son, I am,' she bellowed back. 'Everything okay?'

'My sausage sarnies have gone cold. Would you warm them up for me, please?'

'Of course, son, I'm on my way.'

And with that Ma showed some nifty supply chain dexterity of her own, dropping the washing she was sorting into whites and colours in the kitchen, breezing past the vacuum cleaner blocking the hallway, mounting the stairs – with today's mail still resting across the bottom two steps – and arriving ahead of her ETA in the upstairs back bedroom to meet the ever-fluctuating demands and needs of her number one priority sausage sandwich client.

EIGHT
PEARL'S A SINNER

BARRY HAD ALREADY EATEN a McDonald's breakfast of two double bacon and egg McMuffins, a sweet apple pie (not from the breakfast menu) plus a large Coke – brought to him by Deliveroo – and was now chomping on a cold hunk of two-week-old black pudding whilst standing at the fridge with the door wide open, working out what he would gorge on next. It was 10.11am and he was comfort eating, on account of his gambling.

He had lost another £500 he did not have, this time the £500 Aunty Ruth had lent him last week to 'sort himself out': buy some new clothes for a return to the office to work (big fat lie), stop the electric from being cut off (big fat lie) and clear some of Ma's council tax arrears (big fat lie with knobs on).

He felt bad he wouldn't be able to pay the money back as quickly as promised but he was in a vicious circle, spending more than he was earning on feckless things, mostly betting.

Yesterday, he lost £40 on some unknown American golfer called Chuck Mendonza in an unknown American college golf tournament. He'd had a £50 treble on Philippine basketball but got let down by Blackwater Bossing losing to Phoenix Super

LPG Fuel Masters. He'd ventured a further £70 on Ha Noi to see off Trang An Ninh Binh at 7–1 in the Vietnamese Volleyball A League. The big upset didn't happen. Trang won at odds of 1–18.

On and on it went, including two hours of total madness this morning when he should have been working – chancing his arm on sports he knew absolutely nothing about in countries he didn't know still existed. He travelled the sporting globe to fritter away Aunty Ruth's hard-earned pension money, clicking randomly on brightly lit, flashing buttons in complete anonymity whilst sitting in yesterday's pants, drinking the dregs of a large flat McDonald's Coke with bits of black pudding stuck to his gums, in search of a buzz. It was no way to live.

When he tired of sports betting he lost his last hundred quid in the blink of an eye on Paddy Power's more 'fun' games which weren't much fun at all. He then read Mr Power's helpful safer gambling information, which told him that they wanted to be part of the solution and do their best for people like him with gambling problems. He stopped reading when he was alerted to the fact that Mountfield HK had won him £80 (European ice hockey, apparently).

Barry felt ashamed and disgusted with himself. He felt dirty. He wondered how he would pay Aunty Ruth back. Or if she would mention the loan to Ma. He could offer to do her lawns instead? Polish her brass? Walk her dog? Cook a few meals? Tell her to knock it off future birthday and Christmas presents? Ignore it and hope she never mentioned it again?

Poor old Ma might have to carry the can. Barry had already told Aunty Ruth that Ma liked a drink or three on the sly, hence her difficulties with paying bills. Now he'd have to make out that Ma's gambling was an issue too. He knew Ruth would be uneasy confronting Ma head-on about such things. And once he had the money together to pay her back, he could tell her that old Pearl had successfully overcome her demon vices with a course of online counselling and a few heart to hearts with Reverend Hill – and a little support from her son, obviously – so everything in their orbit was hunky-dory once more.

Barry hated himself for lying to his aunt and blackening his own mother's name but what else could he do? Sell one of his kidneys to an African prince? Quit LesCargo and get a better-paid job in Cardiff? Stop gambling and drinking so recklessly? Nah, he'd win the dosh back, it was just a matter of time. He was on a rough streak, that was all. The Cardiff boys would call it a market fluctuation. His luck would change, his tide would turn. Wouldn't it?

———

At teatime, over home-made chicken curry, rice, chips and nan's bread, as Ma always called it, Barry found it hard to look his mother in the eye. He'd made her out to be this sad, secretly depressed drunk, someone spiralling out of control because of a fictional online gambling addiction. Now, he looked at her and saw her for what she really was, and he felt ashamed of himself.

Barry usually spent a couple of hours sitting with his mother when he finished work, his official finishing time of 5pm not the real one, around 11am. They'd eat the tea that Ma would always cook, in front of the telly together, watching *Pointless* and the headlines of the *BBC News*, switching over before it all got too detailed and too depressing to *Richard Osman's House of Games*. It was always the BBC at teatime, never ITV and the feckless Bradley Walsh. The Bible and the BBC were Ma's most trusted sources of info. The onset of *The One Show* theme tune was the cue for Barry to return to his room or get ready to go out, while Ma gathered up the dirty crockery, carried it all to the kitchen in two or three trips and washed up alone.

Ma did everything for her idle man-child; she scooped up his dirty clothes off his bedroom floor, washed them, dried them, ironed them and put them away again neatly in his wardrobe and drawers. She bought his food and drink – making sure to write down his explicit wants before she went to John John's Mart to do the shopping. If John John didn't have what Barry had asked for, Ma would often take a bus into Monmouth or sometimes even Hereford to get the things on her list. She washed his bedding and dusted and vacuumed his room whilst he was out so as not to disturb him. Her son was her absolute everything. At seventy-eight, he kept her going and made her feel needed. And she was needed, because Barry was a useless so and so who could not be trusted to do much for himself. Ma knew this. She also knew she was partly to blame for making him so dependent on her.

After Barry Senior died, she showered her boy with love and an extra ring of protection, and just kept going. For her, watching Barry stumble like the other kids did, falling off bikes, scraping knees, cutting fingers with penknives or burning themselves making cups of tea or getting pizzas out of the oven, was too painful. She sheltered him from all that stuff and stopped him making the mistakes he needed to make, at the times he needed to make them. Now, she regretted what she had done but it was too late. Her son would probably never marry or even have a girlfriend – and she would have no grandkids – because she had overprotected him and warned him off getting his heart broken.

'You've got a good soul, my love,' she used to say. 'Don't let them gold-digging girls go spoiling it. Stay with me. I'll look after you.'

And she did, all for £50 board a month. The cheapest three-star hotel in the UK. The same price as a typical wager on the Czech table tennis league.

Whilst Alexander Armstrong asked contestants to name the most obscure five-lettered word they could think of by changing only one letter of mince, Barry looked at his ma and felt nothing but gratitude for everything this little old do-gooding, churchgoing, selfless woman with the grey Shirley Temple curls that she put into rollers every night before going to bed, sacrificed for him. She was always giving what was hers to him. Her money. Her opportunities. Her time. Herself. He vowed to put things right with Aunty Ruth and restore his mother's reputation in her eyes.

Ma stared back at her only son, who she adored and would give her life for, and gave him a comforting 'all's well with the world' smile. Barry would take it to mean his Ma was just grateful that he was there. And of course, she was. However, she was also noticing how fat Barry had got and that she would have to check in at John John's in the morning to see if he had any XXL polo shirts, instead of XL ones. She looked at the helpless way he shovelled huge torn-off lumps of nan's bread into his gob, with lukewarm blobs of curry dripping off his chin, rice inexplicably smeared in his eyebrows, and realised he would be with her until the day she popped her clogs.

'MINGE!' shouted Barry, poppadoms exploding from his mouth like hailstones in a thunderstorm. 'M – I– N – G – E, minge. I know it's a bit rude but it's still a proper word, Ma. It's sure to be in the dictionary, and I don't reckon many of the general public would have said it to them *Pointless* researchers, on account of being too embarrassed to say it out loud. But I'm not, Ma. I'm not. M – I – N – G – E, minge, it's a good one, ain't it, Ma? What do you think, do you reckon it will be pointless, Ma? £250 for the pot all day long, I say.'

Ma smiled, pretending to be impressed by the work of the LesCargo content creator sitting in her lounge, shouting obscenities at her, then checked her watch to see how long before that nice Ronan Keating came on her telly in *The One Show*.

My boy is a fecking idiot, she thought to herself. *If only he was more like Ronan. He'll never cope in this world without me, when I'm gone.*

NINE
SHUT IN THE BOG WITH STEPHEN MCQUEEN

DESPITE GAMBLING AWAY MOST of the £300 Uncle Derek gave him up front, Barry had come to a big decision. He was not going to accept his uncle's offer to become his gopher. He was only forty-four, too young to retire from rugby, his best playing days might still be in front of him. Look at Alun Wyn Jones, still in the Welsh national team when he was thirty-eight. Barry only wanted to turn out for Anghofiedig once a week, and he wasn't bothered if he only got half a game. In fact, he would welcome it, because the eighty minutes or so between kick-off and final whistle was the bit he enjoyed the least.

Barry struggled with the violence and brutality of one-to-one combat, where he was certain to come off second best, getting punched in the face or gouged or bitten or stamped upon, be that deliberately or accidentally. He hated too, how he would react to such incidents in the moment, not for him the response of Uncle Derek in his prime or current Anghofiedig skipper Stephen McQueen. If someone was brave or stupid enough to throw a right-hander their way, they'd come back stronger with a 'nip it in the bud' approach, determined to retaliate harder, to wreak immediate revenge then take things up another notch, for the sake of retribution and for justice.

The physical exertion that sapped his strength and the gamesmanship that stripped him of his dignity made Barry feel like a lesser man. He couldn't stand being squeezed so tightly in a suffocating scrum that it felt as if his neck might snap.

And yet – once he got through the eighty minutes of torture – there was so much to love about being a rugby player. The beer definitely tasted sweeter afterwards. Opponents who had revelled and delighted in tramping his face in the dirt suddenly became best buddies, buying him drinks all night by way of apology for their worst misdemeanours, putting their arms around him and laughing, talking and joking with him, mano a mano, encouraging him to keep playing because things would be better next week. Barry loved this environment and the carefree optimism of it. Here, in the clubhouse, he was a champion, not least because he could sink a pint of anything in 4.4 seconds flat to defeat most challengers. However, to get to this place you had to take to the field and pay your dues. You had to get down into the trenches, not stay safe and warm on the touchline. Even Uncle Derek knew this, that if someone was prepared to put their body on the line and accept whatever punishments came their way, they could walk off at the end of a game with their head held high, regardless of the score, and call themselves a rugby player.

That's what Barry loved. At work, in the pubs, even in church, Monday through to Sunday, being able to call himself a rugby player. Rather than the son of one.

Whilst Derek was laying out the kit in the changing room a couple of hours before kick-off, Barry crept in and pushed the door closed. His uncle had his back to him and didn't hear him enter. Barry coughed but Derek still didn't react. So he coughed again. Derek turned around, saw who it was and went back to laying out his matching sets of shirts, shorts and socks in neat little piles.

'Uncle Derek, I've decided not to donate my boots to charity just yet. I reckon the club needs me. I reckon you need me. Especially as you've only got fourteen players for today – thirteen if I do a Tony Bennett and say, "Thank you very much and goodnight, you've been a wonderful audience".'

'But I paid you £300,' snapped Derek.

'You'll get it back,' said Barry.

'When? You owe me £800! And don't think I don't know you've been tapping up my missus for more money on the sly too. It all stops today, you hear? It's getting out of hand. You're gambling heavy again, aren't you?' Uncle Derek's face reddened.

Barry put on his best indignant look, faking hurt like a Premier League footballer. 'No.'

'And pissing too much up the wall. You're not eighteen anymore – it's time you took a long, hard look in the mirror and grew up.'

Somehow, Barry's decision not to quit rugby had quickly turned into a lifestyle counselling session, from someone who had no rightful qualifications to give one.

'You're a bloody fool, son, a bloody fool.' Derek's head swung from side to side and Barry heard the bones in his neck click. 'I've always tried to help you as best I can, you know I have, on account of your dad not being around, but I know one thing for sure – he wouldn't have pussyfooted around you, trying to be nice. He would have told you things straight years ago cos he didn't have a lot of patience and wasn't one for shades of grey. He'd have kicked you out of the house for your own good, made you stand on your own two feet.'

'Does that mean I'm starting the game today?' said Barry.

Derek picked up a pile of kit he hadn't yet sorted and threw

49

it in a heap on the floor. He kicked it across the room. 'I don't know what to do now.' He sat down on a bench and sighed. 'Like you said, we're a bit thin on the ground and Jonah's got sixty-five cows to milk at four o'clock so can only play until half-time.'

Barry started picking up kit off the floor. 'Put me in, I'm feeling good.'

'McQueen won't be happy. He wants you gone.'

'I knew it was him.'

'He wasn't the only one.'

'No, but the others listen to him.'

'He's a leader, that's why.'

'He's a dickhead.'

Derek laughed and snorted with the air appearing to come out of his cauliflower-shaped ears rather than his nose or mouth.

Barry played the full eighty minutes to his usual abject level. Jonah departed to milk his cows at half-time, and Anghofiedig lost 75–0 to The Stragglers.

McQueen was spitting bricks in the clubhouse that night at the sight of Barry on the floor doing the 'Oops Upside Your Head' dance with the opposition, laughing and messing around like nothing had happened. When Barry went to take a leak, McQueen was waiting for him.

He grabbed him by the lapels and yanked him into the disabled toilet for a private chat.

'Steady on, Stephen, people will talk, what the bloody hell you doing?'

'Time for a proper conversation, Whitey.'

McQueen temporarily let go of Barry's collar so he tried to walk away. 'I don't want a proper conversation, not now, I'm going back for more "Oops".'

'Okay, I'll talk and you'll listen. Today, you played your final game for Anghofiedig. You're going to accept your uncle's offer and retire. For good. Forever.'

'And what if I don't want to?'

'Then you need to find yourself some other mug team, except there's no one else soppy enough to want you.'

Barry looked exasperated. He was tired of all these conversations making out he was the scapegoat for the rugby club's demise. 'But we haven't got enough players as it is.'

'Don't care,' said McQueen, sticking his chin out. 'I can handle losing every week. Every club has its ups and downs. We're in a rebuilding phase, I'm a good builder. I can put up with playing a man or two short – as long as everyone on the pitch is together, giving their all, blood, sweat and tears. What I can't handle is people like you giving the club a bad name – crying like a baby, pulling out a bag of toffees and offering them to the oppo in the scrums, tickling people to stop them from punching you, shouting at the ref all game and squealing for protection. You're making us a laughing stock. Not just yourself. All of us.'

'Why don't you quit then?' said Barry, backing off from McQueen's protruding chin.

'Me? I'm our best player.'

'So?'

'I'm Anghofiedig through and through,' said McQueen, inwardly seething.

Barry wasn't backing down. 'So am I.'

'But you can't run anymore. You've got nothing left to give.'

'I've got soul, baby,' said Barry, pathetically.

'I'll give you one last chance. Are you going to walk back into that bar, ask for a moment's hush and announce to everyone that you're packing up rugby to help your uncle on the sidelines?'

'No. I am not.'

'Why don't you show spunk like that on the pitch, eh?' said McQueen, grabbing Barry by the waist and lifting him upside down until eventually he was dangling by his feet. It was quite an impressive show of strength from McQueen, because Barry was certainly the wrong side of sixteen stones. His phone and loose change bounced out onto the hard floor.

'How am I going to get through to you? Would hanging you from the goalposts stark naked do the trick?'

'It might,' said Barry, stubbornly.

'What's going on here, then?' said Jonah, sticking his head around the door.

McQueen dropped Barry in a heap on his head. 'All right, Jonah. Me and Barry were just larking about.'

'That right?' said Jonah.

'Yes,' said Barry, rubbing his head and scrabbling around for his money.

'I came looking for you cos we're doing "Oops" again and our boat just ain't as good without you. Also, Stragglers reckon they've got a bloke who can neck a pint of Strongbow faster than anyone in South Wales so we need you to take him down a peg or two.'

'Happy to,' said Barry.

'He's a big-headed copper who nicked me last year for taking a piss behind the Dylan Thomas phone booth library so I shall enjoy you wiping the smug grin off his face. I'd consider it a personal favour,' said Jonah.

Jonah was one of the few people in Anghofiedig who even McQueen didn't take liberties with. McQueen was much bigger and more muscular than Jonah, half his age too, but the latter was unpredictable. He possessed wild, dark eyes and an even wilder, darker mind. He ate mostly roadkill and Derek reckoned he deliberately went out in his van at night looking for deer, pheasants and wild boar to run over. He worked as a labourer on

Eric's farm but would sometimes disappear for months on end and no one would know where he had been, not even Eric. He lived alone in a ramshackle hut in the middle of the woods. He was grubby and unwashed and wore the same clothes every day of the year regardless of the season, including an old brown mac – indoors and outdoors – a bit like Liam Gallagher.

Jonah had a soft spot for Barry though, and would watch out for him both on and off the rugby field. Again, it probably stemmed back to macho admiration for Barry Senior and a sense of pity for his weird offspring. Barry didn't care what his motives were, Jonah was a usefully ally to have around. Particularly, when you were dangling upside down in the disabled toilet with McQueen about to strip you of all your clothes and suspend you from a goalpost.

'What you boys doing in here? On second thoughts don't tell me, I don't want to know,' blurted out a breathless Uncle Derek, pushing his way in.

McQueen slapped a large hand to his forehead. 'Bloody hell, like Cardiff Central in here. Don't tell me, you need Boy Wonder for "Oops Upside Your Head" cos no one rows a pretend boat better than he does.'

'No,' said Derek. 'Barry, we've got to get down the cop shop pronto cos your ma's been taken into custody.'

'Custody? Ma? What's she done?' Barry tried to tuck his belly back into his shirt but realised he was now missing three buttons.

Derek felt like alien words were spilling from his mouth. 'Not sure exactly, but Sergeant Sargent mumbled something about armed robbery.'

'Shit the bed,' said McQueen.

'What a gal,' said Jonah.

TEN
STICK 'EM UP, THIS IS A ROBBERY

IT WAS the morning after the night before and Ma was understandably sheepish. For years she'd acted out this little charade with John John at the mart where, if she approached the counter and John had his back to her, maybe bent over sorting newspapers, she would hold up her little brolly as a mock gun and shout, 'Stick 'em up, soldier.' John would recognise her voice, laugh, turn around with his hands held up and say, 'Just take what you need, the Polos are on the second shelf in front of you.'

This caper had gone on for about ten years but Ma and John John still laughed every time like they were teenagers. Sometimes, John John would improv and swap Polos for chewing gum or on one occasion, pickled onion Monster Munch, which really tickled Ma. Similarly, Ma might spice things up by calling him pilgrim rather than soldier, or pulling out a loaded water pistol from her handbag and squirting John John's glasses for full fall-over-on-your-face comic effect. She'd done this on the Saturday evening she got arrested.

Except John John wasn't the one behind the counter with his back to her on this occasion. It was Arwyn Griffiths, hardly a doppelgänger for John John seeing as he had a shock of unruly salt and pepper curls and John John was completely bald, but Ma protested that at seventy-eight, her eyesight wasn't what it used to be. Arwyn was relatively new to the village and a self-professed gibbering wreck, working his first unsupervised shift. He screamed like Barry at the bottom of a ruck when Ma pointed her purple pistol at him, and slammed on the panic button underneath the counter to spark 120-decibel chaos. Ma didn't exactly scarper from the crime scene, but she panicked in the moment and didn't hang around to explain anything to Arwyn. In the confusion, she also forgot to pay for a sliced white loaf, a bottle of toilet cleaner, half-a-dozen Pink Ladies and a bag of Maltesers.

Sergeant Sargent was duty bound to call by her house and take her down the station, though he stopped short of cuffing her and sounding his blues and twos.

'I'm not going to elope to Mexico or nothing like that,' said Ma.

'I know, Pearl, it's a pain in the derrière for all of us, but the quicker we sort things out the more chance you've got of sleeping in your own bed tonight. I'm sorry to interrupt *Celebrity Pointless*,' said the sarge, staring intently at the telly. 'Say, is that Dave from *The Royle Family* teamed up with Phil Mitchell off *EastEnders*? Don't fancy their chances if it is.'

Ma didn't even bother looking at the screen. 'No idea.'

Arwyn Griffiths claimed he needed therapy for PTSD and insisted that an ambulance take him to hospital so he could get his nerves and ticker checked over. John John had to close the mart early but corroborated Ma's statement and got her released after several hours in a cell. Ma phoned Derek to round up Barry, pick her up and take her home. They made endless jokes that Ma failed to appreciate on the short hop back to Cerys Matthews Heol.

Around one in the morning it was John John's turn to make Ma jump out of her skin by calling her up on her landline.

'Sorry for ringing so late, Pearl, but I couldn't sleep. I was worried about you. Figured you'd be awake too.'

'I am. I won't sleep a wink tonight.'

'Understand.'

'Quite a day.'

'Yes, quite a day.'

There was an uneasy pause as the pair danced around each other's silences trying to predict what they meant. John John wasn't a decisive man but he seized the initiative. 'I hope today won't change anything between us.'

'It won't.'

'Promise?'

'Promise.'

'I enjoy our bit of banter.' John John's tone was calm and soothing.

'Sergeant Sargent told me not to stage any more hold-ups, fake or otherwise, but I'm sure we can come up with something else, can't we?' Ma loved their little games just as much as John John and didn't want them to end either, despite the embarrassment and further ridicule to come. 'I told the sarge he can keep my water pistol. There was a poster up in the station about a weapons amnesty so I handed it in.'

'I don't want any money for the bread, bog cleaner, apples and chocs,' said John.

'Thank you, soldier,' came the reply.

Like a couple of awkward kids, rather than a pair of almost octogenarians, they both blushed down the line and said it was probably time for them to be settling down.

'Goodnight, Bonnie.'

'Sweet dreams, Clyde.'

Sunday morning. Barry sat for a while at his dad's graveside outside the church and told him all about Ma's exploits the night before. Barry Senior would have mocked and teased her incessantly. Cruelly so. He thought, too, about what his Uncle Derek had said – that Barry Senior wouldn't have put up with his son embarrassing the family name or the rugby club he loved. He'd have sided with McQueen for sure. He'd have probably helped him strip Barry off and tie him to the goalposts. McQueen would have been the son he wanted. A chip off the old block. Tough. Uncompromising. Thick as pig shit.

'Sorry to be such a let-down, Dad,' said Barry to his old man's headstone.

'Who you talking to?'

Barry hadn't heard anyone sidle up and sit down on the bench beside him, but there she was, the love of his life, Angharad Davies.

'Oh, hullo, Angers, I was just talking to the old man.'

'Is he listening?'

Barry shrugged his shoulders and smiled weakly, but said nothing.

'Well, he didn't much listen to anyone while he was alive so why would he be any different now?'

Barry deliberately changed the subject. 'How are things with you?'

'Crap.'

'Greg still living it up in Barry Island with his young flame?'

'Yep. I'll not have him back when everything goes tits up and he runs out of dosh. He's toast this time.' Angharad spotted a small lump of dirt on the arm of the bench and brushed it away with a firm sweep of her own arm. She then flicked her sleeve with her other hand and clapped her hands in a washing motion.

'Glad to hear it.' Barry stared at the lump of dirt now on the ground and imagined it was Greg.

'We're a right pair of knobheads, aren't we?' said Angharad.

Barry could understand why Angharad might view herself in such a fashion: for marrying Greg in the first place; for falling for his lies and street patter; for forgiving him one sordid affair after another, only to be taken for a ride again. However, he couldn't quite see what he'd done to find himself lumped in the same bracket. 'Am I a knobhead?'

'Of course you are, but not in a bad way.'

'In what way, then?'

Angharad could see Barry was offended so tried to backtrack. 'In a harmless way.'

'I don't understand.' Barry pushed further for an explanation.

'Well, here we are in our forties, you still living with your ma and me back living with mine. Neither of us have got any significant others in our lives, no kids, both still living in this dump of a village, doing dull jobs we hate just to get by. We've never lived anywhere worth living, never taken any of the risks we used to say we were going to take. We're just stuck on a boring old hamster wheel, know what I mean? I never thought we'd be here, where we're sat now, on this Sunday morning, not when we were young, free and handsome.'

'Did you think I was handsome?'

Angharad put her hand on Barry's arm and looked him squarely in the eyes. 'Yes.'

'Am I handsome now?'

Angharad laughed. 'You're neither handsome nor not handsome. You're just Barry.'

Holding his nerve, Barry held eye contact long enough for

Angharad to notice. 'I think you're still pretty.' It clearly caught her off guard.

'You're a sweetheart. I hope some kind-hearted woman notices that before it's too late.'

'Too late for who?'

'Too late for you. And too late for her.'

The tenderness of the moment was broken by the sight of Reverend Jacob Hill stomping up the pathway towards the bench where Barry and Angharad were perched.

'He looks a bit hot under his dog collar, don't he?' said Angharad. 'I'm going to go in for the second half of the service. How about you?'

'Second half? Bugger!'

Barry checked his watch and froze in panic. The reverend was marching towards him with a major cob on because *he* was supposed to be playing the organ for the service that morning.

'Lovely talking to you, Angharad, I miss our little chats.' And with that Barry was off, waddling down the path that led away from the church, whilst a red-faced vicar – looking more like Benny Hill than Jacob Hill – chased after him waving an arm in the air and shouting the closest thing to obscenities that a man of the cloth can utter on a Sunday morning.

ELEVEN

JULIET RETURNS FROM SUPER-DUPER-MARE

FRESH FROM HER vacation to Weston-super-Mare, Juliet called an emergency meeting with Barry and Romeo for 8.30am ahead of the morning conference with the rest of the comms gang. Going through her emails on Sunday afternoon to catch up on what she had missed, she'd almost choked on her cheese and pickle sarnie when discovering via an email from Bish that Romeo had bared his arse to all at last week's team jamboree. Juliet had been asked to address the issue by various senior managers but wasn't exactly sure what that meant. She was okay managing cats, but didn't really know how to transfer those skills to people, especially ones like Romeo. She knew his personal quirks had got significantly worse since Covid and that he was basically a loose cannon these days, although he did sometimes listen to Barry – which was why she wanted him to join the meeting as chief arbitrator and translator. She despaired that the level of control she now had over her own team was so bad she couldn't even be sure they would turn up to meetings with their clothes on.

She didn't know this morning whether she should play good cop or bad cop, whether to be sympathetic and listen to Romeo's pathetic excuses or line him up immediately with all guns blazing and hit him hard with a peppering of direct questions and wound-inflicting demands. She wasn't very good at playing any sort of cop. She'd been promoted through the LesCargo ranks because her seniors wanted someone *in situ* that they could easily manipulate and dump on. That was essentially her main strength, her ability to take flak.

When she flicked on her Teams screen for the hastily arranged pre-9am watershed meeting she was left staring back at herself for several minutes. She feared neither Barry nor Romeo would turn up at all because it was too early for them. She'd sent them text messages on the Sunday to say she needed to speak to them urgently first thing – and her phone had alerted her to say the messages had been opened and read – but she knew they hated meetings, especially ones before 11am. She wasn't sure what she'd do if they failed to show. She could just about cope with their idleness but she needed them to at least maintain the charade that they respected her, otherwise they were all done for.

Weston seemed a distant memory now. Paddling in a cold, dirty Bristol Channel with her husband Jerry, walking around the helicopter museum hand in hand, drinking lager shandies in the Jill Dando Memorial Garden most afternoons, eating fish and chips and dodging seagulls on the freezing seafront by evening, strolling up and down the pier with the old couples who came in search of flat terrain for their mobility scooters and their arthritic hips, watching the world go by, thinking this is the life, if only it were warmer and they'd come in July.

Barry logged on to the meeting with Juliet at 8.45am and apologised immediately for his lateness, blaming poor wifi connections.

'Good week at the seaside?'

'Fine,' said Juliet with a straight face, clearly in no mood for jokes. 'So tell me, what the heck happened at last week's comms call?'

Barry explained that his update had actually gone quite well in the grand scheme of things, save for Romeo forgetting to put his trousers on, and then also forgetting that he'd forgot to put his trousers on, when getting up to sort his curtains out.

'I'll give him curtains.' Juliet folded her arms abruptly. 'Look, between you and me, Mr Davies is running out of friends and chances. You both need to buck your ideas up, but Romeo especially. He's hardly producing any content at all these days and what he is doing is substandard. People are actually beginning to notice him and his weirdness. Not just me.'

Barry looked sheepish.

'They wouldn't sack him, would they?'

'Possibly.'

'At the very least, I think they'll want both of you back in HQ working three days per week, maybe four.'

The thought of having to return to office life filled Barry with dread. 'Bloody hell, that's a bit drastic.'

'But there's no reason for you to be working from home now.'

'What about Covid? It's not disappeared. It's still lurking in the shadows. Mutating.'

Juliet was ready for this line of defence and had her response fully prepared. 'The people at the top of LesCargo say it's not lurking anywhere anymore. They don't even want people wearing masks in the office. Handshakes and hugs are back in. Germ spreading is officially permitted again.'

'Will we get a say in what happens to us and where we work?' Barry was almost pleading now.

'Sure, there'll be plenty of meetings and consultations and you'll get lots of opportunities to air your views and opinions. It'll be a considered process, involving the full weight of HR.'

'Then what?'

'Then you'll both be back at your old desks, and expected to work like you did in the old days. Eventually, they want everyone back in. But first of all, it'll be those who are deemed least productive. Which deffo includes you two.'

Barry knew it was checkmate. 'Do we have any other options?'

'Yes, one.'

'What's that?'

'The P45 and the exit door.' Juliet unfolded her arms and leant back in her chair with a smug expression on her face.

A dimly lit square popped into view on Barry's screen, entitled Romeo D.

Romeo looked grey and dishevelled with angry little cut marks all over his face, but at least he was fully clothed.

'All right, Juliet, how was Super-Duper-Mare?'

'Nice to see you've got your action slacks on,' said Juliet.

Romeo missed the sarcasm in her voice. 'Thank you. Last week's little incident could've happened to anyone. I was probably too focused on my work, too keen to get cracking, I actually forgot to dress myself properly. It happens sometimes. Well, it does to me.'

Barry tried not to laugh at his pal's ridiculousness but Juliet wasn't amused. Romeo made things fifty times worse by continuing to open his mouth, allowing words to drop out of it.

'I actually feel a bit ropey this morning, boss, I was hemming and hawing about whether to phone in sick or not. I drank a bottle of Knob Creek yesterday; it was on special offer in John John's place so I thought I'd give it a try. I didn't really know what it was but it said bourbon on the bottle. I don't know what bourbon is, except for biscuits, but it definitely did strange things to me.'

'You're bleeding quite a lot,' said Barry, concerned.

Romeo put a hand to his head and touched a congealed patch of skin. 'That bourbon sent me down Knob's Creek, all right. I drank way too much of the stuff and for some reason felt the urge to put my head inside my hamster's cage and imagine I was staring into the eyes of a lion. I fell asleep with my head in the lion's cage. When I woke up, I had all these red bleeding sores all over my face, head and neck from where the little shit had licked and bitten me senselessly, no doubt having discovered a taste for Knob Creek too, either that or my aftershave.'

Juliet sighed. 'Romeo, I give up on you.'

'It's true, I tell you. Kenny Rogers, that's the name of my hamster, was asleep on his back and actually snoring like a lion when I stirred this morning,' said Romeo, contorting his face.

'Romeo, we'll leave this meeting for now because you were so late joining and we've got conference shortly. However, I want to see you in my office tomorrow at 10am, in HQ, in person, not just dressed, but smartly dressed, and by that I also mean groomed and suited. With shoes on. And socks. And a tie. Around your neck, not holding up imaginary trousers. Understand?'

'Yes,' said Romeo.

Barry interjected quickly. 'What about me?'

'I want the first draft of that Douglas McAllister piece in my inbox by end of play today.'

'Okay.'

'See you both in fifteen minutes for conference. And leave all the talking to me this week. I don't actually want to hear a peep from either of you. I just want you to sit there, attentive and upright, looking like you're listening, with your kit on, your cameras on and your audios off.'

Barry responded with a thumbs-up emoji of agreement before logging off.

Romeo did the same, but swapped the giant, throbbing big thumb for a couple of screaming faces, with cheeks puffed in.

After getting through the dreaded conference, Barry lay back on his bed exhausted. He felt he'd been working too hard lately, doing way too much for the LesCargo cause. He resented the fact he now had to finish off the McAllister piece this afternoon instead of moving it on in gradual instalments and having it done by Thursday. There was snooker on the telly this afternoon, Luca Brecel versus Judd Trump, and he fancied watching a couple of hours. He also needed to sort his bets out. He called Romeo.

'What you doing?'

Romeo was breathless. 'Been pacing around, it's all the stress that Juliet's heaping on me.'

'Things are changing.' Barry's voice was hushed. 'We're going to find ourselves back in the office before too long, Juliet said as much.'

Romeo disappeared out of view as he continued his pacing. 'We need another pandemic,' he shouted.

'I reckon Juliet had a terrible holiday and it's made her crabby. I blame her bloke, Jerry. He don't treat her right,' said Barry.

'I wouldn't want her life.' Romeo dived back on his seat like he was playing musical chairs.

'No, nor her job.'

'Looking after the likes of us.'

'We're pretty lazy sometimes, aren't we?'

'We're quiet quitters.'

'We've moved on from that, I reckon.'

'Noisy quitters.' Romeo sprang from his seat to start pacing once more.

'Do you know the best thing in my life right now?' Barry listened for Romeo's heavy breathing as confirmation he was still there.

'Chico?'

'No,' said Barry.

'Chicken madras and cumin rice with a Bombay potato side?'

'No, your sister, Angharad. I met her in the graveyard yesterday and we talked a lot. She stirred up old feelings in me.'

'Oh that's not good.' Romeo sat back down; his attention grabbed.

'I might ask her out,' said Barry.

'Please don't do that.' Romeo put both hands on his head and tugged at his own hair, a surefire sign his anxiety was rising.

'Do you think she'd go out on a date with me?' said Barry.

'No, she's still married. Her and Greg might patch things up.'

'Yeah, forgot about him.'

Romeo examined a lump of hair in his left hand. 'I got doctors tomorrow, will you come with me?'

'So have I,' said Barry. 'What's wrong with you?'

'It's my pacing. I'm doing it a lot more lately, finding it harder to control, can't stop myself cos I love it too much – I'm losing hours of my life. Weeks even. Mum's worried. What about you?'

'Just feel I'm losing my pep.'

'That's Angharad's doing.'

Barry nodded. 'Could be.'

TWELVE
WATCH OUT FOR BRONSON, HE'S A
WRONG 'UN

ROMEO WAS A DREAMER, a maladaptive one, he did it for several hours a day, losing himself in a heightened state of make-believe that meant he could not control real-life functionality. Two hours of daydreaming – rushing frenetically around the room like an over-gassed balloon released to bounce off anything in its path – felt like ten minutes to him.

Doctor Humphreys said it was probably down to an anxiety disorder. Or ADHD. Or autism. Or something else on the spectrum that people in his profession liked to discuss but didn't really know much about. Being a GP used to be so much easier: prescribe some aspirin or paracetamol, send people to the hospital, lance a few boils, syringe clogged ears, refer the properly sick to specialists, check blood pressure and heart rates, give the odd injection or two, tell people to rest. Nowadays, most came to him wanting to talk about their mental problems and how depressed they were feeling, but he'd never really covered that stuff at medical school in his day. He seriously wanted to tell some of his patients to 'man up' but knew it was wrong and if he ever did so, he'd probably be cancelled and stripped of his house and pension.

Humphreys had never heard of maladaptive daydreaming until the day Romeo rocked into his surgery, with Barry holding on for dear life, trying to slow him down as if he were a wild pony. The doctor googled the symptoms there and then and hey presto. A professional diagnosis, all the way to rural South Wales from Wikipedia.

Romeo's daydreams were intense, detailed and complex. And his daydreaming had become the most important thing in his life. He was addicted to doing it, it was compulsive. As he got older he did it more and more and now it often took over, ruling the roost above eating, sleeping and working. He looked a proper sight, a grown man chanting as he hurled himself into concrete walls, pulling crazy facial expressions, making himself laugh, scream, shout or cry. Afterwards, he'd be covered in bruises and wouldn't realise why bits of him hurt.

Every day, Romeo travelled to a fictional planet called Feelgood where he hung out with his imaginary best friend, a guitarist called Wilko. He'd just crawl inside his own head and escape into the fantasies that consumed him. He'd talk to Wilko, argue with him, fight with him occasionally, swear at him, tease him, defend him. He could snap out of the daydream at a second's notice if he had to, which meant his actions were voluntary and he wasn't schizophrenic. He also knew the differences between planet Earth and planet Feelgood. Which one was real and which one wasn't. Romeo and Wilko would live the same day over and over, like it was *Groundhog Day*. Snippets of reality – a line from a song or a movie or maybe a word from someone around him – could send Romeo running off to Feelgood in an instant. He preferred to go there alone, in isolation, behind closed doors, but if the urge was too strong he'd quit caring about who might see him doing his thing.

Wilko's arch-nemesis – and the villain of Feelgood – was Mr Bronson, who kept turning up at places unannounced, stealing jobs, money, women, gigs, parking spaces, the last bottle of semi-skimmed milk in the supermarket, hotel bookings, anything really... if it could be stolen, Bronson was your man.

'In Feelgood, you don't trust Bronson, not ever, he's a total wrong 'un,' said Romeo to Doctor Humphreys. 'I know because I've seen things no one else has seen.'

'Where exactly?' asked the doctor, pencil poised on paper to write down Romeo's every word.

'The wig shop. He likes a mean syrup,' said Romeo.

The doctor pressed down too hard on the paper, broke his pencil and sighed.

'Told yer,' said Romeo, with a knowing look.

And off went Romeo like a firecracker, chattering, muttering, shouting, down the corridor, as Barry smiled politely at Doctor Humphreys and asked him what he thought Wales's chances were against Scotland at Murrayfield this coming Saturday in the final round of the Six Nations.

The doctor never heard a word because he was too busy working out how many days he had left before he could retire to his allotment, the golf course and being nagged to either death or dementia by the formidable Mrs Humphreys.

———

Two hours later, Barry was back in Owain Humphreys' surgery for an appointment of his own. For a couple of weeks, he'd been having palpitations and feeling agitated for no real reason. He lacked energy – more so than usual – and his skin seemed slightly discoloured, like he'd had a half-hour session down at Jerry Wilson's Tantastic Day salon.

'You like a drink don't you, Barry? I've seen you going hammer and tongs at it in the clubhouse,' said the doctor.

'Yes, I'm sociable,' replied Barry.

'In an average week, how many units would you say you consume?'

Barry deliberated. 'What's a unit?'

Doctor Humphreys checked the chart on the wall in front of him. However, he'd had this conversation so many times with so many different people he knew the information off by heart. 'Well, a single shot of spirits is one unit. A low strength pint of beer, cider or lager is two units – we're talking under 4 per cent strength. A can of stronger beer over 5.2 per cent would be about the same, two units. A pint of strong beer or cider, call it three units.'

'What about wine?' Barry was playing for time.

The doctor glanced at his chart again. 'A small glass of red, rosé or white, about 1.5 units. A standard glass is nearer two units. A large glass, I'd say three units.'

'Hmm, complicated, ain't it? What about a bottle of wine?' asked Barry.

'Around nine units.'

'And a bottle of whisky?'

'That would be thirty units.'

There was an uneasy silence before Barry broke it. 'So what was the question again?'

'Well, in a typical week, how many units of alcohol would you say you consume?'

'Approximately?'

'Yes, approximately,' answered the doctor, checking his watch.

Barry thought long and hard. He was tempted to go for the calculator on his phone but resisted it in case it condemned him. Instead, he went back through the past week in his mind, rounding up numbers and talking to himself via his encouraging internal monologue.

Right, Barry lad, last Tuesday evening you had a few in The

Dragon with Romeo, to console him after Foxy's ice-cream meltdown. Ten pints of piss-weak Midweek Gold cider. Call it twenty units. Wednesday, half a dozen after training and a sherry or two to pep me up beforehand. How much is sherry? It ain't a spirit, more like a shandy. Say fourteen all in. Thursday was a quiet night in. Oh no, I had a bottle of Malbec in me room watching The Apprentice. *Friday, I was in The Dragon with Uncle Derek. About eight pints of beer and half a dozen whiskies. Few shots too but we won't count them. Glorified pop. How many's that? I can't do this in my head. Saturday night I went fairly heavy – must have had sixteen Stellas. I've no idea really, I can barely remember getting home, let alone anything else.*

Barry could feel Humphreys' stare piercing through his vital organs. Judging him. Examining his liver through skin and bone. From nowhere, Barry plucked a random figure out of thin air and blurted it out.

'Eighty-five units, doc. Give or take.'

The doctor's eyes were now out on stalks.

'Eight-five units? In one week?'

Barry rechecked his workings quickly, wondering if he had got it madly wrong. In truth, he reckoned the figure to be somewhere nearer to 120 but had knocked a few off in order to stay on the safe side of the doctor's reckoning.

'Yep, about eighty-five. Like I said, give or take a few.'

'Barry, you're killing yourself!' said the doctor.

'I don't feel like I am. I'm just feeling a bit under the weather. I could do with a little pick-me-up, a little tonic.'

'You could do with a load more tonic than that,' said Humphreys, trying to stay professional. 'You won't see fifty if you keep drinking like that. You'll follow your old man into an early grave.'

Barry took exception to this comparison and couldn't hold back.

'My old man didn't die from drinking. He drove a lorry the wrong way down the M4. Stone-cold sober he was!'

'What you're doing to yourself is equally reckless,' said Humphreys. 'You are careering the wrong way down the M4 metaphorically speaking. It's an accident waiting to happen and it won't be pretty.'

'So what's normal?' asked Barry. 'In units.'

'About fourteen,' responded the doctor.

'Okay, that's about seven pints, isn't it? I can keep to that of a night, I reckon.'

The doctor paused, his brain quickly assessing whether he was dealing with a joker, a madman or a buffoon.

'The recommendation is that you drink no more than fourteen units per week. That's seven pints a week.'

Now it was Barry's turn to stare back incredulously and assess if the shadowy, gaunt Humphreys was joker, madman or buffoon.

'Doc, even my old ma, who goes around telling everyone she's teetotal, drinks more than that a week in communion wine.'

'Then your mother also needs to curb her intake. Barry, it pains me to say this, but you are an alcoholic. And a chronic one. That's why you're not feeling well. It's also why your skin is slightly jaundiced, you can't always remember things, you're struggling with social anxieties and your work is, I suspect, less efficient than it used to be.'

'My work is every bit as inefficient as it always has been,' said Barry indignantly.

'You need to stop drinking and find new things in your life to excite you,' said Humphreys. 'But I appreciate you will probably need a lot of help and support in order for this to happen. Have you tried non-alcoholic beers? There are some very good ones on the market nowadays. I want you to keep an alcohol diary for the next couple of weeks, accurately writing down everything you consume. Be honest, because ultimately, the only person you will be cheating is yourself. I'd also like to get some blood tests done to see how bad things really are. Then we'll reassess and look at how best you can detoxify. Hopefully, you'll be able to do it at home, without too much medication. You might need a course of cognitive behavioural therapy, and probably some chlordiazepoxide.'

'Doc, I'll self-moderate a bit better. I'll be more responsible and just drink at weekends,' said Barry. 'Seven pints max on Friday and Saturday nights, like you said. I don't need any of your therapy or fake Guinness on prescription. I'm not an alcy. I've just been a bit irresponsible lately. A bit lazy. Last week was a tough week – it wasn't typical. Half of what I drank I didn't even want, but I couldn't be bothered to say no to people. But today has been a wake-up call. I'll change my ways. I will learn to "just say no" like good old Zammo and the *Grange Hill* gang used to tell us to when we were kids. I will become a new improved, much less sociable me. I promise. Scout's honour.'

'It's not just the drink that concerns me, let's see how much you weigh – pop yourself on the scales, will you?'

Barry, now sweating profusely and feeling like his brain was going to explode out of the top of his skull, leapt to his feet and made for the door. He was desperate to get away from Humphreys' doom and gloom soothsaying as fast as he possibly could and wasn't going to hang around to be told he was morbidly obese and had to give up chips, pies, pasties, kebabs and curries as well as the grog. He had planned to get his prostate checked by Humphreys – having received a letter about it in the post recently – but there was no way he would cope with that sour-faced puritan shoving his rubber-gloved finger up his boozy arse. Not now, not yet, perhaps not ever.

He'd make an appointment to see Doctor Melanie Epstein

for his backstairs MOT – a sixty-something, semi-retired grandmother and a regular in the church choir. Barry knew she was partial to a drop of Pinot Grigio because he'd seen her in action. And two of her sons used to play rugby and were absolute pissheads. She would understand him better and have a softer touch downstairs. She'd be less judgemental and wouldn't resort to Wikipedia for her medical guidance. A proper doctor, was Melanie, someone from the real world. A Caeau Anghofiedig girl. Born and bred.

THIRTEEN
GENERATION ME, ME, ME

BARRY LAY on his bed as the clock struck ten, wearing just a pair of yesterday's Superman pants. He opened his legs into a Y shape and tried unsuccessfully to touch both sides of his own mattress with outstretched heels. Too weary to lift his head off the pillow he put out a hairy hand into a giant porcelain bowl on the bedside table, stuffed a flabby paw inside and tossed large cheesy balls into his open mouth, catching and gorging on some, whilst watching others bounce away into the sheets and floor around him. Some escaped off his pasty white man-boobs and his oversized belly to leave crumbly orange blemishes on his skin. He smelled of cheese.

He sat up slightly and caught a reflection of himself in his mirror. His overwhelming reaction was one of self-loathing. He patted his big stomach, muttered, 'All bought and paid for' and tried pushing it back inside himself so it disappeared, but it was going nowhere. It had nowhere to go to. He let out an enormous bellowing, echoing fart – which took him straight back to the industrious past of his father and those stinking underground corridors with their whirring, whisking engines that rumbled like ghost trains. From the age of fourteen Barry White Senior worked the Anghofiedig pits, digging for coal. Hard, physical graft, measured in minutes, pounds and tons. Dirty work. Thirsty work. The coal hadn't changed and the pints Barry White Senior and his fellow workers drank through teatime into early evening were hard earned.

Barry could whisk and whirr farts all he liked in his bedroom-cum-office. There was no one to hear him or judge him. No one to tell him to get his act together and stop wasting his and everyone else's time. It was his life, his time, his motion. No one else depended today on the sweats of any of his labours. The world of work had certainly changed for his generation. The Millennials. Generation Y. Generation Me, Me, Me. He was actually a year out on most reckonings to be a true child of Gen Y – having been born in 1980 rather than 81 – but what the heck, he fitted the mould perfectly. He was unmarried, in his forties, doubted his own fertility, never had sex with anyone bar himself and spent too many hours staring into screens and eating cheesy balls. Alone.

His ancestors fought and killed Germans so he could pass his days in such a blissful haze. Was he grateful? Not really. He wasn't really grateful for anything.

He thought about what the doc had said to him yesterday. And Juliet before that. And Angharad on Sunday. McQueen. Uncle Derek. Were they all wrong about him? He wanted to change. To be better. A different shape, inside and out. He didn't want to be known as a good drinker anymore. Nor a bad gambler. He wanted to be more focused about meaningful stuff. To feel inspired. There were even times when he wanted to work harder and be properly creative. To help others. Be less selfish. But it was all too big a project to change. He didn't know how to get from where he was to where he wanted to be. And Anghofiedig wouldn't let him anyway. He was already defined in the cool, black bitten seams of this place. Anghofiedig and all its people had his card clearly marked for life. He was Barry White Junior, the son of Barry White Senior. Bit of a waster. Feckless. Harmless enough though.

So he stayed in his crusty Superman pants that spoke nothing of superheroes, finished off the cheesy balls, put his Teams activity setting to 'red for busy' and had a two-hour kip.

At rugby training that night, McQueen steered well clear of Barry – having been warned off by both Uncle Derek and Jonah.

Barry didn't exactly train, but he enjoyed his Wednesday night socials out on the pitch more than the actual rugby. If it was cold he could layer up. When everyone else ran laps around the pitch, he performed little stretches on the touchline and cajoled the others to 'keep going' as they passed by him. In the contact stuff, most went easy on him. Barry didn't mind knocking over a few static tackle bags, they weren't bony and didn't hit back. He might do a couple of ten-yard sprints to get his blood pumping. The odd press-up or two. A few attempts at touching his toes. Some reach for the sky à la S Club 7.

Tonight's session was extra special because a new player turned up to try out for the team. James was mid-twenties, handsome, well-groomed and English. He was also posh, extremely so by South Walian standards. He walked about at the start of the session introducing himself to all and sundry with a firm handshake and a plummy, 'Lovely to meet you, I'm James, or Jamie, what do the chaps around here call you?'

Most of the regulars were wary of him because he wore a Harlequins training top and aftershave. New players seldom stayed long so there was no point forming attachments. However, Barry took James under his wing and did his best to make him feel at home, showing him around the clubhouse and giving him the lowdown on the club's history and his own family's part in it, as well as providing colourful pen portraits of every potential teammate, their characteristics and qualities, both on and off the pitch. Barry discovered that James had just moved into the area to work as a senior operations executive for LesCargo.

'What position do you play?' said James.

'Tight-head prop,' replied Barry. 'You?'

'Outside centre is my best position but I understand the skipper plays there so I'm happy to fit in where needed. I'm pretty versatile and I've played most positions to a decent standard. Right now, I'm just looking for a sociable blowout on a Saturday afternoon while I find my feet in Anghofiedig. You get my drift?'

Barry's heart was singing 'Sosban Fach' at full volume and he couldn't stop grinning from ear to ear when he saw his new buddy from London run absolute rings around McQueen without even breaking a sweat in a little six-a-side practice match. Best of all was when McQueen tried to outrun him and James floored him with a shuddering, perfectly-timed, thunderous tackle that left the captain winded and properly gasping for breath for a good forty-five seconds.

'I think we've found ourselves a little Jonathan Davies,' said a beaming Uncle Derek in the bar afterwards.

McQueen swished his pint around as if he was reading fortunes. 'Let's wait and see what he does on Saturday in a real match.'

Barry boldly poked the bear. 'Don't worry, Stephen, I reckon you'll still make the starting fifteen for Saturday but you might have to come and join us real men in the pack.'

Ordinarily, saying such words to McQueen would have

been construed as a death wish, but Barry felt safe with James tucked in behind his right shoulder.

'Hope those ribs aren't too sore, skipper, I thought I held back quite a bit on that one,' said James. 'Let me buy you a beer, Stevie, to show there's no hard feelings.'

McQueen glowered. He didn't usually tolerate anyone calling him Stevie but on this occasion, he bit his lip. He'd bitten more lips today than Romeo's hamster, Kenny Rogers.

'Right, who else would like a drink?' shouted James, across the entire bar. 'I'm in the chair for this round, have whatever you fancy, it's my shout.'

'The Milkybars are on him,' said Barry, rather pathetically, in a voice that sounded too squeaky and too excitable to be his own.

FOURTEEN
IT'S NOT FAIR

REVEREND HILL KNOCKED on the door around 11am and caught Barry eating a family-sized hot cheese and bacon quiche straight from the silver tray. It was no way to answer the door.

'Ah, the elusive Mr White, may I come in?'

Reverend Hill was not your typical man of the cloth. He was young for a parish vicar, early thirties, rode a fast motorcycle, smelt of patchouli oil, went to a lot of Christian heavy metal music festivals and bristled with an inner anger that you could see he was battling to contain. He didn't exude peace and love. Barry was a little scared of him.

'Ah, vicar, I've been meaning to catch up with you,' said Barry.

'Really? The last time I saw you, you were actually running away from me and I was chasing you,' said Reverend Hill.

'I'm sorry about that. I got talking to Angharad and the time ran away from me, then I ran away from you without really knowing why. I still don't know why I did that. It was stupid.'

'Yes it was,' said Reverend Hill. 'Barry, I'll cut to the chase, I get the impression that you play the organ in church from a sense of duty, not to me or even to God, but to your mother. Is that correct?'

It was spot on, but Barry stayed silent.

'You never come to any of our evening music practices. In fact, your commitment to the church has waned considerably of late. Is that a fair thing for me to say?'

'Not sure,' said Barry.

'Do you pray? I mean, in your own time?' said Reverend Hill.

'I am actually supposed to be working right now,' said Barry, hoping the reverend would take the hint, shut up and go away.

'This is important,' said Reverend Hill, refusing to leave him alone.

Barry did pray occasionally and he did believe in God, but he'd always stopped short of making the big leaps of faith that Reverend Hill – and Ma – wanted him to make.

Reverend Hill continued to push him hard on all things theological, and Barry figured his annoying dog-collared cold caller wanted to make him squirm for leaving him in the lurch on Sunday.

In the background, Ma had left *Bargain Hunt* on the telly and it was irritating Barry massively. He understood why God might create forests and mountains and volcanoes and sunsets but *Bargain Hunt*? An appalling woman in a blue fleece was bouncing up and down in excitement because she'd just sold a broken antique toilet seat for a tenner. She'd paid £25 for it. Barry wasn't surprised she'd made a loss because there were only a few old pensioners in the auction house and they were buying diddly-squat.

'Why do you believe in Jesus?' said Reverend Hill.

In a more considered moment, Barry might have mentioned his assessment that chance could not have made a universe that was underpinned by mathematical laws, with the earth sitting just the right distance from the sun to sustain life, with just the right balance of heavy elements and organic molecules. Or the miraculous fact that mathematical, physical and human conscious worlds interacted far too seamlessly to be random, with atoms and molecules able to create something that wasn't physical, that only existed in his head. Like the thought that Jacob 'Benny' Hill was not cut out for small-time parish life. Also, he regarded the big bang theory as fanciful horseshit, but he appreciated a lot of very clever people whom he respected greatly, including the likes of Gervais, Fry and Radcliffe, preferred the notion of an accidental creation to a divine one.

He might have confided to Reverend Hill that he felt his conscience judged him and everything he did every minute of every day. Or that doing good made him feel good, even when it was to his own detriment, giving him a pat on the heart from deep down inside to silence the bad voice in his internal dialogues. He could have told Reverend Hill that he thought God was real because there were 400 billion stars and 100 billion planets in the galaxy and no one had ever found a single signal of other life. And then there was DNA, his own personal instruction book with some three billion letters. How the hell could Mother Nature have written that for herself from absolutely nothing?

Barry actually said none of this. Instead he answered, 'Look, rev, that bloody woman in blue is doing my head in and I can't concentrate on anything you're saying right now. She's acting like she's Alan Sugar cos she just bought an ugly china cat for £4.75 and sold it for a fiver. *Bargain Hunt* does my head in. It's Ma's fault, why would she go out and leave this on? She's not been herself lately, I don't know what's up with her. Did you hear she got arrested for armed robbery last weekend?'

Reverend Hill sighed heavily and looked defeated. Saving

souls in Anghofiedig on a drizzly Thursday morning was not a job for those of timid faith.

'Dotty can't make it this week so can I rely on you to play organ for us this Sunday? Will you be punctual so we can run through the hymns beforehand? I really need you to be there by 9.30 at the latest,' said Reverend Hill.

'Count me in,' said Barry, staring right past Reverend Hill's gaze, transfixed by the TV. Unbelievably, the annoying lady in blue was now punching her husband's arm quite intensely because the blue team had lost to the reds by the princely sum of forty-five pence.

———

Romeo called Barry up on Teams right on lunchtime, which was unusual.

'Barry, I've got a cracking idea for a game show. I've spent most of the morning working on it.'

'What's it called?' said Barry.

'*It's Not Fair*,' said Romeo. 'Basically, you have a panel of real clever bastards on one side, you know, like The Beast off *The Chase* and Kevin from *Eggheads* – not Judith the *Millionaire* winner though, cos she knows squit about too many things. And on the other side you have a bunch of dickheads who know nothing about anything, and I mean dickheads, we're talking people like McQueen and Jonah here.'

'Sounds like a mismatch to me,' said Barry.

'Ah, but that's the beauty of it. Cos you ask the clever bastards real hard questions and the dickheads real easy ones. So it's a fair contest, see? I've been working on some questions this morning. Want to play?'

'Sure,' said Barry.

'Clever bastard or dickhead?'

'What do you think?'

'I reckon clever bastard. Okay, here goes, to get you up and running, who replaced Dicky Harris as Dumbledore in the Harry Potter films?' said Romeo.

'Er, that would be Michael Gambon,' said Barry.

'Corrrectamundu,' said an impressed Romeo. 'See, I said you were a clever bastard. What type of food is pumpernickel?'

'Pumpernickel? Never heard of it. Is it some sort of cabbage?' said Barry.

'Nah, it's bread.'

'That's too hard. This quiz ain't fair.'

'Ha, you said it – cue pandemonium,' said Romeo, and with that he ran around his room making pretend whooshing sounds, shouting, 'Gunge the clever bastard,' and chanting, 'It's not fair, it's not fair,' over and over again.

Barry waited for him to calm down and return to the screen.

'Anyone who says the words "it's not fair" gets plastered with all kinds of gunk for whingeing,' said Romeo. 'Adds extra spice to the game, don't you think?'

Barry nodded in agreement but said nothing.

'Let's give you a few dickhead questions,' said Romeo. 'Who is the current president of the USA?'

'Too easy. Biden.'

'A lot of dickheads would say Trump or Obama and some would even go Bush, Carter or Tony Blair. Blimey, some might even go Lionel Blair,' said Romeo.

On and on Romeo went.

'What is the capital of Wales? In which continent is Australia? What nationality was Bill Shakespeare? Who sang the Christmas hit 'Fairytale of New York'?'

'All too easy,' said Barry.

'Not for the people I'm having on the show, I promise you,' said Romeo. 'On *Tipping Point*, Ben Shephard asked someone what day Christmas Day fell on and they said Wednesday. And someone on *Pointless* answered JR when asked who shot Lee Harvey Oswald in Dallas.'

'Really?' said Barry.

'Straight up. They'll be racking their brains for the answers and that's the beauty of it, see, the clever bastards will sit there all smug and knowing, looking down their noses at the oppo and so will we. Good, eh?'

'Where did you get this idea from? It seems a bit cruel and not very PC to me,' said Barry.

'Watching you play rugby.'

'Huh?'

'Yeah, you were getting stuffed in the scrums real bad by someone who was actually half decent, whilst you didn't have a clue what you were doing as normal. Yet there you were, on the same rugby field together, doing your own things, having a competition of sorts.'

'Glad I could be of some assistance,' said Barry.

'And you kept saying it's not fair to the referee as well,' said Romeo.

'Then I want half the money if anyone buys the rights.'

'Naturally,' said Romeo.

'Who you got hosting this little caper, not Walsh I hope?'

'No way, nor Armstrong, nor Osman and definitely not any of the Kemps,' said Romeo. 'I was thinking Gervais if he was interested.'

'Interesting choice,' said Barry.

Romeo beamed and logged off without warning.

FIFTEEN

GORGING BROCCOLI FOR ZERO FOLLOWERS

ROMEO'S IN-PERSON meeting with Juliet never happened. He failed to turn up, so Juliet consulted with Bish and they decided to escalate things. Romeo's behaviour was inappropriate at best. Over the years, Juliet had tried reasoning with him, pleading with him, even bribing him, but none of it worked. She didn't overly care about what he got up to, but she was concerned that the bigwigs in the senior offices on the fourth and fifth floors were now noticing what he was doing, or rather, not doing, and that the buck would stop with her as his line manager. She had to protect herself. Everyone was expendable and she'd had her own run-ins with HR and the disciplinary bods over some of her old-fashioned phrases and colourful ways of speaking, which she blamed on her upbringing across the border in the Dean. She wasn't sure what words she was allowed to use to describe Romeo's antics nowadays so preferred not to use any. She needed her job if she was going to keep on living the high life with Jerry and enjoying those winter breaks to Weston and Anglesey plus summer ones to Tenby and Paignton.

Bish said the company would call Romeo's behaviour

insubordination because he consistently refused to do what was asked of him, namely work. He said he wasn't sure what category 'baring your arse in a comms meeting' came under but was confident it qualified as gross misconduct. It was certainly misconduct. And gross. Bish said he would double-check with HR just to be on the safe side.

Because trying to resolve things informally – and amicably – hadn't worked, Bish instructed Juliet to itemise all of Romeo's misdemeanours in writing. Then the company would call a disciplinary hearing. Bish told Juliet it was important she did her best to look after Romeo's well-being during the process as it was likely to stress him out and make his mental and emotional issues worse. She had no idea what that meant or what she was supposed to do, but she nodded her head in agreement anyway. There was a look of horror on Bish's face when Juliet referred to Romeo in their discussions as 'the defendant'.

Romeo was past caring about LesCargo. He welcomed the income that a regular day job provided him, but everything else about being an employee got in the way of his daily trips to Feelgood and hanging out with Wilko, or his more earthly hangouts in pubs with Barry. Angharad said she would support her brother in any hearings with the company and reckoned that if he played his cards right, he might be able to apologise to them, get a course of paid treatment or therapy and just carry on. She told Romeo to get something in writing from Doc Humphreys confirming that he had anxiety issues, ADHD, autism, or maybe all three. She reckoned there was a counter claim to be made because her brother's maladaptive daydreaming had definitely got a whole load worse during Covid and the lockdowns. She said LesCargo had not looked after him responsibly enough during this period so his negative traits were a by-product of their failings. She was good at all this stuff; she'd had enough practice on account of being married to Greg for so long. She reckoned Romeo could spin things out for a while, until everyone got fed up and life went back to normal. Or, in her brother's case, whatever form of normal was deemed just about acceptable in the crazy world of logistics.

Barry felt some sympathy for his buddy but also recognised that his problems took the heat off him. He could kick back, safe in the knowledge that Juliet was far too incompetent to do simultaneous battle with both of the lazy bastards in her sub-team. Besides, Barry knew how to play the game better than Romeo and could usually stay on the right side of her lines. He knew how to produce just enough work at just the right times. He'd delivered his Douglas McAllister piece before the cut-off so that would earn him enough Brownie points to see him through to summer. Minimum effort for maximum effect. The LesCargo way.

Mid-afternoon, Barry revelled in a little cheeky Chico time, happily watching his favourite gorilla munch his way through a small box of fruit and veg. As one large primate to another, Barry was proud to share some of the physical characteristics of one of nature's finest specimens. He watched Chico open a banana with a little nip on the side to rip the skin apart before sucking and scooping out all of the fruit in a single sideways swallow. It would be impossible to invent a machine that could do the job with such precision. Chico repeated the feat four times before moving on to several giant broccolis.

Something inside Barry stirred and he strode downstairs to the fridge to raid his ma's vegetable drawer. He carried two large broccolis back to his room and lay on his bed, restarting the video. He watched Chico confidently and effortlessly tear a strip of broccoli off with his large right hand and place it into the side of his mouth. Chico chomped down five or six times with an open mouth, spraying pieces everywhere, before it was gone. The gorilla worked himself up into a frenzy, devouring larger pieces of broccoli each time, the chomping getting noisier. Barry began to emulate his hero, imagining that he too was a world-renowned silverback with more than 600,000 followers across every continent on TikTok. Barry shoved large lumps of broccoli into his gob and worked his jaw ferociously from front to back and side to side. He felt the green stems smear across his face and drop into his chest and bed but didn't care a jot. He was an animal, a wild thing, his carpet was his jungle floor, he spat out the bits that didn't taste so good and loudly savoured the parts that did. He contemplated the madness of a world where a leading global logistics company would pay him £14 an hour to eat last week's broccoli with a complete disregard for good manners and his own dignity.

Unlike Romeo, the majority of Barry's eccentricities usually went undetected. Sure, in ten minutes' time Ma would walk into his room unannounced and uninvited with a cup of tea to find her son gorging himself on a bed of broccoli, with his spittle all over his cheeks, crunching through the stems, looking slightly demented with his eyes glazed over, physically in the room but somewhat out of body. She'd politely ask him what he was doing and he would say 'snacking' – but she would see the video of Chico playing on his laptop by the side of his bed, and she would know some of the things that were dancing around his head. Barry reasoned she would say nothing to no one but she would know. And surely she would judge him too?

My forty-four-year-old son is wasting his life in a cage of his own making.

My forty-four-year-old son is actually pretending to be a gorilla.

My forty-four-year-old son is finally eating something healthy. I'll pop into John John's later and pick him up a few more broccolis, some peaches, two or three cabbages and a bunch of the finest, yellowest bananas the store has to offer.

SIXTEEN
THE WORLD MAKES NO SENSE

£82,466.98.

In the online betting account of Mr B White, Esquire.

Barry re-read the emailed message from Paddy Power himself, congratulating him on his winning bet. Paddy was joking around and seemingly excited for him but he was a bookie; deep down he'd surely be pissed off and want to get it all back as quickly as possible?

It was a Saturday. Match day. Best day of the week, but Barry never made it to rugby. Today, his world changed completely. It threw him a pass that he didn't know what to do with. He caught the ball and the space in front of him to the try-line completely opened up with no defenders close enough to stop him. He just had to run for the line and dot the ball down. It was all in his hands for once. It was a strange feeling. He had thought about this moment all his life but now it was here he didn't know what to do. He wasn't sure how to be a winner. A voice in his head – either one of his own or the gruff, rasping bark of Barry White Senior – was still throwing doubt into the mix.

You can't make it to the line on your own, you'll screw it up somehow, I know you will. You'll drop the ball or trip over your own massive feet or get a stitch that will sink you to your knees and the opportunity will be gone forever. Maybe you'll just freeze and not move. A statue. Going nowhere. Like your life. You know what happens, don't you? You know who you are and what you are, don't you? You understand how this all plays out from here, don't you?

Barry had been dozing in bed when his phone bleeped to tell him that the Hawke's Bay Hawks had defeated Steelformers Taranaki Airs in what turned out to be a basketball match in New Zealand. The odds were lousy, just short of even money, but it didn't matter. Barry had no idea why he'd thrown the Hawks into a bet he couldn't even remember placing. A ridiculous £20 accumulator apparently put on at 2am several months ago, probably between coming home from the club half cut and falling asleep in a bowl of Frosties, where he was saved from drowning in milk by Ma, who always liked to stay awake and listen out for her boy coming in. She couldn't rest until she knew he was home and back in his bed and PJs.

Twenty quid of hard-earned pension money, either belonging to Uncle Derek or Aunty Ruth, he couldn't be sure which, was the catalyst for all this. He would pop to theirs tomorrow and pay back everything he owed them with interest aplenty, £800 for his uncle and £500 for his aunt. He would give them double at least. Maybe treble. He'd also give Romeo a few grand to pay off Foxy's vet bills plus have a bit for himself. He'd speak to Angharad and see what she needed to clear this month's mounting bills. He might even offer Juliet a bit towards her next holiday. And then there was Ma. She mentioned yesterday that the washing machine was on the blink and she was having to do things by hand. And the grill on the cooker had packed up. She needed some new clothes. She didn't say as much or ever complain, but Barry had noticed the patched-up bits in her cardigan sleeves and the small holes in her shoes. He would sort her out. He would be a proper son for once. He'd give her five grand and tell her to do whatever she wanted with it. He would happily give her more but he didn't want the hassle of having to provide bigger explanations. He could pass £5k off as a sizeable LesCargo bonus for the success of his interview with Inverness celebrity Douglas McAllister.

In the blink of a sleepy eye Barry had spent fourteen or fifteen grand as easily as that. Throw in another £3,000 to pay off his various debts and that left him with a cool £64k or so to spend or save as he wished. He picked up his phone and looked at the balance on his Paddy Power account once again.

A mighty seven-fold accumulator lay behind this life-changing moment, an accumulator full of all things bright and beautiful, all things weird and wonderful, and every single one had come up smelling of roses. You little beauty.

Rugby: Wales to beat England, odds 5–1.

Snooker: Mark Williams to become world champion again, 10–1.

Eurovision: Tom Jones to win outright for the UK, 20–1.

Football: Neil Warnock to become the new manager of Real Madrid, 33–1.

TV: Archbishop of Canterbury Justin Welby to win *I'm a Celebrity... Get Me Out of Here!* 6–1.

Politics: Boris Johnson to return as leader of the Conservatives, 13–2.

New Zealand Basketball: Hawke's Bay Hawks to defeat Steelformers Taranaki Airs on March 16, odds 4–6.

Reflecting on his triumph, Barry couldn't believe he'd staked real money on such random happenings. And the basketball? He must have accidentally hit a button, there could be no other explanation. Maybe he'd accidentally smacked on seven buttons?

There was so much to think about. However, one thing he decided upon fairly quickly was that he wouldn't tell a soul about his winnings. He didn't want his life or his friendships to change. He didn't want people telling him to move out of Ma's and buy a flat of his own, or learn to drive and splash out on a fast sports car that he didn't even fit in. He didn't want gold-diggers coming onto him in The Dragon like he was Hugh Hefner just because they knew he had a few quid in his pocket to pay for their expensive curries and Jägerbombs.

His biggest problem would be thinking up believable reasons for giving those close to him big wads of cash in crisp notes. He'd worked out what to tell Ma and was confident she'd keep counsel. Romeo was easy too, he already went around telling anyone who would listen that his best pal Barry was a rich bastard, on account of how little board he gave Ma. Uncle Derek was shrewd, he wouldn't gossip but he could detect bullshit from a mile away. Barry reasoned he'd tell him the truth and ask him not to say anything to anyone. Except he'd tell him he'd won £20k not £82k. Derek would also take care of any explanations to Aunty Ruth. That left Angharad, again reliable as she wouldn't want people knowing she'd accepted charity handouts from him. She cared about her public image, which is probably why they'd never dated.

Barry decided to take Juliet out of the equation and give her zilch. He must have been half asleep when he'd contemplated donating to her holiday fund. If she could afford four weekly excursions per year, she didn't need any extra assistance from him.

A few more clicks on his phone and Barry had transferred all of the money from his Paddy Power account to his Lloyds Bank current account. He was officially rich. Loaded by Anghofiedig standards.

Everything had changed. And yet everything seemed exactly the same.

———

The rest of the day passed by in a blur. Come early evening, Barry decided to go down the rugby club because he was desperate on two fronts: to find out how Anghofiedig had got on against All Greens fourth XV and to load himself up with a skinful of ale. Greens won the game 54–30, but it was a cracking result for Anghofiedig and a cracking game by all accounts. Standing on a chair, downing the giant glass shoe of beer for player of the match, was new boy James who scored six tries on debut and single-handedly stopped Greens scoring ten more.

'You should come and play for us, you'd get in our firsts,' implored the Greens' coach. 'They'd pay you. Reckon you'd get a decent contract.'

James was having none of it. 'Awfully kind of you but I've got a good job and don't need more money to play rugby. I'm old-school, a bit of a Corinthian if you like. I just play for fun.'

His new teammates, including Uncle Derek and even McQueen, could not have loved anything or anyone more in that moment because someone with real talent was putting Anghofiedig first. Like the old days.

Barry stood at the bar, oblivious to everyone, feeling like a bystander, full of regret that he'd missed today's match because the faces around him had never looked rosier. The most miserable rich man in Anghofiedig was cheered up by the sight of Pricer walking into the bar with a mohican haircut.

'All right, Pricer, how's the bollock?' Barry asked.

'Shrinking.'

'What's with the hairdo?'

'Fancied a change. Young lad at Kenny Wick's barbershop came up with the idea.'

Barry gawped at the glistening shark's fin cutting through the room's sea of grey. 'What's the missus think?'

'She don't like it, says I'm too old for it. Kids are taking the piss too.'

'It'll grow back at the sides, won't it?' said Barry.

Pricer turned his head and looked at his reflection in the mirror behind the bar. 'Hope so, though might be a different colour than before.'

'Didn't know you were into the punk stuff. Who do you like, Sex Pistols? Clash? Bit of Sham 69 and The Ramones?' asked Barry.

'Oh hell no, none of that old tosh, I likes me Glen Campbell and me Dolly Parton, me Kenny Rogers and a bit of Tammy Wynette,' replied Pricer, affronted by the slur on his taste in music.

'Ah right,' said Barry, still mesmerised by the gravity-defying construct upon his middle-aged friend's head. 'I'm gonna get my haircut on Monday.'

'Mohawk?' enquired Pricer.

'Don't think so,' said Barry.

SEVENTEEN
OH HAPPY DAY

ON HIS WAY TO CHURCH, Barry called by the office of the local rag, *The Bugle*, and pushed the handwritten match report he had cobbled together for yesterday's game through the dilapidated door. *The Bugle* printed absolutely anything anyone sent to them. In one sense it was disconcerting but in another exciting. As rugby club press correspondent, Barry was able to transform his terrible performances on Saturdays into something altogether more favourable with a few lusty strokes of his powerful pen and the occasional 'Everything's All White' or 'It's All White on the Night' headline. He was careful not to stretch his own personal truths too far, lest the boys down the club get worked up, but he could raise the level of his own game umpteen notches by the careful use of adjectives such as 'powerhouse', 'warrior' or 'stallion'. Invariably, he'd prefix these with 'dependable', 'resolute', 'unselfish' or 'dedicated'. Equally, he knew how to damn his teammates without resorting to outright character assassinations.

Although he hadn't watched yesterday's game, he went to town on superlatives for new boy James who he described as a 'deadly, explosive, fleet-footed gift from the rugby gods, parachuted from heaven to land on his feet in Anghofiedig with a Brylcreem bounce and a swerve and a sidestep to die for, a rugby ball tucked under his arm and the stride of a lion who knew – instinctively – that the jungle belonged to him and him alone'.

Okay, it was well over the top but what the heck, James was good and people needed to know it.

Barry's organ-playing survived all scrutiny in church and he didn't murder 'Great is Thy Faithfulness' like the last time he'd performed it. Barry could see Reverend Hill was holding his breath until halfway through the hymn when he started to relax a little.

Though not a great organist, Barry was competent, certainly more so than on a rugby pitch. Playing the organ didn't give him as much joy but the pleasure came from looking across and seeing the smile on his mother's face in the front row. She loved to see her boy making himself useful and serving in God's house.

The trick to organ playing, according to Reverend Hill, was proper articulation, making sure notes were released as smoothly as they started. Reverend Hill also drummed into Barry the importance of gathering up notes with one-beat pauses on the first note, to give the congregation enough time to open their mouths and breathe a little. 'They're like baby sparrows,' Reverend Hill would say. 'You get them to open up their little beaks, you pop a morsel of bread straight in and you wait for the little flicker of their tonsils to follow as they burst forth in song.'

When it was time for Reverend Hill's sermon, Barry moved to the seat next to Ma and tried to concentrate earnestly.

However, it was impossible; the sermon was too dull, too long and too difficult to follow, with tangents left, right and centre. A wandering mind in church when Angharad was sitting just across the way was also problematic when it came to glorifying God. Barry felt ashamed of his sinful, lustful thoughts but he had noticed a lot of old stirrings awakening inside him lately, as if he was a teenager all over again. Maybe it was the fact that Angharad was now living apart from Greg and potentially available once more, something she hadn't been for donkey's years. Of course, all logic said she wouldn't be interested in him but where was logic when his ridiculous accumulator bet came up trumps? And where was logic when Real Madrid came knocking for Neil Warnock?

Today, Angharad was wearing faded blue jeans tucked into long leather boots, with her large bust held in shape by a strongly wired bra and a tight see-through sweater. He imagined peeling it all off and writhing in the aisles with her naked to the strains of 'Oh Happy Day', until Reverend Hill brought him back to reality with a hard, noisy thump of his Bible.

Barry often had good cop, bad cop conversations going on inside his head simultaneously. Sometimes he wasn't even sure which cop was which. On the way to the rugby club last night, he was feeling kind of spiritual after his good news, so he said a little prayer of thanks as he walked. He felt good, in touch with his positive self and his Lord and Maker. Then a woman he didn't know walked out of a side street right in front of him so he had to pull up ever so briefly. She glowered and tutted at him. In that fraction of a second, his serenity was interrupted by an internal voice pitching up on the scene unannounced and screaming, *Oi, thunder tits, watch where you're bloody going.* Thankfully, he did not voice these words aloud, but it shocked him that they should even enter his head at that precise moment when he was in touch with aspects of a higher plain. Another voice inside him, a lot more sympathetic, expressed confusion by enquiring, *Where did you come from? Were you there all the time, just waiting for your chance to pounce?*

Bollocks to you too, came the rapid reply.

Barry wondered if an inner angel was going rogue. He felt like a squatter inside his own head.

Is this what it's like for Romeo all the time? he reflected.

Maybe I have Tourette's of the soul because I seem to yell 'fuck off' in my head at random people and random things an awful lot these days?

Barry had tried to discuss his inner rogue angel with Reverend Hill a while back, with little success.

'Reverend, I think I have a maniac hiding within me, posing as the Holy Spirit.'

The reverend threw Barry a sympathetic look. 'My friend, it's absolutely normal to feel that way. What you're describing is nothing more than the struggle of the human condition. The fight to win the war with oneself.'

Barry wasn't convinced. 'But it made me linger longer than I should have done when I accidentally upskirted Dora, the barmaid down at The Dragon.'

Reverend Hill was not a Catholic and not au fait with the mechanics of the confessional box. 'Do you have feelings for this woman?'

Barry felt insulted. 'Hell no. She's nearer sixty than fifty. I don't find her the slightest bit attractive. She just bent down to pick something up off the floor and there it was, growling at me.'

Reverend Hill appeared to be getting hot under the dog collar. 'So it was accidental?'

'Yes, reverend. Completely.'

'Then what's the problem?'

'The problem is I lingered. For a split second. And she was commando.'

Reverend Hill must have wished he had not ventured into this discussion with Barry, of all people.

'But you looked away?'

'Yes.'

'Not immediately. But immediately enough?'

'Suppose so.'

'And you're sorry? For this momentary linger?'

'Oh abso-bloody-lutely! She's a grandmother of six, rev, though saying that, she's not that much older than me. What a thought, eh? I didn't get a kick out of what I saw and regretted finding myself in such a predicament. I accidentally downbloused her too. About half an hour later when she went round collecting beer glasses. Again, I didn't go searching for it – it just arrived on my doorstep. Put me in an almighty internal pickle, I can tell you.'

Reverend Hill had had enough. 'Barry, I must be going, but rest assured, God will forgive you. Is that all?'

Barry bit his lip. 'There is one more thing. I keep having this recurring dream involving a waterbed and Nadine Dorries.'

Angharad cried when Barry stopped her on the way out of church and thrust a hefty envelope in her hand.

'I know you're struggling. Take this. Call it a loan if you must but it's actually a gift.'

It had been a while since anyone had shown Angharad such kindness. 'You realise you're the answer to my prayers?'

Barry thought she could be the answer to his but wasn't brave enough to tell her so.

'How about I cook you a meal as a proper thank you? Can you make Thursday night? Please say yes. Let me do something for you.'

Barry beamed. 'Sounds lovely.'

Romeo was cock-a-hoop too when he received his windfall, which rescued him from the wrath of both Betty and Foxy. Uncle Derek and Aunty Ruth were grateful to get their money back in triplicate. Aunty Ruth said she'd keep some of it to one side in case Barry – or Ma – ran into difficulties again. Uncle Derek probed his nephew over where the loot had come from and wanted a concrete oath that Barry would knock the gambling on the head once and for all.

'Any crap fighter can have his day in the sun with a lucky swinging punch,' he said, shadow-boxing. 'Quit whilst you're ahead, Barry boy. Cos you ain't a fighter. And you ain't lucky.'

Barry's most enjoyable moment came when he sat Ma down that evening and thrust a large brown envelope full of £50 and £20 notes into her hand. She tried not to accept the money. She said she didn't need it but they both knew she did.

'I love you, son, more than words can ever say, and whatever happens in the coming weeks and months I want you to always know that and to always remember it. You understand what I'm saying?'

Ma had tears in her eyes as she spoke and she gripped Barry's hand tightly as if holding on to the edge of a lifeboat on a rocky sea.

Unfortunately for her, Barry was oblivious to her tenderness. *Antiques Roadshow* was on the telly and Fiona Bruce was trying to work out 'basic, better and best' between a ceramic frog, a 250-year-old original mahogany bureau and a collection of empty biscuit tins from Huntley & Palmers.

EIGHTEEN
YOU ARE NOT IRON MAN

THROUGHOUT HIS LIFE Barry had been blessed with luxurious chestnut-brown hair but now he was almost bald. He made the mistake of walking into Kenneth Wick's barbershop for a £5.50 haircut. Kenneth wasn't there so Barry found himself in the hands of a skinny but incredibly vain young man in narrow jeans which hung loosely around his hips to show off some faded, well-worn red Calvin Kleins. He discovered this was Kenneth's grandson, Olly. He spoke minimally to Barry in an accent that sounded like it was from the West Country. He draped a sheet around his customer and without even a casual glance in his direction enquired, 'What's it to be, boss man?'

Barry stared at the photographs of handsome models all around him. 'Well, Oliver, I think I'd like a scissor cut, blended at the back, with a parting to the right and a generous amount of hair left on top. At the back and the sides, I'm looking mainly for more blending. It's all right if you cut the grey bits out around me Shirley – that's temple to you.'

Olly smiled quizzically before picking up his clippers and diving straight in to give him what is known in the trade as a number one all over. It seemed futile to Barry to try to argue or protest over the misunderstanding as Olly didn't seem to understand a word he said. Besides, what could Barry do to rectify the situation, with most of his hair sitting on his chest, shoulders and the stained laminate floor? He sat back to smell the Nescafé and let Olly carry on with his extravagant flicks of wrists and elbows, designed to tell any girls passing by the window that here was a master craftsman at work (with a devilish glint in his eye and the Calvin Kleins to back it up).

Occasionally, Olly would remember that he was cutting the hair of a live human being rather than a dummy and throw out a short question which required only a nod or a shrug in response.

'Hot shave, boss man?'

'Eyebrows?'

'What about those hairy ears?'

'Did you want a hot drink, boss man? We do tea and we do coffee.'

'Some wax and a slick-back to impress the ladies?'

'What about hair gel? Not today? Scented perfume then?'

'Why aren't you at work today? You're your own boss, aren't you, boss man?'

Barry declined all offers and ignored the last question completely. He didn't fancy having his eyebrows shorn off or his ears invaded by razor blades or worse, fire, whilst there seemed little point putting wax, gel, or even scented perfume on his now egg-shaped head.

He yearned for Olly's grandfather, Kenneth, to step into the shop with calm assurance and quickly assess the situation, dressed immaculately in a clean white coat and perfectly scrubbed with shiny fingernails. A real pro was Kenneth. An old-school Hai Karate or Mandate kind of guy. Sure, Barry would probably have ended up with the same scalped haircut that £5.50 affords you, but at least he would have enjoyed some pleasant conversation about the Welsh rugby team's frailties, the pros and cons of holidaying in Tenby for a week in August or whether he needed anything for the weekend.

Barry wanted to be called 'sir', not 'boss man', which made him sound like the owner of a late 19th century tea plantation. Kenneth Wick was not the world's best barber but he knew how to carry himself. The irony was that he was the boss of no one whilst sat in the barber's chair. He didn't even have the power to order the haircut he had walked in for. Instead, he got what he was given and had to be thankful for it, paying by cash rather than card because Olly didn't know how to work the machine.

The men of Anghofiedig deserved better than this. Kenneth's shop had stood on the corner of King Henry Street for over fifty years but now Barry feared for its future. He vowed never to set foot in the shop, or any other hair salon, ever again. He would get himself a proper pair of scissors off Amazon and do his own hair, with Ma finishing off the bits he couldn't reach. That method worked well enough during the lockdowns.

Had Kenneth's shop been on the internet, Barry would have left a one-star review and advised the old owner to send his grandson back to Shepton Mallet, Taunton Deane, Midsomer Norton or wherever it was he came from. At the very least, young Olly deserved a few more terms at hairdresser college and a strongly worded warning on a par with what Romeo was about to receive for baring his arse in a comms meeting.

His severe haircut put him in a bad mood for the rest of the day. That and not knowing what to do with over £60,000 that was burning a hole in his bank account – money that no one else knew he had. Barry felt guilty to have so much cash secretly stashed away. He didn't deserve it. He certainly didn't need it. His requirements were small: beer, food, a warm bed to lounge in day and night, a bit of Chico time, the love of his ma, the respect of his peers. He felt he was lying to all of them by not telling them about the money, but if he did a whole load of things would change immediately. Even something as simple as taking it in turns to buy a round of drinks after rugby would become more complicated. People would look at him and think *come on, put your hand in your pocket again. You can afford it.*

Back home, he looked around his bedroom and noticed how little had changed in over twenty-five years. Longer probably, going back to when his dad died. It was essentially a child's room with a few mod cons added on. He could use some of his money to properly modernise and update it. New furniture, different bedding, fresh carpets, curtains and wallpaper. Better lighting. A proper bachelor pad with a popcorn machine and a new TV as big as the facing wall could hold. He'd go for bolder colours and grown-up tones. Geometric patterns.

Maybe he could get the kitchen and the bathroom done for Ma as well whilst he was at it. The living room too. The whole house was badly in need of a *DIY SOS*. He'd always fancied a walk-in shower in the bathroom, with a seat so he could take a little rest when he wanted. Solid teak vanity units everywhere, with built-in serenity. Lots of curves and glass but not too many mirrors – he didn't want to see himself butt naked if he could help it. In the kitchen he liked the idea of shiny new appliances wherever you looked and Ma had always dreamt of marble worktops. Wooden flooring, well-camouflaged additional storage space, boiling water on demand, a dishwasher, plus grease-free, non-stick pots and pans – the frying pan Ma used for bacon and eggs was almost as old as her!

There wasn't really room for a floating island but they could integrate space better to include a pressure cooker, a coffee machine, a fridge freezer, perhaps even a wine cooler. He'd get Angharad to help with the designs and plans, she had an eye for all that stuff and Barry could help keep her afloat by employing her. Ma would be made up when it was all done. She would probably get emotional again, like she had last night.

Mid-afternoon, Barry returned to the health surgery for his follow-up appointment with Doctor Humphreys to get the results of his tests. He'd still not got around to booking a prostate examination with Doctor Epstein.

Barry remained annoyed with Doctor Humphreys because he'd called him both obese and a chronic alcoholic. He braced himself for another dose of bad news worse than anything you'd find on the BBC's six o'clock bulletin. He half expected the doctor to casually pronounce, 'Mr White, I'm afraid it's worse than we expected, you're going to die next Friday.'

All the more reason to get cracking on those house renovations, he thought.

Having got past nosy-parker receptionist Brenda Howells with the stealth of a safecracker, Barry waited for his name to be called.

'Barry White to room four, please. That's Barry White to room four.'

Barry knocked on the door and Humphreys called him in abruptly. He sidled in sideways and stood guiltily in the doorway as Humphreys carried on staring at his computer screen for around a minute. Either he was building the suspense or he was downright rude and in need of a course on bedside manners.

'Ah, Barry, thank you for coming in today, I've received the results of your tests and wanted to go through a few things with you. I must say I found them extremely enlightening,' said the doctor, eventually.

'Bugger,' said Barry, slumping himself down on a seat. 'Okay, give it to me straight. How bad is it?'

'Well, your blood pressure is a little on the high side, I might put you on statins but it's not essential just yet. Your blood sugar

ROB HARRIS

reading was also slightly elevated, around 9.7, but nothing to be overly concerned about. Your cholesterol was remarkably good for a man who eats and drinks so excessively. In fact, your heart, liver and kidney all seem to be holding up to the strains of your lifestyle quite well. The state of your liver surprised me most, we found very few enzymes in the blood. Which is good news for you at any rate.'

'Then I'm healthy?' Barry perked up.

'No, you remain morbidly obese and an alcoholic, I would never say you were healthy,' said the doctor.

'So I'm not going to peg it?'

Humphreys looked down at his notes. 'Wouldn't expect you to. Not today.'

It sounded like good news being delivered through gritted teeth. 'Can't you be happier for me? I mean, you're telling me I'm fine in one breath, then bigging up the warnings in the next.' Barry was annoyed by the doctor's demeanour.

'Well, it appears you have the constitution of an ox and that your appalling way of life has not, thus far, seriously impinged on your physical well-being. However, you are not Iron Man. If you continue to drink in excess of one hundred units of alcohol per week, eat far too much fast, fatty food and refuse to exercise properly you will be back here in six months' time or twelve months' time, or maybe even two, three, or five years' time if you are fortunate, receiving very different news. You have an opportunity to change direction and change the path of your life. I strongly urge you to take it,' said Humphreys.

'Still don't sound like you're being very cheery,' replied Barry.

The doctor looked up and finally made eye contact with his patient. 'How is your ma?'

'Ma? Oh, she's like me, strong as an ox. Why do you ask?'

'No reason,' said the doctor, suddenly looking

uncomfortable and returning to his paperwork. 'Make an appointment to come back and see me next week and we'll look at getting a plan in place to help you with your boozing. I'd like to keep an eye on you for a while.'

'Anything else?' said Barry.

He watched Doctor Humphreys theatrically get up and move to the large cabinet by the window. Humphreys put on a latex glove and pulled the end of the fingers tight, so the rubber snapped back sharply like a teacher's cane on flesh.

'Yes, while you're here pop your trousers and pants down and lie on that couch, please, on your left side with your knees up towards your chest. No more messing me and Mrs Epstein about – I'm going to have a little rummage in your back passage and make sure that prostate of yours isn't too lumpy or hard. Now relax will you, you'll just feel the mild sensation of my index finger entering your rectum. I expect I will need to loosen you up with some lubricating gel first. The gel isn't harmful but I must warn you it is cold. As are my hands.'

When Barry was at peak vulnerability – feeling completely helpless and somewhat violated, with a cold bony finger wriggling around inside his arse – the doctor stood up straight and stopped what he was doing.

'What is it?' said Barry.

'May I ask you something personal?' said the doctor.

'Sure, I can take it,' said Barry.

'Well, excuse me if this offends, but who on earth gave you that haircut?'

'Olly from Somerset,' said Barry.

'Did he do Pricer's mohawk?' said the doctor.

'Yes,' said Barry.

'I see,' said the doctor.

NINETEEN
A FESTIVAL OF DREAMS

THE RUGBY CLUB'S annual sojourn to the Cheltenham Festival was one of the highlights of the year. A party of seventeen met at 7.30am in the club car park for the ninety minute coach ride to poshest Gloucestershire. Romeo didn't play rugby but he was always invited, along with a few other non-rugby-loving, horse-racing fanatics from the village. Uncle Derek, McQueen and Jonah weren't much into racing but loved a day on the drink, whilst new boy James had no idea what he had let himself in for, but thought it would be a good way to bond with his new teammates.

'Right, lads, let's get this show on the road,' said Uncle Derek, lobbing cans of Guinness to each and every member of the crew from a gigantic crate that would need six to carry it to the coach. James looked horrified.

'Sorry, Del, little bit early for me,' he said.

'Drink it,' said Derek sternly.

When Derek wasn't looking Barry crept over to James, took the can of Guinness out of his hand and swapped it for his empty one, which he had necked in a couple of gulps.

'Stick with me today, Jamo, I'll look after you,' said Barry.

'Thank you!' said James, looking like someone had just carried him to safety from a battlefield.

The drinking continued all the way to Cheltenham, so by the time they drove down the promenade some of the older guys were already pretty well oiled. James drank one can of Guinness and did two more swaps with Barry. On arrival, Derek led them to a dirty café to eat a huge fry-up to line their stomachs – Anghofiedig on tour. Then they'd hit the Cheltenham pubs for a couple of hours of drinking and studying their *Racing Posts*, eavesdropping for any Irish voices proclaiming they had an absolute sure thing.

Around one, they'd make their way to the course where they would splinter into sub-groups among a crowd of pilgrims and lost souls just like them. Some would search for hospitality tents to gatecrash, whilst others – like McQueen and Uncle Derek – would simply find a good bar with comfy seats where they could sit and drink all day long, relatively oblivious to the horse racing going on around them. Barry and Romeo would make a beeline for the betting ring, studying the bookies' boards, looking for the best prices, sussing out the value, talking to fellow punters just like them, then darting for their hallowed vantage point, the place they made for every year to watch the racing. It gave them a good view of the horses as they headed towards the long uphill run to the line and there was also a big screen close enough to fill in the gaps where they couldn't see a thing.

'Did you remember to book today off as annual leave?' said Barry to Romeo.

'No, I'm technically working.'

Barry frowned. 'That's not good.'

'I can handle it.' Romeo climbed up a step to get a better view of the horses circling the parade ring.

'What about tomorrow?' asked Barry.

'Working again.'

'No rest for the wicked.'

Romeo dismounted the step and gulped ale from his pint glass. 'Too right.'

James was the first casualty of the day. He only managed six more pints of fizzy lager before he fell asleep in a corner of Wetherspoons around midday.

'What we gonna do with him?' said McQueen.

'Stick him back on the bus until he wakes up,' barked Derek.

'The boy might be Billy Whizz on a rugby meadow but he's a bloody lightweight off it, ain't he?' said Jonah.

'Modern day rugby player for ya,' snapped Derek again, rolling his eyes.

By the time the rest of the party entered the Cleeve Hill course they'd had a proper skinful. Even Barry, arguably the most hardened drinker in the group, was aware he'd had a few. Or to be more precise, thirteen or fourteen. Romeo had matched him drink for drink and was now wobbling.

'Come on, let's concentrate on the racing for a couple of hours, give our livers and bladders a break,' said Barry.

The Cheltenham Festival betting ring was a proper jungle. And a pickpocket's dream. Drunken red-faced men mostly, past caring about anything in life and relishing a day free from the clutches of bosses, wives and kids, jostled with each other, their fat wallets sticking out ready to be plucked like plums from a bush.

Romeo made the mistake of carrying on drinking through racing hours. He started making less and less sense. To calm him down a little, Barry joined him in a few easy ciders, though at £8 a pint he considered it the most sinister form of pickpocketing on show that day – along with £6 hot dogs that weren't hot, comprising a cheap bun from Lidl and a slimy wet German sausage from a Lidl tin.

The roar of the crowd when the tape went up for the first

race of the day, the Supreme Novices Hurdle, was always something to savour, like the roar of a Millennium Stadium rugby crowd when the English were in town. However, few were roaring a few minutes later when a little known Irish horse with no form to speak of came in first at odds of 33–1.

The next few hours played out exactly the same. One Irish long shot after another triumphed. And just when the punters thought they had every possible Irish angle in a race covered, up popped a little-known animal from Welsh trainer Ceri Thomas. Racing could be a truly cruel mistress sometimes.

By 5.15pm, the time of the last race of the day, Romeo was legless and sleeping on the bus in the arms of the still-slumbering James.

Barry found himself alone in the betting ring with no one to talk to and the drink had made him a bit depressed. His bank card was burning a hole in his pocket and the temptation to smack the plastic was overwhelming. Ever since his accumulator had come up, he'd felt the money was a weight around his neck that he didn't need, a burden of responsibility he didn't know what to do with. That feeling had grown inside him today with every pint downed. He loathed himself and what he was. He wanted to be recognised for being good at something besides drinking. He didn't want to feel different from the other guys on the bus, he didn't want to be secretly rich and living a lie. Even his best pal, Romeo, didn't know the truth about him.

Barry walked up to the first brightly lit bookie's pitch he came to. He'd already lost about £300, which was sensible going for him on a Festival jolly. Now, he was going to do his absolute nut on the National Hunt Steeple Chase Challenge Cup, a grade two free-for-all for amateur riders, a true gambler's graveyard. He spied a tall, thin man, about sixty-five, standing on a box. The name on the pitch told him he was Pete Redfearn.

'I want a bet, Pete. I mean a proper bet,' said Barry.

'How much?' said the bookie.

'Twenty grand.'

'Okay, fella, big boy stakes. What do you want to bet on?'

Barry looked at the electric board and plucked a name from the nether regions of the list. 'Brecon Beacon Boy.'

'On the nose? To win? All twenty grand of it?' The bookie looked around to make sure none of his competitors were listening in.

'Yep,' said Barry.

The bookie climbed down off his box and spoke briefly to a woman in her forties, probably his daughter. The woman looked at the old man and he at her. There was a pause before he nodded her way. They both smiled. They tried not to let their smiles collapse into all-out grins. The woman produced a cash transfer machine. Barry put in his card and tapped in his pin number. The transaction went through successfully.

'Right you are, fella, you taking the price? 50–1? Can't say fairer than that now, can you? I mean, everyone else around here is going 45s. They don't call me Honest Pete for nothing.'

The man and the woman started to laugh uncontrollably. This was the day they had always dreamt of. An idiot from the valleys dropping thousands in their lap on a complete no-hoper called Brecon Beacon Boy, whose form guide read nowhere, nowhere, nowhere, pulled up, refused to race, pulled up, eighth. The nag shouldn't even be here, he belonged at Bangor or Ffos Las on a wet Wednesday, or maybe even a point-to-point meet at little off-the-map venues such as Bredwardine, Howick, Lydstep or Bonvilston. The horse was only running because his rich American owner wanted a day in the weak English sun.

Barry felt disgusted with himself for throwing so much money down the drain. He had never disliked himself more. He yearned for a life more meaningful. A sad displaced refugee

THE ABSURD LIFE OF BARRY WHITE

would say he'd been blessed to have been born in Anghofiedig, a peaceful paradise in comparison to most countries, without searing 365-day suns or vain, puff-faced dictators. He was fortunate to live amongst people who were able to laugh at their own ridiculousness and sorry plights. However, he felt embarrassed talking about the fragile state of his own mind from the comfort of a safe, warm bed, just feet from a loaded fridge, because he knew beyond his front door – or rather his ma's front door – there was a frightening world of raging tornados, wars, earthquakes and misery. Peasants fearing a 3am knock on the door from the state police had a right to doubt their existences, he didn't. At least those same peasants, despite being scared shitless, knew they were alive and didn't have to watch *Love Island* every night with a glass of wine in one hand and their own manhood in the other, fretting about their singleness or the fact that time was running out and they were less butch than Jayden from Romford, currently cavorting with Alicia from Stepney on the TV screen in front of them.

Barry would have liked to have lived for a cause and something more purposeful. To have fought Hitler and all he stood for and to have been prepared to lay down his life for such a fight. To have sacrificed himself for others. The freedom of the next generation. He thought he might have made a decent soldier once.

He didn't even bother to watch the last race. He found the bar where McQueen, Jonah and Uncle Derek had spent the entire afternoon getting blotto and decided to join them in their slow plod to unconsciousness.

'Had a good day, son? We all have, haven't we?' said Uncle Derek, three sheets to the wind.

Giving away a huge sum of cash to Honest Pete had suddenly sobered Barry up, but in the company of his pals he felt more at peace with what he had done. He was now reunited with his people. He could buy and receive a round. And he still had forty grand in the bank, a lot more than most, and more than enough to do all the house renovations he'd planned for himself and Ma. His boat wasn't rocking anymore. He knew who he was. What he was. What he would always be. Barry White Junior. Son of Pearl and Barry White Senior. An okay sort of guy but nothing special.

In another corner of Cheltenham, loud-mouthed trainer and former scrap-metal dealer extraordinaire Grenville Grayson was saying 'I told you so' to all who had ever doubted him when he was a nobody who crushed cars for the council.

And not so far away from him, Honest Peter Redfearn Junior, son of Honest Peter Redfearn Senior, the now deceased long-time turf accountant of Pontefract, was taking down his pitch, whilst his daughter Avril, the apple of his eye, sobbed her heart out in the passenger seat of the Audi Q8 car she loved but was now about to lose. She'd lose a lot more besides, along with her dad: their houses; their cottages, both in the countryside and on the Costa del Sol; their entire life savings too – the money they'd built up steadily over cold days and nights driving up and down motorways to and from the likes of Hexham, Folkestone, Chepstow, Hereford, Cartmel, Catterick and Lingfield.

Brecon Beacon Boy, like his jubilant trainer Grenville Grayson and mug punter Barry White, were the true winners of Cheltenham's 'get out of jail' stakes, the National Hunt Challenge Cup.

It was much later that night, whilst drinking shorts in a Montpelier pub with his back-from-the-dead pals Romeo and James, that Barry overheard an inebriated Irishman bending the ear of the barman over the biggest shock of all in the last race, on a day of giant upsets.

'I mean, you can't possibly predict results like that – there's no form book anywhere in the world that can give you clues to solve problems like them. There's no rhyme or reason whatsoever, is there? Nothing in this world makes sense anymore. Not even Cheltenham!'

The sullen barman had given up dishing out pretend smiles to people he despised, people who seemed to forget that whilst they were merrily betting and losing hundreds and thousands of pounds, he was being asked to listen to their pathetic sob stories for minimum wage.

'Horses are even more unpredictable than women if you ask me and that's saying something,' continued the Irishman. 'They get together and they whisper and they conspire to bring us down.'

The barman handed the Irishman his tumbler and he raised it toward the roof. 'I dedicate this drunken haze I'm about to fall into to you, Brecon Beacon Boy... you sneaky little Welsh fucker, destroyer of mighty coups.'

The Irishman drank the contents of the tumbler down in one.

Barry turned and patted the man on the shoulder. 'I'm sorry, what did you say won the last race?'

The Irishman looked Barry up and down. 'You Irish?'

'No, Welsh.'

'Ha, my nightmare is complete. I'm being tortured, so I am. Tortured. Two Welsh ghosts visited earlier to rob me of my winnings and bring me despair and now you're the third. You're a vision, aren't you? From the wilds of the Brecon Beacons. It's you, isn't it? You're the Brecon Beacon Boy himself! In human form! Come to goad me once more!'

'Did Brecon Beacon Boy win the last race?'

'Aye, he did. With Jacob Marley in the fucking saddle. Robbed my Darling Ruby up the hill like a highwayman from the valleys. As if you don't know.'

Barry didn't know what to say or do. He tapped some numbers into the calculator on his phone and worked out that if the drunken Irishman was right – and there were certainly no guarantees there – his £20k bet at odds of 50–1 had netted him exactly £1 million. He pulled out the betting slip from his pocket, a crumpled, grubby piece of paper now worth more than Cheltenham Hospital.

He roared like a lion in pain and passed out on the floor as the blood could no longer make it to his brain.

'Hey, I don't believe it, I never thought I'd see the day, but our Barry's fallen down pissed!' said Derek.

Everyone in the pub laughed with approval.

'He's not real... he's all apparition,' screamed the Irishman.

Derek, James, Romeo and Jonah scooped him up, carried him outside through the cool night air and loaded him into the back of the bus to sleep – or maybe dream – a route back to sobriety and the real world.

The betting slip now worth £1 million fell out of Barry's trousers as they raised him up and manhandled him onto the bus. However, Romeo, without even pausing to look at it, picked it up and shoved it back into the pocket where it had come from.

TWENTY
HOMEBASE HERE WE COME

A THUMPING HANGOVER ALMOST MADE Barry forget that his life was changing beyond all recognition, whether he liked it or not. The crumpled betting slip on his sideboard reminded him of the truth. *Who wants to be a millionaire? Do I?*

Barry didn't know what a millionaire ought to be doing with his morning, apart from contacting Honest Pete Redfearn asap to arrange the speedy BACS transfer of his loot and to make sure he hadn't fled the country. Pete was surely nursing a thumping hangover of his own for very different reasons.

Barry was now one of the richest, most eligible bachelors in South Wales (on paper, at least) but he'd won his life-changing loot, attempting – and failing – to self-destruct. Maybe it was God's doing. Fate. Karma. It made his simple existence suddenly very complicated; he knew that much.

Lying in bed, eating a tin of pilchards with a spoon, he watched the race for the first time on Racing TV. He was much luckier than previously imagined, because Brecon Beacon Boy was a distant third going to the last fence. However, the horse in front, Love Prevails, came a cropper, almost bringing down the unfortunate hot favourite Darling

Ruby, who'd been cruising easily and had plenty left in her tank at the time. Brecon Beacon Boy flapped to the line like a tortoise outstripping fallen hares, his inelegant, uncoordinated amateur jockey Dr Phillipson P. Montague, doing his best to mess things up, but just about holding on from a posse of perked-up horses who all seemed to find their wings half a furlong too late.

Barry picked up the phone and rang the number on his slip. A man answered.

'Hullo, Peter Redfearn speaking.'

'Ah, Mr Redfearn, Barry White here – the Brecon Beacon Boy. Can you transfer my money over, please? You've got my bank details.'

'I can. I will. Except I can't do it all at once. Not today, I mean,' said Honest Pete.

'When?' Barry had an in-built mistrust of all turf accountants, even ones called Honest Pete.

'I can do £150k today. Then another £350k next week maybe.'

'And the other half a mill?'

Honest Pete didn't have it. 'You'll get it, don't worry, I don't want to end up in the clink. It's just an awful lot of money. I've got to liquidise most of my assets. You'll have to give me a month.'

'Okay.'

'How the hell did you know that horse was going to win?' asked Honest Pete.

'I didn't. I thought it would lose,' said Barry.

Honest Pete sounded confused. 'You mean you wanted to lose?'

'Not sure. I wasn't thinking straight.'

'You'd had a few sherbets, I could see that.'

'Is that why you took my bet?'

'I broke my own rules. I got greedy,' said Honest Pete, clearly feeling sorry for himself.

'You saw a drunken Welshman staggering around with more cash than brains and thought it was your lucky day?'

'Yes,' said Honest Pete, honestly.

'What you gonna do next?' enquired Barry.

'Don't know. I'm done on the pitches though. Fifty years man and boy and you've finished me off. Got to start again at sixty-five, from the bottom up I suppose. Might try Homebase, on the tills.'

Barry was a sucker for a sob story. 'Listen, keep twenty grand for yourself, for your new start.'

'Thanks, that's very generous.'

'Be lucky,' said Barry, before hanging up.

Within a couple of hours, true to his word, the now former bookmaker of Pontefract had transferred the first instalment of £150,000 into Barry's account, giving him a balance of more than 190k.

To distract himself from everything going on inside and outside his head, Barry decided to start work on the house renovations immediately. Without giving Ma any prior warning – and waiting until she was out – he began stripping the front room of its gaudy 1970s yellow, brown and white floral wallpaper, ready for painting at a later date in more soothing tones of magnolia or alabaster white.

His track record in DIY was not encouraging. He'd once painted the kitchen Day-glo yellow but Ma had been unimpressed by the fact he'd gone around her Michel Roux and Raymond Blanc cookbooks, so that when she took one off the shelf to read, the old grey paint screamed '*sacre bleu*' at her.

Worse still, he once convinced Aunty Ruth he knew how to bleed radiators. He removed the cap off the end rather than just loosening it – whilst also not realising that he should've turned the central heating off first. Hot water gushed out of the radiator flooding the place and destroying the Axminster carpet whilst Aunty Ruth fussed, panicked, screamed and yelped. Barry suffered minor burns to both hands but managed to get the cap back on the radiator before Uncle Derek came home to forcefully shove it somewhere dark, musty and warm where no additional heating was required.

Barry's DIY therapy session began well enough and he managed to tear off most of the wallpaper at eye level relatively easily. It came away from the wall without putting up much of a fight, probably on account of the damp hidden behind various appliances. However, the bits higher up were harder to shift. Here was an accident waiting to happen; a sixteen-stone man with no sense of balance, stretching and tugging at firmly fixed wallpaper, whilst standing one-legged on a rickety wobbly stepladder that hadn't seen action for years.

When the inevitable happened, Barry lay on the floor dazed, unsure if his headache was concussion or hangover. He managed to get himself to his feet but felt shooting pains down his wrist. It hurt a lot. He pulled his phone out of his pocket with his other hand and called Aunty Ruth.

'Aunty, what you doing right now? Would you be able to run me down to the community hospital? I've fallen off a ladder and think I might have broken something besides Ma's coffee table.'

Aunty Ruth had a golf lesson so she dropped him off at the entrance to the hospital and said she'd pick him up later if he needed a lift. Barry didn't mind sitting in the hospital waiting room on his own for three hours, it was strangely therapeutic and probably just what the doctor ordered. It gave him a space and some time to think – whilst watching various poor unfortunates come and go with an assortment of limps, rashes, black eyes and bleeds.

He saw children who had fallen off bikes and climbing frames and one with a saucepan stuck on his head. There were wheezing babies and wheezing old folk, plus plenty of casualties just like him – Do It Yourself experts in the art of self-harming. One had swung a large hammer 360 degrees and whacked himself unconscious. Another had fallen through his own shed roof whilst trying to replace the felt. There was a guy who had smashed his own hand into bits in sheer frustration because he was struggling to assemble a flat-packed wardrobe. His creation was obviously a lot sturdier than he realised. Most embarrassed of all was the fellow who had dropped a tin of green Dulux paint all over his own head. The potential risk to his health was nothing compared to the shame of having to drip his sticky way through the hospital corridors like the creature from the deep lagoon.

Eventually, a pretty, middle-aged nurse entered the waiting room and shouted Barry's name. He followed her through a set of double doors into a small cubicle tucked away from prying eyes and the carnage of everyday life on public display.

'Hello, Mr White, my name's Diana, I'm an A&E nurse. I understand you've had a little mishap with a stepladder?'

Barry was mesmerised by Diana's eyes, which were greener than Mr Creature from the Dulux Deep.

'Call me Barry,' he said.

'Okay, Barry, I'm guessing the problem is that left arm which you're holding tight to your chest?' Diana tenderly took hold of the arm and began to examine it.

'It's my wrist that hurts most.' Barry winced.

'Okey-dokey, let's take a little look. Did you fall far?' Diana pressed into the wrist in search of bones.

'No, not really, but I'm not as light on my feet as I used to be. I landed awkwardly.'

'That's what I say to my sister when she keeps nagging me to do a skydive with her. It's not the jumping out of a plane that I'm scared off, it's the potentially awkward landing at 120mph I'm bothered about, particularly if my parachute doesn't open.' Diana stopped assessing Barry's wrist but continued to hold on to it.

'I reckon the speed of my fall from the ladder was around 5mph, a bit like a three-toed sloth in the January sales,' said Barry. 'Or you could say I went down like the council tax – in instalments, each of them painful.'

Diana laughed a proper belly laugh. 'You're funny.'

'Thank you,' said Barry.

An X-ray confirmed that Barry's wrist wasn't broken, just sprained. Nurse Diana Fenwick told her patient to ice and rest his wrist and tenderly wrapped it in a splint for him. She handed him a packet of paracetamol and advised him it would probably be wise to leave the DIY alone.

'There you go, soldier, right as rain. Nice meeting you,' she said.

'You too,' said Barry, walking into a desk on his way out of the extremely tight cubicle. 'Ouch, me privates.'

Nurse Diana laughed. 'I'm not wrapping them in a splint,' she said. 'Well, not today.'

———

Barry expected to find Ma all worked up about the state of her front room when he got home, but she didn't even mention it. She was sitting in her favourite chair in the lounge, reading *Take a Break*.

'Ma, I've sprained my wrist, I decided to make a start on

decorating the front room cos I wanted to surprise you but I fell off a ladder and look…'

He held up his bandaged wrist for Ma to see.

'What's going to become of you, son?' she said.

'It'll be okay, just a bit sore for a few days, that's all.'

Ma said nothing.

'I'm sorry about the front room, I'll call Pricer later – get him over straight away. He told me he's not got much work on at the moment and his bollock is almost back to normal size so he can bend down and dip a brush again. We won't stop at the front room, either. I'll get him to decorate right through the whole house, you said yourself it all needs doing. I can pay him, don't worry about that, the money isn't an issue. You can help choose the colours and everything, we'll get some new furniture too. It'll be my treat. I want to do this, Ma, don't say no – I want to say thank you to you, properly. You do so much for me. I know I let you down quite a lot,' said Barry.

Ma wiped a tear from her eye and it was obvious she was working hard to stop a whole load more from following.

'That all sounds lovely, son. Just lovely. And just so you know, I'm proud of you. Always have been. Always will be.'

Ma went to the kitchen to put the tea on. Unannounced, Romeo shoved his head through the open window of the lounge.

'Barry, you won't believe it, I've been cancelled.'

Romeo's ongoing escapades and his failure to either work, or justify his lack of work, had finally caught up with him and he'd been unceremoniously fired by LesCargo.

'I told you to book yesterday off as annual leave, didn't I? Was Juliet cross?'

'Tamping, though I reckon she was putting on a bit of a show for Bish's sake. He said I was an embarrassment to the company and that I'd let him down personally. The cheek of the man. I'll tell you what's embarrassing, a guy of his age having blond highlights and a ponytail.'

'What you gonna do?' asked Barry.

'Chillax.' Romeo laid his head on the windowsill.

'Can you manage financially?'

'Nope.'

Barry knew he was in a position to help out. 'Listen, you've got a car and I could do with having someone drive me around sometimes. Fancy doing some work for me?'

'You gonna pay me?' asked Romeo, lifting his head and pushing it in closer.

'Does £500 a week sound okay?'

'You bet! What am I, your chauffeur?'

'Call it PA. I might need other stuff doing.'

'Cool! Have you won the lottery?'

'No, but I need you to be discreet. You're not to tell anyone about our arrangement. Not Ma and definitely not Uncle Derek. Not even your mum or Angharad. Got that?' Barry made the universal 'zip-it' sign across his lips.

'My lips are sealed,' said Romeo, repeating the zip-it charade. 'I feel like a spy.'

'You're not a spy,' said Barry, matter-of-factly.

'Are you a spy?' asked Romeo.

'Maybe,' replied Barry.

TWENTY-ONE
TONIGHT, TONIGHT, TONIGHT

'WHAT HAPPENED TO YOUR WRIST? And your hair? Oh my God!' was Angharad's opening salvo as she let Barry in.

'I fell off a ladder. And Olly from Somerset attacked me with a pair of clippers,' said Barry.

Barry could smell something good cooking in the kitchen of the family home where Angharad had grown up. The nest she couldn't wait to escape from at seventeen but had now flown back to, to lick her wounds and mend her pride after being dumped for a younger model by her philandering husband.

'Mum's at her friend's and Romeo's off wandering the streets somewhere, probably in fantasy Feelgood, so we won't get bothered. Would you like a glass of wine? I've only got red. Merlot okay? We're eating Greek. I've made stifado, or beef stew to you. Sticky toffee pudding for afters. Sound all right?'

'Lovely. Your dress looks nice by the way,' said Barry.

'Thank you,' said Angharad.

Barry had known Angharad nearly all his life and was generally comfortable around her, but this felt different, a bit like the night of Davey Fisher's party all those years ago. He wasn't exactly sure what was expected of him. Did Angharad just want to say thank you for the money? Or was there something else? She'd started drinking without him and had obviously had a few before he got there.

'Thank you for bailing me out with the loan,' said Angharad.

'No problem, and it's not a loan. You don't need to pay me back.' Barry helped himself to a big glass of red.

'You are so sweet, thank you. I've decided to try and keep the house if I can. I'm just about staying on top of the bills but it's too painful for me to be there at the moment. Too many reminders. And I don't want to be on my own.'

Barry demolished half the contents of his wine glass. 'I understand.'

The stifado was delicious, chunks of tender beef cooked with tomatoes, onions, cinnamon, vinegar, red wine and a pile of other spices and herbs, most of which Barry couldn't identify. It came with rice and a slice of brown Hovis, not quite all the way from Athens.

'You always used to ask me what I saw in Greg,' said Angharad, out of the blue. 'The honest answer, which I've only just admitted to myself, is I just wanted to change my name from Miss to Mrs and he came along at the right time. It didn't really enter my head that he might not be a suitable person to spend the rest of my life with. I should have said no when he proposed but I didn't want to be a party pooper,' said Angharad.

Angharad looked wistfully into the distance so Barry finished off her sentence in his own head.

And you liked the idea of a big and proper party with all your friends and family together, a real Anghofiedig shindig. Plus you knew, deep down, it would never be 'until death do us part', not with bloody Greg. He couldn't keep his pecker in his pants for two minutes. You knew you were signing yourself up for more conflict further down the line but you figured you'd cross that bridge when you came to it. You basically nagged Greg to death to get him to ask you to marry him. And he did so to shut you up. Just for a bit.

Barry had a theory that this was probably how most marriage deals got brokered. Forget the hands of fate, Cupid's arrow and the words of the great love poets and pop balladeers, millions of incompatible couples throughout history and time have limped through life with their ball and chain, resenting, squabbling, bickering and pulling faces behind their partner's back because one of them – or both – didn't have the heart or the fight to do the right thing and rock the boat, floating and swishing on a mildly pleasant and interesting summer sea that was known to get choppy once July was out.

'We had some humdinger rows and I let myself down, but it was the 2000s,' said Angharad. 'I hit him a few times, I'm ashamed to say, with plates, cosmetic bags, handbags, laundry bags, gym bags, teabags, garden gnomes and, best of all, a dustbin. I struggled to lift it up and he laughed and said, "Need a hand?" We ended up making out on the kitchen lino with the smelly old bin next to us.'

Barry choked on his beef stifado and had to spit some of it out into a tea towel. The discovery that Angharad had a violent streak was a shock to his system. He thought he'd known her all his life. All her life. Yet how well did they really know each other?

'Greg wasn't all bad, he was just lousy at being faithful. He saw a side of me I didn't know existed. An angry side, a side I never want anyone else to see, ever. When he left me, he got all the stick off people but I wasn't entirely innocent was I? There are two sides to every story aren't there?' said Angharad.

Barry refilled his wine glass and skilfully emptied the stifado dish of all its contents with his one good hand. He had no idea how to be Oprah Winfrey but he knew how to keep quiet and eat.

'I never really loved him and he never loved me, but we both liked the idea of being loved by someone. I didn't have much family and his were mostly bastards,' continued Angharad, head in hands on the table. 'We were never honest with each other. He lied to me about something pretty much every day, instinctively, randomly, convincingly sometimes, over things big and small. He said he discovered early on in our marriage that lying was the only way to survive with a woman as passionate, unpredictable and volatile as me. Of course, life wasn't all bad, for either of us. We had loads of tremendous sex, and I mean tremendous. Greg truly knows how to pleasure a woman but then I suppose, he's had a lot of practice.'

Barry was now in the realms of checking windows and doors for an escape route. The Angharad before him was not the Angharad he had mooned and lusted over these past few weeks. She seemed more insecure than usual. She was normally good at making decisions and thinking on the spot but not tonight. He really hoped she'd quit talking about Greg and start eating her fancy stew. She'd hardly touched it. If she didn't eat it soon, he'd go for it himself and see if she noticed.

'No one knows this, but I attempted suicide once. Greg found me,' said Angharad, matter-of-factly.

Barry was way out of his comfort zone. Listening to Angharad speak had become too painful, so he turned on his internal radio and focused hard on mentally singing each and every word to 'Bohemian Rhapsody'.

'I got some proper help and Greg was great throughout that dark period, really supportive. I'm telling you this now because if we're going to get together you need to understand. I don't want you to feel sorry for me.'

Barry had no idea. Romeo had never mentioned it, maybe he didn't know either? And what was that bit about 'if we're going to get together'? He needed to hear that part again. He didn't know what to say or do. His inner voice was shouting 'run' but he wanted to be supportive.

'I always struggle to cope when I feel like I'm a let-down, sometimes Greg reacts as if I deliberately go out of my way to hurt him.' Angharad had tears in her eyes but did not wipe them. 'It's when I feel judged, unheard or misunderstood that I overreact. I don't know which way to turn. I guess I never felt free to speak honestly and openly with him because he didn't want to hear it. I had to carry it alone. There was no one in my corner, no one willing to be in the hardest part of my life with me, no one who really accepted all of me, no one who really knows all of me. Greg couldn't love what he didn't want to know, could he?'

'No,' said Barry, sympathetically, his downcast expression made genuine by the fact that he'd just finished off the last of the wine.

'Do you know what I said to Greg when he left me for that young girl? I told him I was tired of being made to feel like a failure. I told him I could, and would, do better than him and that he would rue the day he left me. And I've already found something better, haven't I? Something – and someone – that was there all along, right in front of me, but I couldn't see it. Now I can, clear as day. Greg would never listen to me the way you listen to me.'

With that Angharad reached in and squeezed Barry's hand. She leant forward close enough to kiss him but stopped herself to make the moment last. He felt her warm wine-infused breath on his cheek.

'To hell with Greg and sticky toffee puddings. My sweet, sensitive Barry, take me to bed. Tonight, I want to be yours!'

Angharad lunged forward to kiss him. Instinctively, he turned away so she missed his lips and got his neck. Again, she'd managed to throw him. Of course he wanted to go to bed with her but why had she tossed in the word 'tonight'? Did that mean that tomorrow she would no longer be his? How long did he have her for, exactly? He was no good at this game and he didn't know how to play it. A real man would have zoned in on the words 'take' and 'bed' instead of 'tonight' and whisked her upstairs, oblivious to everything else in the sentence. Why was he so different? Why did 'tonight' matter?

Also ringing in his ears were Angharad's words about Greg being a tremendous lover and knowing how to truly pleasure a woman. There was no way Barry was going to measure up to that kind of yardstick. He didn't know his way around well enough. He didn't even know for sure if he was a virgin or not. He'd had some fumbles and a few whey heys, but he wasn't sure if any of that constituted a loss of virginity? He didn't think so. He'd studied the theory long and hard but hadn't gotten around to the practical. He was bound to disappoint 'tonight'. And what then in the morning?

He didn't want to disappoint Angharad. He didn't want his prowess between the sheets, or lack of it, to be compared to Greg's. And he didn't want the woman who dominated the life he led in his head to think he was less of a man than her fault-filled husband. And actually, if they were going to go to bed together, he'd quite like his sticky toffee pudding first!

'Angharad, I'm really sorry but your stifado hasn't agreed with me. I think I need the toilet urgently,' said Barry.

'Eww, that's a passion killer,' said Angharad, recoiling from her swoon position. 'Well you'd better go quickly.'

Barry shuffled from the table to the hallway, impersonating a man who had half-shit himself.

'Be back down in a bit, but might have to borrow a pair of Romeo's kegs. I know he won't mind,' said Barry. 'I'll be right as rain in a jiffy, I just know I will. Tell you what, when I come back down how's about we open another bottle of Merlot and you warm up those sticky toffee puds? Custard and cream on mine, please.'

TWENTY-TWO

FIRE UP THE QUATTRO

THE SMELL of the LesCargo offices brought back a lot of memories; Dettol disinfectant and sickly vanilla mixed with strong coffee beans to produce a kind of hospitalised tiramisu aroma that permeated throughout every floor of the entire building. Walking through the place it was hard to believe people still worked here; that human beings actually sat at desks all day long staring into computer screens, with telephones at their side, sitting upright, freshly showered, smartly dressed. This was a world Barry forgot existed. For those being held captive within it there was a new resentment, because they realised that somewhere else, people like Barry were beating the system, getting paid the same as them to sit in their undies and T-shirts and watch *Flog It!* Still, a few more hours and they could join them too. Hybrid working meant that Monday to Wednesday they belonged to LesCargo. Thursdays and Fridays? Time to go off-grid and play a little.

Barry hadn't come to HQ to work, though Juliet was looking forward to finally getting in the same room as her elusive content creator for the first time in ages. Instead, he'd come out of loyalty to Romeo, to help him clear the last few remaining things from his workspace and to sit with him through the painful exit interview, which he had to attend in order to get a few extra quid and some sort of reference that didn't condemn him as unemployable.

'Romeo, I understand things have been difficult for all of us recently but the goal of this meeting is to have a short, amicable and open reflection so that we can all go our separate ways with a semblance of understanding of why what happened, actually happened,' said Bish, sounding like a member of the Tory Cabinet.

'You're not coming back whatever you say.' Juliet's staccato words bypassed all politics and social niceties.

Bish struggled on, steering the LesCargo ship alone. 'What Juliet means is, today is not about decision-making. It's about gaining fresh learnings on both sides.'

'Mostly on yours though,' said Juliet.

Bish turned to scowl at his colleague, then returned to face the front with the smile restored to his features like it was a company logo. 'I'm just going to ask you a series of questions, Romeo, if that's okay with you, and Juliet will stay quiet to note your responses. Won't you, Juliet? These will be typed up and sent to you to authorise and sign as a true and accurate record of this meeting. Whatever you say will remain totally confidential – this exercise is purely for your benefit and ours – as a company – so we can assess how we handled things and what we might do better in future.'

'All sounds reasonable,' said Barry.

'Romeo, do you understand why the company ended your contract?'

'Because I bared my arse on Teams.'

'Not exactly, though that incident was a contributing factor to you getting a warning.' Bish shuffled his papers and looked downwards to make sure they were still in the right order.

'You don't like *The Sweeney*,' said Romeo.

'Your tattoo is irrelevant,' replied Bish, calmly.

'Not to me it ain't.'

Juliet was finding it impossible to sit quietly. 'There's a million things we could have fired you for, Romeo, but they all boil down to terrible or non-existent work and an attitude that stinks like a cow field.'

'And for the record, you're a terrible team leader. There, write that down, please,' demanded Romeo, jumping out of his seat and slamming his hand up and down on Juliet's notepad.

'You say Juliet's a terrible team leader. What makes you think that?' enquired Bish.

'Well, I don't trust her, never have. She's too keen on brownnosing you and your lot, she don't care about us. She acts like she's the law, too. When I got my first warning, she actually told me that I didn't have to say anything, but that it might harm my defence if I didn't mention something that I might later rely on. She said anything I said might be used in evidence against me.'

'She said that?'

'Yep.'

'Did you?'

Juliet squirmed. 'Can't remember.'

'Go on, write it all down,' screamed Romeo, tugging at his own hair.

'At this rate you'll be getting your job back,' said Barry.

'Don't want it back, I work for you now.'

Bish had another go at restoring civility to the proceedings. 'Okay, but you understand that the company could not tolerate you being at Cheltenham races on a day when you were supposed to be working?'

'I was still working.'

'From Cheltenham?'

'Yeah.'

'How could you be?' piped up Juliet. 'I saw you on the telly with a glass in your hand, shouting down the camera, behind a live interview with Tony McCoy.'

'Aha, say no more.' Romeo flew out of his seat and danced towards the window.

'What do you mean?' said Juliet.

'Well, how come you saw me? If you were working, how come you saw me?'

'He's got a point,' said Barry to Bish.

'What's good for the goose is good for the gander,' exclaimed Romeo.

'I'm not on trial here, you are,' replied Juliet.

Bish finally lost his patience. 'For goodness' sake, Juliet, please! No one's on trial.'

'No, cos I'm a free man at last.' Romeo perched on the sill of the window, looking like a man who might actually jump.

'Why don't you just pay Romeo what you owe him, give him a reference that doesn't say anything too bad and let's all go our separate ways?' said Barry.

'Actually, let's do that,' agreed Bish.

'Fine by me,' replied Romeo.

'Me too,' said Juliet.

'Anything else either of you would like to add before we wind this meeting up?' Bish put his papers neatly away in his briefcase.

'Yes,' said Barry.

'What's that?'

'I quit too.'

Barry's lobbed grenade definitely hit its intended target. Ordinarily, Juliet wouldn't have been too bothered about his resignation but now this reflected badly on her and raised more question marks about her ability to manage anything besides her ongoing holiday plans.

'But why? And why now?' she asked.

'Had enough.'

'Enough of what?'

'You,' said Romeo.

Barry shook his head. 'Logistics.'

'Have you thought this through properly? Your Dougie McAllister piece is beginning to get noticed in high places,' said Bish, putting his briefcase back on the table and wondering if he ought to get his papers out again.

'How many people have looked at it so far?'

'Seven or eight.'

'How many to go?'

'Seven or eight more.'

Barry threw out his hands in front of him. 'Say no more.'

'What you gonna do with yourself?' said Juliet.

'No idea.'

'How will you manage for money?' asked Bish.

'I'll get by.'

'He's a spy for the FBI,' sang Romeo, to an imaginary reggae beat.

'We'll need your resignation in writing,' confirmed Bish.

'No problem.'

'And your notice period is one month,' added Juliet.

'No, I'm finishing up today. Don't worry about paying me anything more.'

'You can't just walk out when you feel like it!' said Juliet, enviously.

'I'm sure we can sort something out,' said Bish.

'Shall I fire up the Quattro so we can get the hell out of here?' Romeo cleared the table of two plates of chocolate Hobnobs, stuffing them all in his pockets.

'Yep,' said Barry.

'You drive a Quattro?' Bish was impressed.

'No, I drive a sporty French classic, but I call her Quattro cos I like saying it,' said Romeo.

'It's a Citroën Dyane,' revealed Barry.

'Racing green,' said Romeo, defensively.

That evening, Ma invited Dotty around for tea. They had been friends most of their lives and even met their husbands on the same evening in 1964, at the Hereford May Fair. Dotty's husband, Lionel, was a rough and ready miner who worked, drank and played rugby alongside Barry Senior. Too much coal in the lungs did for him when he was still in his forties so Dotty had been a widow for around half of her life, just like Ma.

Her approach to widowhood was very different, though. Dotty was much more outgoing than Ma and said yes to almost any invitation, which was why she usually dined at other people's houses every night of the week and had been out with most, if not all, of Anghofiedig's single pensioners at one time or another. Uncle Derek wasn't her biggest fan and called her 'the black widow' or 'silicosis' behind her back – because she was working her way through the old pit boys and finishing them off one by one.

Barry thought Dotty was harmless enough. Sure, she was seventy-eight and on Tinder, but she didn't have kids and got lonely on her own. She'd had a pretty tough life but still looked for the joy in things, taking her pleasures where she could find them. And she was good company for Ma, dragging her out to places and events that she wouldn't otherwise go to on her own. When Ma wanted to walk down memory lane Dotty would happily go with her, even if her own preference was to always look forward rather than back.

The three of them sat around the table in the lounge eating sausages, mash and peas and drinking orange squash.

Dotty watched Ma struggle to load her fork with peas and turned to Barry. 'Your mother's looking peaky. I told her she needs to stop doing so much for you.'

'I don't ask her to.'

'I like doing,' protested Ma.

'And anyhow, she cooked tea tonight for you, not me. I was gonna call by the chippy on my way to The Dragon.' Feeling picked on, Barry shoved a whole sausage in his gob to show his dissent.

'That's right,' said Ma.

Dotty realised it was two against one and she had no chance of winning any arguments away from home. 'Well, I appreciate it right enough, Pearl, thank you.'

'How are your sausages?' said Ma to Barry.

'Fabulous.'

'Got them from the new freezer section at John John's.'

'Wow, that man sells everything.'

Dotty fixed her eyes on Barry's head. 'What's going on with your bonce?'

'Olly from Somerset cut it.'

'Oh I see.'

'He's getting his hands on a lot of heads lately,' said Ma.

'Thought something weird was going on,' replied Dotty.

'Bumped into Dicky Bridges from Honeywell Farm this morning and I didn't even recognise him,' said Ma to Dotty.

'Funny business.'

Ma lowered her voice, as if Dicky Bridges was lurking in the next room. 'He's got the sides all long and a straggly grey mullet at the back but the top of his head is completely shaved out like some sort of alien crop circle landing zone.'

'I thought he couldn't make his mind up whether he wanted to join a monastery or Duran Duran,' whispered Dotty.

'Poor Richard. You went out with him, didn't you?'

'Yes, for a while.'

'Why only for a while?' asked Barry.

'No chemistry.'

Ma pulled a face. 'What's chemistry got to do with anything at our age?'

'Plenty,' said Dotty.

'You still think you're twenty-one, that's your problem,' said Ma.

'Don't call that a problem, eh, Dorothy?' Barry began to laugh to himself.

'Thank you, dearie. How's your love life any road?'

'Er...'

'He's waiting for the right girl to come along, aren't you, love?' said Ma.

'Don't wait too long,' said Dotty.

Ma defended her boy. 'It'll happen when it happens.'

'Suppose so.'

Barry took his empty plate to the kitchen. Ma seized the chance to talk to Dotty without her son in the room.

'Me and you married much too young, didn't we?'

'Yes, and we buried them too young as well.'

'I was lucky our Barry came along when he did. I was thirty-five at the time and thought I couldn't have children. He was my little gift from God. He's kept me going.'

'I'd have liked a son, but Lionel never wanted kids. He reckoned they'd slow us up.'

'We've all got to slow up sometime.'

Dorothy was uncomfortable with Ma constantly reminding her how old she was. She watched Barry return with his second big plate of food.

'And what about work, Barry? You back in the offices yet?'

'No, not yet.'

'Why not?'

'Because he can do everything he needs to do here at home, can't you, son?'

'Yes,' said Barry.

'All he needs is his brain and his laptop,' said Ma.

'Bit different to our day, eh, Pearl?'

'Very.'

Dotty looked wistfully at the table lamp which had outlived both of the women's husbands. 'I wouldn't have wanted my Lionel around me all day, getting underfoot. He didn't like being at home in the daytime.'

'My Barry was happier underground with all his pals,' said Ma.

'They were made for the dark, weren't they?'

'They were.'

'Do you miss him?'

'Sometimes. But more often not.'

'Really?' said Barry, surprised at his own mother's revelation.

'Really,' said Ma.

Dotty nodded. 'Same for me with my Lionel.'

TWENTY-THREE
IF ANYONE ASKS, I'M HUNKY-DORY

PERHAPS IT WAS ALL the talk about Dad or Ma's revelation that she didn't miss him that much. Or it could have been the overdose of late-night cheese, on top of a skinful of beer, half a packet of Gaviscon and a handful of painkillers for his aching wrist. Or maybe it was down to a panic attack from the stark realisation that he was actually a secret millionaire. Whatever the reason, Barry awoke with a sharp pain in the centre of his chest that took a good forty minutes to shift.

Much of last night's conversation around the tea table had troubled him. He realised he didn't possess savage, competitive genes or the desire to reproduce and leave the world a legacy of mini Barrys. He didn't necessarily want to be a winner in the game of life. Doctor Humphreys was also right; he was killing himself with bad food and too much alcohol. He'd sunk enough grog since the first lockdown to drown multiple battleships but his constitution was the strongest part of him. The booze hadn't decked him. Drinking was his refuge, his safe place, his happy place, his hobby, the thing he was good at. He loved walking up to a bar and proudly announcing his poison. However, he knew that both mind and body could not take much more.

His morning chest pain scared him. He felt and looked a lot older lately. He wasn't so different from Lionel, Dotty's dead husband, who drank ale by the bathtub and ignored all the signs of his failing health until it was too late. Dotty said Lionel had been encouraged to suck on twenty Players a day by his old man, who even bought him a stash of fags for Christmas when he was about fourteen to get him started. Apparently, his father, in his infinite wisdom, thought smoking would make a man of him. Lionel never blamed his old man, or the booze and ciggies or even the perils of pit life for his own demise when things all started to go wrong. By all accounts, when the cancer came and stopped him in his tracks he looked it squarely in the eye and didn't flinch.

Ma might not miss her husband much, but Barry sure as hell missed having a father figure in his life. He might have turned out differently. He knew he should have left Anghofiedig years ago; he should have run for his life, kept going and not looked back. This village, these streets, they'd dragged him down and suffocated him – they judged him and never allowed him to escape from who he was, or to be more accurate, who the people round here said he was. Good old Barry White, likeable pisshead. Old-school waster. Occupier of pub snugs, purveyor of bullshit stories. Lazy layabout. Daft as a brush. Soft in the head and soft in the heart. Harmless enough.

He could have called anywhere home. Turkey, Tunisia, Greece, Cyprus, Thailand, USA, Italy, Germany, France, Hungary, Austria, South Africa, Portugal, Spain. Why Anghofiedig? Dark, depressing and wet. Damp and empty. Squeezing the juice out of him slowly. This was the place where Ma and Dad came from. These were his streets because they'd also been their streets. As a kid, when the old men caught him nicking apples from their gardens, they'd always ask the same question, 'Who are you?' And the correct answer was 'I'm Barry

White Junior – you know my old man, strong in the arm and thick in the head.'

The umbilical cord to past connections that he hardly knew proved hard to sever, but he should have cut them all the same. Now, it was almost too late. Not quite, but almost...

In the afternoon Barry watched his beloved rugby team do the unthinkable: win a game. One man doesn't make a team but James was certainly a rare talent on the pitch, and he somehow managed to galvanise those around him so they were doing things they never knew they could do. James scored all the points in a 20–18 defeat of Crusaders and was head and shoulders the best player on the park. However, his most impressive skill was getting the likes of Jonah, McQueen et al to work as a team, do the basics well and play to a plan. He'd effectively come in and replaced McQueen as captain and Uncle Derek as coach without them even realising.

'Systems and tactics work,' he said. 'Trust the process and the rest will follow.'

He sounded like Peter Jones off *Dragon's Den*.

LesCargo had done well to bring in a man of his calibre and Barry wished he had been led by him rather than the rudderless Juliet. Things might have turned out differently.

Barry decided not to stick around after the game but James saw him walking across the car park and ran over to have a word. 'Hey, Barry, not seen you much lately, not staying for a drink?'

'No, got to get off, meeting Romeo tonight.'

'Ah right. How's the wrist?'

'Much better.'

'Glad to hear it. Listen, why don't we do some one-to-one

training when you're fit and ready? I'd like to help you get more out of your rugby.'

'Er...' Barry's stutter spoke volumes.

James didn't get to where he was in the LesCargo management structure without being able to give short motivational pep talks to disgruntled, disinterested foot soldiers. 'You know, we really do need your enthusiasm and I've got an idea to get you playing to your strengths a bit more.'

'What's that?'

'Well, I want to help you get a bit fitter because that alone would make a world of difference to your Saturday afternoons. But on top of that, I think you need to forget this tight-head prop thing, it's not you.'

'So what am I?' said Barry, half-wondering if James was going to persuade him to take another off-field supportive role.

'I think you should play inside centre, number twelve, close to me.'

'In the backs? Me? I'm overweight and slow as a donkey.'

'Doesn't matter, not at this level anyway.' James was getting excited for no apparent reason, like a children's TV presenter. 'You can actually run a straight line, you kick okay from hand and you read the game better than anyone in the club. I've watched you and I've listened to you. You often see what's going to happen before it happens. That's a talent. We need to work on your tackling a bit but you'll have a lot more protection around you at twelve. I'll look after you. Promise. I'll be right next to you throughout the game so all you've got to do is get the ball off McQueen – who's playing great at ten – and give it to me. Think about it. Give it a go and if it doesn't work out, well, you can always switch back, can't you? You've nothing to lose.'

'Guess not,' said Barry, still trying to take everything in.

In the space of a couple of weeks, he'd won a million quid on the horses, Angharad wanted to sleep with him and now the best rugby player in the district by a country mile was telling him he had all the credentials to be Anghofiedig's answer to Jamie Roberts or Sonny Bill Williams. What was happening to Barry and his world?

Just when he thought he might have a normal evening...

Romeo had persuaded Barry against his better judgement to catch the bus into the Forest for a night out.

Barry wore his Anghofiedig rugby shirt, with the number three emblazoned on the back. His number. His father's old number.

The pair of them sat in The Buck playing the Pac-Man machine, an original that no one had ever bothered to get rid of. It took old ten pences so you had to exchange real money for the old stuff with Maggie at the bar.

'Hello, soldier, how's the wrist?'

Stood behind him, in jeans and a pink hoodie, was Diana, the A&E nurse, and her incredible green eyes.

'Oh hello, what you doing here?' said Barry.

'Having a drink, same as you,' said Diana.

'Yeah, but why here? *In bear country?*' said Barry, whispering the last part.

Diana laughed. 'Because I live here, that's why.'

'What? You mean you're a Forester?'

'Yep, and proud of it.'

'I'm Romeo,' said Romeo.

'Are you now? I can see I'm going to have to watch you,' said Diana.

'No really, that's my name. Romeo Davies.'

'Your parents big fans of Shakespeare?'

'No, Showaddywaddy,' said Romeo.

147

The rest of the evening was a blur but that had little to do with alcohol. Diana and her friend Sarah sat at a corner table with Barry and Romeo, until Sarah decided she'd had enough of scrolling through Instagram on her phone and made her excuses. Romeo departed for the Space Invaders and Pac-Man machines and lost himself in primitive 1980s gaming heaven, shooting wave upon wave of descending aliens or gorging himself on all in front of him, like Barry at a wedding buffet, whilst avoiding a few friendly ghosts in the process.

Barry found the chat with Diana easy. She was divorced with a fourteen-year-old son called Eddie. She'd always been a nurse and loved her job in the community hospital. She liked riding horses but didn't get much chance to do it these days and no longer had a horse of her own. Her father had run a successful haulage company but dropped down dead two years ago. Her estranged mother left them around the time *Shirley Valentine* was popular, for a toy boy called Christos. Incredibly, they were still together and living in Corfu. Diana was only three or four when her mother ran out on them. She'd tried to forgive her but found it difficult. Now, they got along okay but they didn't really know each other and that was unlikely to ever change. Her mother was full of remorse and regrets, but there was no going back. Diana had effectively been raised by her grandmother, who lived with her and her father until she died in 2002.

'Just your everyday life story,' she said. 'Mistakes, let-downs, bad luck, wrong turnings and dead ends. But I'm okay, really I am. I'm happy with my lot. I wouldn't change much about my life, I'd just tinker with some bits around the edges. How about you?'

Ordinarily, when asked such a question, Barry would play a defensive straight bat. If anyone enquired how he was doing, how life was going, how his day had been or even what he thought tomorrow's storms might bring, his response was the same. 'It's all fine. Hunky-dory.'

But right here, right now, in this backwater pub that stood frozen and preserved in 1981, where previously he'd never felt safe, he found himself opening up completely to someone he hardly knew.

'Actually, I would change quite a lot about me if I could.'

'Like what?' said Diana.

Barry held his belly in both hands. 'I'm too fat for a start. And I drink too much. My doctor told me I was an obese alcoholic and he reckoned he was being kind.'

'What else?'

'I wish people didn't laugh at me when I walked into a room. My name doesn't help, especially with older people. When they get past that, I'm always Barry White Junior. I'd like to be Barry White Senior one day. My dad's been dead almost as long as you've been alive yet I'm still living in his shadow. I don't think I've grown up and now I don't know how to. I used to gamble heavily as well but I think I've quit that one. Do you know how? Because I've become frightened of winning.'

Barry paused and drank a mouthful of beer, wondering whether he should carry on or not. He realised he was at a bit of a crossroads. Diana might start laughing at him. However, it was a risk worth taking.

'I spend most of my days lying in bed watching TikTok and YouTube videos. I watch a gorilla called Chico eat fruit on a livestream every day. I even send him money for bananas via a standing order. Or I watch videos of the Welsh rugby team from the 1970s and imagine that I'm Charlie Faulkner or the real Graham Price, or sometimes Gareth Edwards or JPR Williams. Hard as nails. A proper man's man. Socks down round my ankles and blood spurting from my forehead. I live in the same place I've always lived. I've never been anywhere else, except in my head. I'm lost, Diana. I'm lost. Even now, a voice in my head is shouting at me "what right do *you* have to talk to her? You're gonna mess it all up".'

'Oh, soldier, I don't think you see what other people see.'

Diana leaned forward and kissed Barry on the lips.

Instinctively, he kissed her back.

TWENTY-FOUR

CHIN UP, VICAR, GOD'S ON YOUR SIDE

IT WAS difficult at first but they both handled the awkwardness with maturity.

'Sorry about the other night,' said Barry.

'Sorry about the stifado,' said Angharad.

'Tasted great on the way down.'

'Romeo hasn't noticed a pair of his pants have gone missing.'

'Wouldn't expect him to.'

'I know you didn't really need them.'

'Thought as much.'

'Thank you anyway. For not taking advantage of me when I was low.'

'You're welcome.'

Once they got past the forced silences, Angharad confessed that she was finding the break-up with Greg and the rejection hard to handle. Barry said he understood, though he wasn't sure he did. James was right about one thing, however, he had a talent for reading the game even if he couldn't always play it. Angharad kissed Barry on the cheek and they agreed to stay just good friends. Nothing more, nothing less.

'You know you still mean the world to me,' said Barry.

'Good to hear,' said Angharad.

'And I've got a proposition for you, one that I think you'll like.'

'Go on.'

Barry told Angharad about his plans to renovate Ma's house from top to bottom – new designs, new décor, new everything – but he needed help with colour schemes, ideas and project management. Angharad was genuinely excited. She loved watching all those *DIY SOS*-style house makeover programmes and always dreamt that one day she could have a go at overseeing a big project like that herself. Barry knew this because she'd mentioned it to him once in the pub a year or so ago. She'd said the same thing more directly to Greg a thousand times over, but he'd never actually registered the words or their meaning.

Barry told Angharad he'd give her £10k for her work and that she'd also get a sizeable budget to finance the project from start to finish. He made out that an investment policy he'd taken out as a teenager had finally come to fruition and Angharad believed him. It was sort of true. He first got into gambling when he was eighteen or nineteen. More important than believing him, she believed *in* him. He was just what she needed right now, a male friend who wasn't on the take. She skipped away down the church path like a teenager with a new spring in her step and fresh, clean, wholesome things in her head to repaint the stained, grubby grey walls of her thoughts with perfect whites of Moon Shimmer, Frosted Dawn, Barley Twist and Milky Pail.

Angharad might have found going to church that morning hugely rewarding but Reverend Hill looked like he was carrying the whole world on his shoulders when Barry and Ma bid him a cheery 'see you next week' in glorious stereo.

The mood of his sermon – and the service in general – had been unusually downbeat.

'Chin up, vicar, your preach wasn't your best but it wasn't the worst either,' said Barry.

'It was hard going this morning.' Reverend Hill thumped the front of his Bible.

'Why?' asked Ma.

'Money,' said Reverend Hill.

'Oh that ol' chestnut,' said Ma, disappointed.

'Our books just aren't balancing,' explained Reverend Hill.

Ma tutted, almost insensitively. 'God will provide, he always does.'

'Hope so,' said Reverend Hill.

'Hope?' Ma emphasised the word to make a point and the reverend looked ashamed of himself for not choosing faith, or even charity, as the central basis of his response.

He told Ma that donations were down almost fifty per cent on last year and whilst 'bums on pews' weren't exactly in freefall, the spirit of revival was hardly infusing the Anghofiedig air. Reverend Hill, being relatively young, took most things to heart. His church relied on the generous giving of its parishioners, along with the odd wedding or legacy. He wanted to open a food bank and organise new ways to support those badly affected by the cost-of-living crisis but he feared that if he did, he might find himself at the front of any queue for free squirty cream and tins of peaches.

'People don't understand what it's like to lead a church in today's broken world.' Reverend Hill was clearly feeling sorry for himself.

Barry saw it as his responsibility to lighten the mood. 'Aww come on, revvo, always look on the bright side of life.' He began whistling the chorus to the Monty Python song.

'Reverend, forgive my boy, he's an idiot.'

'Maybe it's me, Mrs White, perhaps I'm not getting through to people. Are my sermons dull?'

'Not where I sit,' said Ma.

'But she likes *Countryfile*,' added Barry.

'Am I dull?'

'Absolutely not, quite the opposite,' said Ma.

'I'd say you were more intimidating than dull.' Barry took a backward step as a precaution.

'Do I come across as real?' Reverend Hill worked hard to be the kind of man his congregation wanted him to be, but sometimes he felt this detracted from who he really was.

'You're young, that's all. Give yourself time,' said Ma.

'How much time?'

'Hard to say – but look at my Barry, here. He's a lot older than you and he's still waiting for God to reveal His plans for him.'

'I don't know if I can wait that long.'

'Thanks a bunch, both of you,' said Barry.

The reverend smiled. 'It's always reassuring to know there's someone with needs greater than your own.'

'Things will work out just fine – for you and for this church,' said Ma.

'I just need to trust God more, don't I?'

'You do. Things happen in His time, not yours.'

'Bless you, Mrs White, you're very wise.'

'I can be.' Ma looked pleased with herself.

'I'm glad I bumped into you. The Lord truly works in mysterious ways,' said Reverend Hill.

'And rev, remember the bright side. Always...' chirped Barry, with a big self-satisfied grin on his face.

Ma cuffed him across the side of the head with her handbag. 'It's Sunday, this is God's house, the reverend is being serious and that's blasphemy.'

Sunday teatime, Barry went for a walk through Lincoln Park on his own and sat by the lake to feed a tin of Jolly Green Giant sweetcorn to the ducks. He watched families come and go with their shrieking children and barking dogs, their laughter and angry outbursts, domestic power struggles and sulky tensions. Kids wanting to be heard and parents demanding order, thanks and respect. They'd have to wait until they were old and grey before they got some proper thank yous and then it would hardly matter to them anymore. Barry wished he had a family of his own but that was something even money couldn't buy. He was still struggling to comprehend that he was rich. No one else knew and his way of life certainly didn't reflect his new status quo, unless you factored in his secret arrangement with Angharad over the house renovations and putting Romeo on a salary to make sure he didn't go completely off the rails. At some point, brother and sister might talk to each other and start to ask more questions but that wasn't a concern for today.

Barry had no idea how to live a normal life, let alone the life of a millionaire. He felt uncertain about his future and having lots of money in the bank didn't make him feel any happier or more secure. He now felt guilty on top of everything else because plenty of others deserved the money so much more than him.

He left the park and walked around the streets of Anghofiedig for a while, this derelict mining town, carved out of coal, in need of a good wash with its endless rows of two-up and two-down terraces, old sofas in front gardens, gates that didn't fit their latches properly and dustbins flipped upside down, blowing crisp packets on the breeze. Away from these estates Anghofiedig's ruggedness was masked by green fields, rooted oaks and streams that gurgled. On these estates, where people gathered dust in tired-out yellowy living rooms, you could not hide their everyday struggle to put food on tables and shoes on feet. This old-fashioned, long-forgotten Welsh village that no one else cared about, this bizarre centre of logistics that went and led nowhere, this heart attack capital of South Wales, this land of boozers and smokers and drug takers and scrappers, this sprawling jungle of chip eaters and daytime telly watchers, watching their lives pass them by.

None of them had any idea that they had a rich man living in their midst.

And what would they do if they ever found out?

TWENTY-FIVE
TRANSFORMATION STARTS BETWEEN THE EARS

IT WAS EASIER for Barry to lie in bed with a laptop on his knee, pretending to work, than tell Ma the truth. She brought him a mug of coffee and two hefty rounds of bacon sandwiches slathered in brown sauce. The cause of his chest pains at the weekend still bothered him so he put one of the sarnies to the side and ate the other – removing all the fat and rind off the bacon first. For the first time in his life, he genuinely wanted to lose some weight. For himself and his own health, to impress Diana and to silence the cruel matter-of-fact tongues of Doctor Humphreys and others. However, when Ma popped back into his room to collect his dirty crockery, she put the other sandwich back on his bed and told him to 'eat up' because bacon now cost almost £4 a pack and her name wasn't Rockefeller. Grudgingly, he ate it, reflecting that he might have to go to the grave in order to prevent his mother from being offended.

Feigning work was not a new experience but lying about stuff so blatantly was, and he didn't like doing it.

'Good luck with morning conference today, son. Got much on?'

'Pretty rammed today, Ma, better not disturb me until lunchtime.'

'I'll be quiet as a mouse downstairs, promise. What do you want for your lunch?'

'Maybe a salad?'

'I'll do you a nice shepherd's pie with some treacle sponge for afters.'

Barry watched an episode of *The Professionals* on ITV4 with his headphones on but fell asleep and woke up coughing, unable to breathe, with Cowley shouting out instructions to Bodie and Doyle to 'finish him off'. Barry had visible red tractor lines across his throat where the headphone cables had half-strangled him. What a way to go that would have been! He consoled himself in the knowledge that at least his trousers were fastened all the way up and his hands weren't tucked away down the front of his pants – pants he'd stolen from Romeo, which had elephant ears either side of a prominent trunk. Try explaining all that to Anghofiedig's modern-day answer to CI5.

Regaining his composure, Barry typed '*What do millionaires do all day?*' into the search engine. He was shocked to discover that millionaires generally slept less and worked more. He would certainly be an exception to that statistical wonder. He also discovered that millionaires commonly invested their cash in property and low-cost index funds – whatever they were – and were frequently frugal in public. They busied themselves with side hustles, using hobbies and interests to generate even more revenue streams, and they also spent a large proportion of their day researching and playing the stock market. In Barry's world, that was called studying form and it involved a *Racing Post*. A lot of millionaires also, apparently, invested heavily in their own personal growth: listening to classical music, drinking classical wines and driving classic cars. They read biographies by the likes of Alan Sugar or Theo Paphitis, or books about history and wars. And they collected things to challenge their thinking, such as young girlfriends or paintings by Andy Warhol.

'Screw all that,' said Barry to himself. 'It's Chico time!'

Chico was in fine fettle today, wearing Alan Carr-style glasses, watching videos of himself on his keeper's phone as they sat together kissing and eating raspberries. Chico then started showing off to a female gorilla called Grace, trying to wow her with a display of strength and some of the loudest farts Barry had ever heard in his life. What impressed Barry most was the way Chico owned them, with complete and utter pride. He didn't look around shiftily or surreptitiously, hoping no one had heard him. No, his whole demeanour said to the world 'this is me' and 'those are mine' – 'they are part of my power, do you hear what I can do?'

Barry vowed to try this himself the next time he felt the urge to pass violent wind, though it would largely depend on where he was and who he was with at the time. If he was with Diana, for instance, she might not be as impressed as Grace was. Doctor Humphreys might consider him either psychopathic or sociopathic as well as obese and alcoholic. Reverend Hill, were they in church, might ask for others to pray for him. The guys at the rugby club? They would understand. He would definitely get a big Chico-style chest-beating thump of approval from them.

Barry ate lunch with Ma, though she didn't touch a morsel of food herself. 'What's up, Ma, you seem to be off your tucker lately?'

Ma waved his concern away. 'It's just my age.'

'You spend all your time looking after me, you've got to look after yourself too.'

'Don't you worry about me, boy. I'm strong as an ox.'

Barry decided to cheer Ma up by telling her all about his

plans for the house. He thought she'd be more pleased than she was.

'This place doesn't need sprucing up, it's clean, it's tidy, it's all we need,' said Ma.

'But everything's faded, Ma, you wait until it's done, you'll love it. Angharad's working on the ideas. We'll make the place sparkle again.'

'Again?'

'Okay, we'll make the place sparkle.'

'All sounds expensive.'

'I can afford it.' Barry was torn. He desperately wanted to tell Ma about his windfall and share both the good news and the money with her, but he knew it was a secret he had to keep from her. For her sake. So she didn't see who he really was.

'You won the lottery? You seem to be spending a lot of cash lately.'

'No, I haven't won the lottery.' Barry was relieved she mentioned the lottery rather than the horses. 'But you can't take it with you when you're dead, can you?'

'Guess not, son.' Ma could feel her eyes filling up so she carried some plates through to the kitchen to wash them up.

That evening, Barry met James at the rugby club for what he thought was going to be a spot of extra training to aid his conversion from prop to centre.

'Right, today is the first day of your new life.' James told Barry that they wouldn't be doing much ball work for a few weeks, instead they'd concentrate on general fitness. They started with three laps of the pitch to loosen up but Barry was on his knees and fighting to get air into his lungs by the end of it.

'It's okay, you can walk the next three laps.' James didn't have a bead of sweat on him.

'How... many... are we... doing?' Barry was gasping for oxygen.

'Ten or so?'

'If I'd known I was coming to boot camp I wouldn't have had Ma's home-made pizza for tea,' said Barry.

'I'll sort out a diet sheet for you this week,' said James, stretching his calf muscles as he spoke. 'Ideally, you'd cut out the crap food and the booze completely but that's not going to happen, I know. So, we'll do our best and try to make good swaps that you'll hardly notice.'

The words sounded so familiar to Barry. 'Is your old man Doc Humphreys?'

Barry huffed and puffed and moaned his way through a ninety-minute training session, which James repeatedly called a 'low-key intro'. In addition to jogging, Barry tried his hand at skipping, squats, jumping jacks, mountain climbers, burpees, froggy jumps, push-ups and sit-ups.

Showering together afterwards in the rugby club changing rooms, James looked at Barry stark naked and grimaced.

'It's going to take a lot of work to shift that baby.'

Barry cradled his own stomach gently. 'Maybe I should have a caesarian. Or perhaps I should just stay at prop.'

'Rubbish. I worked you quite hard tonight because I needed to gauge where you're at.'

'So where am I at?' asked Barry.

James made a swooping roller-coaster gesture with his hand. 'The start of a beautiful ride.'

James told Barry that he'd train him on Mondays and Thursdays and they'd do club training with the rest of the lads on a Wednesday. With matches on Saturdays, Barry would effectively be working out four times a week.

'It's too much, I'll die,' whimpered Barry, pathetically.

'We'll go steady. Cardio on Mondays and weights in the gym on Thursdays. Your goals won't be complex because you're so...' James curtailed himself from finishing his sentence so Barry did it for him.

'Unfit?'

'Yes.'

'We'll work on your cardiovascular fitness and muscle strength, your body shape and your flexibility. I'd like to do a few simple yoga sessions with you too if you'll let me.'

'Yoga? Me?'

'When you start seeing results, you'll want to do more.'

Barry did want his clothes to fit better so his bum didn't pop out of his jeans when he tried to bend down, and he liked the idea of a new dawn as a rugby player at the grand old age of forty-four.

'Are you in? We won't achieve anything unless you commit,' said James.

Barry nodded to seal the deal.

'Great, any questions?'

'Yeah, this changing-my-diet malarkey, will you speak to my mother?'

'Your mother? Why?'

'Because she won't let me cook for myself and she's the Queen of Stodge,' said Barry.

'I'll have a word,' said James. 'What about the beer? Think you can restrict yourself to just a couple on Fridays and four or five on a Saturday night?'

'It'll be tough but in a weird kind of way I'm looking forward to trying.' Barry knew he could kick the booze if he wanted to. The problem was, he'd never actually had a reason to do so.

'Good man,' said James.

'I might have a proper bender every so often for old times' sake but you're looking at a new me.' Barry puffed out his chest and sucked in his cheeks.

James rabbit-punched him on the chest affectionately. 'Every transformation starts in the head.'

'I feel my head needs transforming most,' said Barry.

TWENTY-SIX
CONFRONTING THE FEEL-GOOD FACTOR

THERE WASN'T a bit of him that didn't ache. It was worse than any hangover he'd ever had and he couldn't drag himself out of bed. So much for exercise giving you the feel-good factor. An all-pervading stiffness smothered various other aches and pains, and his vital organs – and those less vital – marched up and down Barry's body in loud protest, waving placards saying '*Running kills*' and shouting 'What do we want?... The death of James... When do we want it?... Now!'

Ma knocked at the door.

'Are you decent?'

'No, and I definitely don't want any breakfast this morning, nothing at all, so that means nothing, not even a cheeky full English you leave on the side.'

'Someone got out of bed the wrong side this morning.'

'I'm not out of bed,' said Barry. He barely had the energy to backchat Ma.

'Well you need to be, you've got work.'

'I'm not working today. Day off.'

'Oh! Well that's not what Romeo thinks. He was trying to

ring you but your phone was off so he called the landline. He says he'll be round in ten minutes for a business meeting.'

'A bloody what?' Barry regretted telling his friend that his pity handouts constituted a job.

Romeo pitched up on time, wearing a shirt and tie. Ma showed him into Barry's bedroom so he sat on the edge of the bed with Barry still in it, naked and aching. His training session with James had left him feeling so rough he wondered if his limbs would ever move freely again.

'Wos all this about? I'm not in the mood for your messing about,' said Barry.

'Sorry, but we need to sort out a few things about my contract,' said Romeo.

'You haven't got a contract.'

'Exactly!'

Romeo came prepared with a long list of questions and demands. He wanted to know how he would receive his £500 per week and whether that figure was gross or net? He also enquired if he had to pay any tax or national insurance contributions and if there was a pension scheme? If so, how much was Barry putting in? He asked about holidays and holiday cover. Was there a private medical scheme and could he enrol straight away or was there a probationary period and if so, how long? What were his actual hours? And what did Barry want him to do exactly? Did he have a proper job title? Could he have a name badge? If there was a lot of driving involved, would he get a new company car or was he expected to use his Dyane? If the latter, how much would he get for mileage and general wear and tear and how should he go about claiming expenses? Were there any forms? He asked about training and inductions and uniforms. Was there a luncheon scheme? What about maternity and paternity allowances? A proper sick-pay scheme? A flexible working scheme? Could he have a new work phone? And a laptop too, because he had to give the only one he had back to LesCargo. Where was his place of work? How should he go about raising any grievances? When would he get a pay review and would it be in line with inflation? Would he have to attend regular meetings? Did he have any colleagues, for example, was Ma also on the payroll? Would there be a Christmas party? And at the end of it all, he said, 'By the way, don't suppose you've seen a pair of elephant underpants? They've gone missing from my top drawer and they're my favourites.'

Barry barely had the energy to sit up so he waited until Romeo had talked himself dry.

'Listen, you'll get £500 a week and that's it, nothing else. If anyone asks, especially anyone official from HMRC, you don't work for me and never have. I don't actually expect you to do anything for your £500. If you must have a job title then call yourself a Lazy Bastard Executive, in charge of the Lazy Bastard Department. Your function is to help me be a lazy bastard. I will get you a new phone and a laptop. I might even get you a new second-hand car. You call me Barry, like always, so drop the boss or I'll start deducting pay. We're equals. Though I'm probably more equal than you. As for the underpants, have you checked the filter of your mum's washing machine?'

Romeo looked like someone had just popped his balloon. 'Sorry, Baz, didn't mean to upset you.'

'Nah, I'm sorry – it's not you.'

Romeo stroked the dragon on the cover of Barry's bedspread. 'I just wanted to make things right, even though I knew all along it wasn't a real job. I know you're just helping me out cos you feel sorry for me.'

Barry suddenly felt like a shithouse for crushing his mate's feelings. 'We're besties. We're equals.'

'Yeah,' said Romeo, trying not to turn his nod of agreement into a question.

'Are you okay?' asked Barry.

'Not sure,' said Romeo.

The pair seldom had grown-up conversations, most of their exchanges were silly, childish, superficial and banal, but Romeo suddenly lifted the lid to some of the things going on inside his own head that no one else knew about.

'Do you think I'm weird?'

'In what way?'

'Hard to talk to. Hard to predict.'

'Yes.'

'In what way?'

'You never used to pace around like you do. You never used to daydream and go missing so much.'

Romeo admitted that he sometimes felt the daydreaming was taking over his life. From the moment he woke up to the time he went to bed, he had this urge to exist in Feelgood. When he was there, things felt real. He felt real. Everything else felt like the dream. And the slightest thing would send him running back there, a line from a film, a song, a picture, they were all fuel for his fantasies. And when he stopped dreaming, everything felt bad again so he'd go back to dreaming, back to Feelgood, to get away from the stress and the conflict and the emptiness.

'Am I nuts?' said Romeo, blinking fast, craving reassurance.

'No,' said Barry, realising he could just as easily have answered yes.

'Do you think I'm normal?' Romeo reverted to hair tugging – always a sign he was feeling anxious – and Barry noticed a bald spot emerging in a straight line above his right ear, as the lazy crow might fly.

'Who's normal?' Barry fudged an answer.

'Then what am I?'

'You're somewhere in between the two. Like me. Like most people,' said Barry.

'Do you ever think about ending it all?' said Romeo.

'Bloody hell, no.'

'I do, sometimes.' Romeo looked exhausted, worn out by all the competing thoughts fighting for air and space in his head.

He poured it all out. He said he felt like his life was stuck on a terrible loop, as if he was a frightened rat sprinting on a wheel with no end. The only way off was to jump. For a while he thought about walking out to sea and telling himself he wasn't actually doing anything bad – he was just planning to swim to the other side, however far that might be. The fact that he struggled to swim a length of a swimming pool was neither here nor there. It was all about intent and, if he said it often and loudly enough, he could convince himself his intent was to swim to Ireland via his steely resolve and the merits of his untested and unproven doggy paddle.

'What if I signed up for the Ukrainian army? Say I got myself to the front line, determined to defeat the entire Russian Army on my own, with my Swiss Army penknife and a home-made petrol bomb. Am I a fearless war hero or a lunatic? Where's the line between caring too much and not caring enough? What if I climbed K2 in my replica Gareth Bale Wales shirt and a pair of flip-flops? Or attempted to be the next Harry Houdini, covering myself in chains and padlocks inside an airproof tank, submerging myself deep in shark-infested water, to see how long it would take me to escape? I know how to ride a pushbike, what if I tried leaping fifty red London buses like I was Evel Knievel? "Dare to dream", Juliet had that written on her coffee mug at work, remember? Who's to say I'm not actually Jason Bourne? Or James Bond? How will I know unless I test myself? Can I catch a bullet from a revolver in my teeth from twenty-two yards? Why not? I know how to trap peanuts in my mouth when I throw them up in the air so it's only an extension of the same principles, ain't it?'

Barry listened to Romeo talk and felt bad for not noticing just how much his friend had changed these past years, probably since the first lockdown. They'd been pals all their lives and spoke most days. How did he miss so many signs? He should have noticed. He should have helped sooner.

'On Feelgood, we've got buttons in our arms which we can press to end our lives whenever we want,' said Romeo. 'There are no comebacks for doing that. We just start again the next day. That's why there aren't many people over the age of twenty, bar a few deranged attention-seekers like Mr Bronson. The thing is, I don't think killing myself is the right thing to do at all. I'm just not sure how to live anymore. Do you get that? I don't know how anything is going to get better for me? Is this as good as it will ever be from here on in?'

'Let's make an appointment to go back and see Doc Humphreys. I'll come with you,' said Barry.

'Thanks.'

'You'll be okay.'

'I know.'

'And don't worry about money or any of that stuff, I will look after you.'

'I know.' Romeo stopped tugging at his hair but didn't know where to put his hands.

There was a pause with neither man knowing what to say nor do next. Eventually, Romeo broke the silence.

'Barry, why did you steal my elephant underpants?'

'Dunno,' replied Barry, embarrassed.

'It's okay. You can keep them,' said Romeo.

'Thank you.'

TWENTY-SEVEN

WE'RE PROPS AND HOOKERS, IT'S IN OUR GENES

ROMEO WAS EVEN MORE fidgety than usual, but that was a classic symptom. The last time he sat in Humphreys' surgery, the doctor promised to arrange a proper test for autism but then forgot to do it. When an invitation finally arrived in the post, Romeo didn't bother replying to it. Today though – once Barry had told him about all the stuff Romeo had shared with him – things went up a notch. The doctor said he'd make sure an assessment got done within a couple of weeks, following things up personally if necessary. He said he was now almost certain that Romeo was somewhere along the autistic spectrum – and likely to have ADHD as well. It was stating the bleeding obvious really, except no one had bothered doing it before because there hadn't been any point. Such a confirmation wouldn't have changed anything and probably still wouldn't. However, some of the thoughts living in Romeo's head were no longer ones a GP could ignore. Romeo was no longer functioning beneath the radar. The system was catching up with him.

Few had even heard of autism or ADHD when Romeo was a schoolboy and his teachers just labelled him quirky and a bit boisterous. Changes in his routine over the last few years meant he no longer went out to work every day, which made him more unpredictable. He became ruder, more blunt in his responses to people. He found it harder to understand what people were asking of him and spent a lot more time alone. Since the lockdowns, he no longer understood social rules and had little structure to his days or nights. People getting inside his personal space bothered him more. Life bothered him more. He'd spiralled downwards.

Hearing Doctor Humphreys offer a likely explanation for some of the things he did and thought came as a massive relief to Romeo.

'See, it's not my fault,' he said, over and over.

'No, it's not your fault,' said Doctor Humphreys.

Once they were out of the surgery and sat in the Dyane, Romeo acted like a weight had been lifted off his shoulders.

'Baz, you do know I would never do anything stupid to hurt myself, don't you?'

'Yes,' said Barry.

'Or anyone else.'

'I know.'

'What do you reckon they'll do to me?'

'Therapy, probably.'

'Talking?' Romeo dropped his head back against the seat's headrest.

'Lots of,' said Barry.

'Drugs?' enquired Romeo.

'Quite possibly.'

'Can they fix me?' Romeo turned sideways to find Barry winding down the window.

'No, but they can help you.' The whirring window drowned out some of the words.

'Fair enough, I'll take going back to how I used to be.'

'Me too.'

Romeo expressed both relief and surprise that Doctor Humphreys had been quite gentle in his manner – and hadn't taken the opportunity to call Barry a fat alcy again. Barry told his friend that he was in the process of going on a diet and restricting his drinking to Friday and Saturday nights only.

'Really?' said Romeo.

'Really,' said Barry.

'Wow, today's a landmark day for both of us, isn't it?'

'Guess so.'

As they were laying all their cards on the table, Barry considered telling Romeo his million-pound secret, which he was desperately struggling to carry alone.

'Romeo, I've got something massive to tell you, something life-changing,' said Barry.

'What is it?' said Romeo, attentively.

'I've had a proper stroke of luck, something you'd never believe in your wildest dreams.'

'Go on...'

'Well, er... umm... it's just, you know, erm, that woman I met in the Forest last week? I'm going on a date with her on Friday night.'

Club training night and Pricer – with mohawk neatly gelled and glistening – was back in action.

'Bollock one hundred per cent?' asked McQueen.

'Yep, perfect, big and bouncy – but a good big and bouncy, human big, not elephant big,' said Pricer.

'Pleased for you,' said McQueen.

Uncle Derek was putting out cones on the main pitch when Barry sidled over for a word.

'Uncle Derek, I've got an announcement.'

'What's that?' said Uncle Derek, counting yards in his head so he knew when to put down his next marker.

'I'm on a diet,' said Barry.

'Nice one,' said Uncle Derek.

'Two more things, I'm only drinking weekends now.'

'That's one thing?'

'And I don't want to play prop no more. I want to play inside centre from now on.' Uncle Derek's instinctive response was to laugh. Not just from the back of his throat, but a full-on bowels-of-the-stomach explosion. Not for him the response to a smart Jimmy Carr one-liner or a shrewd John Bishop 'my wife doesn't understand me' observation. No, this was the kind of laughter saved for an epic Billy Connolly gig, it was the response you'd expect for an on-the-money, machine-gun tirade of wit. It was wet yourself, fall-to-the-floor laughter. It was a swallow your own tongue and choke on it, what a good way to go kind of laughter. Barry watched his uncle sink to his knees and waited patiently for the old man's sanity to return.

'Ah you crack me up,' said Uncle Derek.

'Don't know why. I'm being serious.' Barry was not amused.

'Oh, son, you're forty-four and built like a second-hand wardrobe. You run the 100 metres in thirty minutes and pass a rugby ball about as badly as you pass a betting shop or a kebab van.'

Barry pushed one of Derek's cones over in frustration. 'Speak to James, he'll tell you. It was all his idea.'

Barry bellowed across the field, 'James, come over here a second will yer.'

James was doing stretches near the corner flag when Barry summoned him over.

'James, tell Uncle Derek about my conversion to the dark side.'

'Come again?' said James, confused.

'Tell him how you're turning me into a number twelve. An inside centre.'

'Ah right, that. Yes, I think it's a better spot for him.'

'But the boy's a prop. Always has been. He's a terrible one, admittedly, but he's a prop,' said Uncle Derek.

'But why?' said James.

'Why what?'

'Why is he a prop?'

'Cos he's a White.'

'So?'

Uncle Derek didn't believe what he was trying to say needed an explanation. 'So what?'

'So why does being a White mean he has to play prop?' asked James.

'Because that's what Whites do. We're front-row forwards. We're props and hookers. It's in the blood. In our genes,' said Uncle Derek.

'But you said yourself he's not great there. You even wanted him to quit rugby altogether a few weeks ago.' James was not giving up.

'He isn't. And I still do. But he's not great anywhere. And he won't be bloody great at number twelve either.' Barry gave his uncle a withering look, which he didn't catch.

'No, but he'll be better, especially with me and McQueen close to him,' said James.

'McQueen doesn't want to be close to him. McQueen doesn't want him on the same field as him. McQueen doesn't even want him in the same village. McQueen would be quite happy if he emigrated to England,' said Uncle Derek.

'Don't worry about McQueen, he'll come around when he sees the improvement. He's just frustrated by failure.'

'Are you saying I'm a failure?' Barry felt like he was

eavesdropping on a conversation that was about him, rather than for him.

'No, course not,' said James.

'I am,' said Uncle Derek.

There was a silence. Barry looked his uncle in the eye and Derek realised what he had done.

'Look, that didn't come out like it was supposed to.'

'I reckon it came out just right,' said Barry, sulkily. 'Uncle, I don't care what you think about me anymore. And I'm done with trying to live up to all this White rugby hardman hero rubbish. And get this, from all I've heard about him, I don't think my old man was that special. He ain't that special from the things I can actually remember about him as a kid and he ain't that special from the stuff Ma says about him. She says I'm worth ten of him. Now, I know he was your brother and you idolised him and all that but he isn't my hero, never was and never will be. To me, he's just a stupid bloody idiot with a thick head and an even thicker temper who was so brainless he drove a lorry the wrong way down a motorway.'

Derek wasn't laughing now. This lump of Welsh granite who men of a certain age still had nightmares about, dropped his head to the floor.

And for once, 'never flustered' James, LesCargo's master arbitrator and go-to problem solver, didn't have a clue what to say or do for the best either.

TWENTY-EIGHT

CONTEMPORARY SCHEMES FOR THE EXECUTIVE LIAR

MA NEEDED to sit down because the bombs were too loud and too frequent. She felt like she was trapped underground in a Tube station somewhere in the east of London in 1940 sheltering from the devastation. The air felt thin and she could hardly breathe. First off, Barry told her what he'd said to Uncle Derek last night and how he'd almost made him cry. Then he announced he was quitting booze, except for weekends. The deepest cut came next; news of his diet and his intention to do his own shopping and cooking from now on. Or if not cooking, exactly, his own chopping, prepping, unwrapping, grilling, microwaving and arranging on a plate, including snacks. Out were Ma's suet puddings, spotted dick, steak and kidney pies, fried breakfasts, Yorkshire puddings and roasters, chunky chips topped with both cheese and gravy, onion cakes and fatty faggots. In were porridge, salted popcorn, chicken breasts, tins of mackerel, green beans, baked beans and broccoli.

'You're Welsh not Greek, so why do you want to start eating yoghurts? Protein shakes aren't even food. And fancy avocados ain't for the likes of you and me. You're mining stock. You need proper grub in you.'

Barry held up his hands so Ma could see his palms. 'I've never been down a pit in my life.'

'Don't matter, you still got coal in your veins.'

'Aww not that again. I lie on my bed with a laptop on my knee all day.'

'It's still manual labour of sorts, sometimes you look like you're lying twisted in a seam,' said Ma, realising as she spoke that she was losing the argument.

'With pillows and fluffy cushions around my head and feet.'

'Then you need brain food. Carbon hydrates.' Barry smiled at Ma's use of words.

'My personal trainer, James, is doing me some proper diet sheets and meal plans. He'll go through them with you.'

'Ooh get you. Personal trainer?'

'Yeah, I'm seeing him this evening. He's helping me get fit.' Barry hadn't finished with his derring-do sortie. He circled around the skies once more before reducing height to tell Ma he had a date with a Forester called Diana tomorrow night and that she had a fourteen-year-old son. Could he go the whole hog and tell her he just happened to be a millionaire as well? 'And another thing, I've had a promotion at work. I'm now a Senior Communications Executive.'

'You are?' said Ma, her eyes lighting up.

'I am.'

'What does that mean?'

'It means I don't have to work so hard and I get paid a shedload more.'

'It's a lot to take in all this. Do you get your own office?' Struggling to keep up, Ma picked up a cushion and held on to it for dear life.

'No, work from home, just the same.'

'D'you get a name badge?'

'Not bothered about that, I work in a bedroom. I know who I am and so do you.'

'Is that why you've got a personal trainer? To look after you, now you're important?'

'No, though I do get a PA-slash-driver.' Barry realised the timing was perfect for dropping in news of his arrangement with Romeo.

'Do yer?' said Ma, cooing.

'Yeah, it's Romeo.'

'I can't wait to tell Dotty.'

'Which bit?'

'The fancy job title with executive in it and you getting to boss Romeo about and the adopted family bit – when do I get to meet my new grandson?' said Ma, tossing the cushion onto the sofa.

'Go easy,' said Barry.

'I wish you'd let me carry on cooking for you,' said Ma.

'You can do me a boiled egg.'

'Soldiers?'

'Go on then. Brown 'uns.'

'Can you say brown 'uns now you're a VIP?' said Ma, scuttling happily off to the kitchen, safe in the knowledge she would live to fight another day and her boy still needed her to boil his eggs, butter his army of soldiers, cut their crusts off and line them up symmetrically on the front line ready for battle.

Angharad came around later in the day to go through her plans for the house renovations so Barry pretended to finish work early. Being an executive would give him much more freedom to lie to Ma, who thought later starts, longer lunchbreaks and knocking off at two in the afternoon were just the perks of a regular executive's daily diary.

Angharad had put a lot of time and thought into the project

and brought folders full of drawings, plans, cuttings from newspapers and colour charts.

'Look who it is, it's Sarah Beeny,' said Ma.

Angharad's plans were clean, sleek, modern and creative with a focus on adding space, increasing storage and removing clutter. She really went to town on the playful bits; choosing carpets and curtains and tiles and artistic pieces from her IKEA catalogue to bring a touch of cool Scandinavia to South Wales. She chose a round bath and lots of glass so Barry and Ma would be able to see themselves naked getting in and out of the tub – independently, of course.

Swish fitted fixtures and fittings and a sense of style would run throughout this former council house. Ma's room would be fit for a queen with painted white floorboards and an old fireplace reinstated to attract the dance of the eye. Bespoke shelving would give her somewhere to put all her knick-knacks and the addition of a skylight would mean she could lie in bed of an evening and look at the clouds or stars to dream. There would be chic shutters and a beautiful new bed, freshly framed photos of loved ones on a facing wall and splashes of colour with rugs and lanterns.

Barry's bedroom would finally be a space for a grown-up with an up-to-date, modern workstation incorporated into the corner of the room to reflect his new pretend executive status. The Welsh dragon bedspread that had comforted him through most of his life would head for the skip, along with the poster of the 1990s Welsh rugby team and the dirty, stained pillows, now grey or off-magnolia. A new TV would be fitted onto the wall and stereo speakers hidden into the internal landscape. The room would be a place of serene calmness and tranquillity. A place where Barry could truly hide from the world and imagine it was no longer there. Barry felt a pang of sadness that his old room would no longer exist, apart from in his head, but he knew all this was the right thing to do. And, despite occasional feigned protestations and mini grumbles, so did Ma.

'I can see you being happy here, son, when I'm gone.' Ma stared wistfully at Angharad's plans, not really understanding what she was looking at.

'Do you like it?' said Angharad.

'I do,' said Ma.

'And you?' Angharad turned to Barry.

'It's amazing.'

'Thank you, son,' said Ma. 'Angharad, did you know my big lump of a boy is now a senior executive and your brother is his something-slash-PA?'

———

'What's really going on, Barry?'

After they'd finished going through the house plans, Barry and Angharad went for a stroll around Lincoln Park. The discovery that Barry was now employing her brother to effectively do nothing, as well as funding her little DIY dreams, told her that he'd come into more money than an old investment plan would pay up.

'You're right, but I can't tell you. Not yet,' said Barry.

'It's nothing dodgy, is it?' said Angharad.

'Course not.'

'Okay,' said Angharad. 'You will tell me one day, won't you?'

'Yes. One day.'

Barry told Angharad about Romeo's visit to Doctor Humphreys and he also told her about the stuff her brother had owned up to. Angharad felt ashamed that she'd been too preoccupied with her own life to notice. She imagined her and Romeo, sat in their childhood bedrooms across the landing, smiling kindly at each other through open doorways, before shutting themselves in to simultaneously contemplate terrible things. She was relieved neither of them were dead but felt guilty because she'd always protected her little brother and had no idea what he was going through. She also wondered why both of them – independently – had turned to Barry, of all people, for support – this middle-aged man who did little for himself and could barely operate a washing machine without causing a flood?

Whilst they were out strolling Ma phoned Derek.

'Heard our Barry upset you last night.'

'It was nothing,' said Derek, giving little away as usual.

'He said he made you cry.'

'I don't cry,' said Derek, sniffing.

'He's changing.'

'I know.'

'It's a good thing.' Ma's tone made it obvious she was looking for confirmation.

'It is,' said Derek, saying the right words but somehow failing to give Ma the affirmation she wanted.

'I'm glad it's happening now.'

'Not before time, eh?'

'Long as you're all right.'

'I'm good, Pearl. We're good. He just caught me on the hop. Stuff he said about our Barry, Barry Senior. Stuff he said you said about him too.' Derek's voice got stuck halfway through the sentence.

'I loved your brother once,' said Ma.

There was long pause. 'I know. Once.'

TWENTY-NINE
BILLY RAY WINSTONE AND THE BLACK PIG

HUNGER HAD NEVER REALLY BEEN a factor of Barry's forty-four years on this planet. He came from a family that wasn't rich, but they all loved their food and made sure there was always plenty of it on the table and in the cupboards. Telling himself that he had to overcome his love of eating by going cold turkey was not exactly smart. He imagined a brown crispy bird on a silver platter, packed with sage and onion stuffing, surrounded by sprouts, roast potatoes, mashed potatoes, red cabbage, pigs in blankets, dripping in cranberry sauce and Ma's own secret recipe gravy (she added every bit of fat and juice from the roasting tray plus a bit extra, along with Marmite, brandy and a dollop of squirty cream).

He refused to call himself a food addict, just like he didn't consider himself addicted to drink. Only Hollywood celebrities and people from Cardiff would ever call themselves food addicts in public, and they probably only nibbled on a few cashew nuts or the odd pasta salad. Barry knew what he was. A greedy git, yes. But he was also Welsh and proud of it. Being Welsh meant he was a connoisseur of fine foods and appreciated taste and quality in the same way the French, for instance, appreciated taste and quality in fine wines. No one ever had a pop at a smooth-talking wine expert from Burgundy or Bordeaux for being a bit of a pig around the red sauce, regardless of whether they spat it out or not. Beefy ridged crisps just happened to be his Pinot Noir. Wotsits his Merlot. Monster Munch his full-bodied Cabernet Sauvignon.

Barry refused to give in to temptation and made himself a giant bowl of unsweetened porridge topped with raspberries. It sated his appetite, almost, and he felt pleased with himself afterwards for not caving in and polishing off the three giant Toblerones whispering his name seductively from the back of his sock drawer, before heading downstairs for a pan full of bacon and sausages.

Of course, today was Friday, the start of the weekend, which meant he could have a few drinks if he so wished. Except Barry had not clarified in his own mind whether Fridays counted as a drinking day or not, along with Saturdays and Sundays. He knew James would say it didn't, that three days of drinking were too many and that he should restrict his booze intake to either Fridays and Saturdays, or Saturdays and Sundays. Barry wanted to please James and show him he could be strong-willed. He decided he would lay off the beer today because he was also seeing Diana and wanted to impress her too. Or maybe, if he really did get the urge for a couple of pints later, he'd stick to stout because it was almost like fruit and veg and full of antioxidants. Well, that's what his Uncle Derek always reckoned. He reckoned that when he was a kid of thirteen or fourteen, both sets of grandparents made him drink it because it was good for him. Like red meat. And burnt toast. And sitting in the sun. And the cane.

Barry showered, shaved, brushed his teeth and even changed the underpants that he'd only put on that morning. Normally underpants survived for a twenty-four-hour life cycle. He spent longer than usual messing with his hair, trying to get it just right, but it was still way too short to do anything with. He applied a blob of gel from a pot that was almost congealed from lack of use, but it just stuck to his skull and made it shiny. On went the Lynx Africa, all over, including the nether regions. Fresh white socks. A clean white shirt that Ma had ironed. Clean blue jeans, still warm, with creases down the sides because Ma had annoyingly ironed them too. Leather boots. He looked in the mirror and saw Billy Ray Cyrus crossed with Ray Winstone. Billy Ray Winstone.

Diana picked him up just before seven in her tidy dark-blue Ford Fiesta. Clean inside and out. No fluffy dice for her. A good little runner. Beyoncé's greatest hits in the CD player. If you like it then you should've put a ring on it, eh?

Nurse Fenwick had worked a twelve-hour shift that day, six till six, but she still looked bright and zestful in a pretty green dress that matched her vivid eyes.

'How was your day?' enquired Barry in the car.

'Oh fast,' said Diana, taking a corner at too much speed, as if to prove the point. 'It was the usual really, changing dressings, mopping up sick, putting on slings, lancing boils, you know.'

Barry said nothing because he *didn't know*. 'Where's your son tonight?'

'He's at a mate's house. He was in a bit of a strop cos he reckons everyone in his class has got the latest Xbox apart from him. Teenagers, huh?'

Barry shrugged as if he understood but again, didn't. 'You look a million dollars by the way.'

'Thank you. That's a surprise because I only had fifteen

minutes to get ready.' Diana checked her hair and teeth in the rear-view mirror.

Barry looked at her and wondered if she was Superwoman, too good to be true. Where were her faults? Did she leave toenail clippings in the bathtub? Armpit hair on the sideboard? Was she an avid *EastEnders* watcher? Did she have hidden psychotic tendencies? If Barry came home late from the pub, a bit worse for wear, would she give him an ear-bashing and tell him he was grounded for a fortnight like Jimmy Coen's missus?

Diana drove them to a Monmouthshire country pub called The Black Pig where she'd booked a meal for two. Barry wanted to take the lead – to ride into town confidently, galloping up to the bar like he was John Wayne minus the horse, announcing himself and his date, loud and proud. He wanted to be the one steering the conversation but he was well out of his comfort zone.

Instead, he followed sheepishly behind Diana as she held the door open for him and he said 'thank you' like he was Bridget Jones. He watched her walk easily through the negotiations and chit-chat with a large man with a grey beard, a dubious stain on his tie and an even more dubious stain on the front of his trousers. They were taken from a desk in the middle of a dark foyer to their table in the restaurant, in lovers' corner, with views overlooking a garden with wilted roses, an unkempt bird table and a crowned cherub urinating on anyone who got too close. Diana saw Barry looking at the cherub and smiled to herself.

'Suppose that's you on a Saturday night in the rugby club car park after you've had a skinful?' she said, poking him in the side.

Barry almost fired back immediately with a 'how dare you insult the size of my manhood' retort but stopped himself at the last moment.

'I'm cutting down on the drink.'

'Well, good for you.'

Barry scanned the wine list, looking at prices first. 'Suppose you see a lot of drunk blokes in your line of work, not that I'm a drunk.'

'I do, it's amazing the things pissed-up people do to themselves and to others, and it's not just men either.'

'I'm cutting down on food too.'

'Oh,' said Diana, flatly.

'You seem disappointed?'

'A bit. Would you rather we just had a quiet drink? We don't have to eat tonight?'

'Heck no, all that dieting has made me famished,' said Barry, rubbing his hands together.

Diana giggled.

Without realising he had even done it, Barry grabbed Diana's hand. 'Tonight's a treat night.'

'Treat for me too,' said Diana, squeezing back.

The conversation was unforced and effortless. They talked about things big and small: the state of the NHS today; where they would go if they could time travel (Barry went backwards, Diana forwards); favourite ways to spend birthdays; best Christmases; dream holiday destinations; are dogs better than cats?; favourite songs, favourite films; is Keir Starmer trustworthy and does God exist (Barry said definitely, Diana was more on the fence). They also discussed the pros and cons of being named after a love walrus called Barry White.

Before they knew it, they'd worked their way through three courses of so-so food plus instant coffee and chocolates, it was 10.30pm and both of them were physically stuffed, emotionally exhausted and spiritually uplifted.

'So one more question, what would you do if you won the lottery?' asked Diana, as they strolled back towards the car.

'Have a lie-in,' said Barry, looking away, only to find himself eyeing up the naked cherub.

'That all?'

'I'd like to make a difference somehow.'

'Difference to what?' said Diana, grabbing his arm.

'People.'

'Doing what?'

Barry bit his lip. 'Dunno – I always get stuck on that bit.'

'What would you like to change?' said Diana, stopping them both from walking so she could see Barry's expressions.

'Loads – and nothing,' said Barry, trying not to give too much away.

Diana kept pressing. 'You need to start with something small and go from there.'

'Yeah, you're right.'

'Often am, I'm a woman.'

Barry faced Diana head-on and couldn't help thinking she was beautiful. 'Noticed.'

'Want to see me again?' said Diana, revealing the teenage girl she used to be.

'You bet.'

Diana smiled another broad smile and flashed her bright green eyes in his direction.

'Come on, soldier, let's get you home to your mother. She'll be starting to worry about what I'm doing to you.'

THIRTY
TILL TOUCHDOWNS BRING ME
AROUND AGAIN

HE KNEW he wasn't ready for it but James fought Barry's corner with Uncle Derek. And keeping star man James happy was the number one priority for Anghofiedig Rugby Club and its coach nowadays.

With only fifteen available players, Barry was picked in the starting team for the home clash with The Mighty Titans. However, today, he wouldn't be packing down with the other front-row lumps in painful back-wrenching, neck-twisting scrums. Instead, he'd be stood out amongst the backs, breathing in clean country air rather than the stale farts of men full of the gas of Friday night's lager. He'd be next to James in the midfield with a gleaming number twelve on his back. His hair, what little Olly had left him, would be in place and his knees would be free of mud. No one could quite believe it, not the line of supporters and hangers-on spaced out down the touchline like they were still adhering to Covid restrictions, nor the opposition, nor the rest of the Anghofiedig team who looked at each other with darting eyes and raised eyebrows as Barry squeezed into a shirt designed for a smaller, sleeker man than him. His old muckers in the front row were relieved they didn't have to do the usual extra pushing and shoving to make up for the lightweight in their midst.

'Just enjoy it. I'll talk you through the game so follow what I say and you'll be fine,' said James, as they lined up in the changing room waiting to run out for the start of the match.

'Don't get in my way and don't fuck anything up,' said McQueen.

Ten minutes into the game, Titans led 19–0 with three tries to nil, each of them coming from mistakes by Barry.

He didn't understand this position at all. Admittedly, he was a terrible prop forward, but his main issues there were all about not being able to do what he knew he wanted to do. Here, in this foreign piece of territory on a part of the pitch he seldom encountered, he didn't have a clue where to stand or what his objectives were. The opposition soon got wind of this fact and their tactic became apparent: run at the big tart in the shrunken shirt.

Even James was starting to doubt the merits of his own decision-making when Barry attempted to kick the ball clear, only to see it slice sideways off the outside of his boot into the hands of the gleeful Titans winger who strolled in for the simplest of tries.

An exasperated McQueen shouted across to Derek. 'Can we make a sub?'

'We haven't got any,' said Derek.

'Well, can we play with fourteen? Your bloody nephew is playing for them anyway.'

'Stephen, let's encourage each other and focus on positives,' said James.

'Shove it, Clive Woodward,' said McQueen.

In his last midweek one-to-one training session with his new mentor, Barry remembered James trying to get him to act as a decoy runner in order to create space for others to exploit.

He couldn't remember exactly how he was supposed to do this but decided to take the bull by the horns and have a go anyway. As the Anghofiedig forwards recycled the ball and sent it out to their waiting back line, Barry left his position nestled between the safe bosom of James and McQueen, tucked an imaginary rugby ball under his arm and sprinted as fast as his little legs would carry him straight through the opposition's defence with a loud cry of 'I'm on the burst, Jimbo.'

The only problem was, he'd ripped his shorts, which were a size too small for him. And he wasn't wearing any underwear. He truly was on the burst.

He had hoped the Titans defenders would track and follow him, but they didn't. They just stood and watched him run through their ranks like he was Forrest Gump with his pecker out. The game stopped as everyone stared in bewilderment at this bizarre half-naked figure running for the hills. Barry careered through the posts and kept on going – now aware that his manhood was flapping in the breeze. He leapt through an open clubhouse window, where he landed in the lap of Beryl 'the peril' Davies, who'd been quietly sipping half a cider next to her husband, Llewellyn, whilst playing dominoes.

Out on the pitch, McQueen could not hold back an expletive-ridden exhortation of oaths and incredulity. The referee and the opposition were on their knees crying with laughter. Jonah was singing 'Rocket Man'. James said nothing but felt like this was his fault. For once, one of his special projects had unravelled and gone haywire.

This day would go down in the annals of Anghofiedig rugby folklore. Uncle Derek knew this immediately – everything he and his brother had worked so hard to create over so many years had been dismantled, quite literally, in a flash. The White name was no longer one to fear. It was one to ridicule. They – Barry, his family and the club itself – were a laughing stock. It was official.

'Remember that day when the crazy White boy picked up a pretend ball and ran the length of the field hollering and whooping to score a mock try with his meat and two veg bouncing all over the place? Well, I was there.'

The mood in the clubhouse after the game was strangely sober – the Titans squad boarded their minibus and sped off back to their own clubhouse to celebrate a memorable 52–10 victory and laugh about the opposition behind closed doors. A few players from the home side, led by McQueen, were bristling for a fight so it was a smart getaway from the visitors. Barry just wanted to slope off home and never play rugby again but James made him stay for a pint.

'Look, you'll laugh about this yourself in years to come,' said James.

'No I won't,' said Barry.

'It could have happened to anyone.'

'No it couldn't.'

'You're right. I'm sorry.'

Llewellyn Davies used to be a formidable second-row forward, playing behind the White brothers, in the club's halcyon days. Now an old man, with shot knees, a walking stick and a dodgy ticker, he remained a nasty piece of work and was also bristling for a fight of sorts, with Barry.

'Oi, White, what you still doing here? You don't belong here no more. This club doesn't need you.'

The place fell silent. No one said a word.

'My missus could sue you for assault. If I was ten years younger, you'd be sucking that pint through a straw and searching for your teeth over a five-mile radius. You're a bloody embarrassment. We've put up with you all these years cos of your old man but enough is enough. We don't want you here no more. No one does. Not one single bloke – apart from your posh English pal – has any respect for you, as a man or as a rugby player. Not even your own flesh and blood. So why don't you do everyone a favour and piss off and don't come back,' said Llewellyn Davies.

More silence.

Barry looked around at people he considered to be friends and saw each of them avert their eyes to the floor and their feet. No one was willing to stick their head above the parapet for him. Most stood behind Llewellyn, either physically or metaphorically. Even James knew it would be futile to try and take this angry lot on in this moment. Uncle Derek sat in the corner of the bar alone, swirling the dregs of a pint around. He said nothing. He did nothing. He looked at no one.

'Go on then, run back home to Mammy,' said Llewellyn, sneering.

The bar roared with laughter.

'And don't set foot in this place ever again, you hear?'

Barry got up to leave, moving quickly because he could feel the tears welling up inside of him. That would be the final public humiliation, the cherry on the cake of catastrophe – walking out of the crowded bar, crying his heart out whilst so-called pals laughed at him.

'Stay where you are, son. Don't budge an inch,' came a booming voice.

Uncle Derek had put down his pint glass and now stood between Barry and Llewellyn and his cronies.

'Sit down, Derek, you old fool, you can't fight his battles no more,' said Llewellyn, leaning on his one good leg with his stick in the other hand.

'I'd die for this club and I'd die for him,' said Derek.

'Bring out the violins.' Llewellyn turned around to play up to the crowd, encouraging them to laugh.

'You always were a bully,' said Derek, ignoring everyone bar Llewellyn.

'What you on about?'

'You were a decent enough rugby player, I'll give you that. Some reckoned you were a hard man but not me, nor our Barry – cos we knew what you really were. We watched you dish out a sly hiding every few weeks to some spindly kid, just to keep your reputation going. We backed you cos you were one of us. Turned a blind eye. But we knew how you operated. Who you really were. And we didn't like it. We didn't like you. Picking on easy prey and going in heavy. Punching people when they were off guard or not looking. Fighting sneaky. But that's where our Barry here is different. He's a White. He doesn't pick easy targets. He gets thumped, bitten, stamped on, abused, beaten and ridiculed every week, almost without fail. Everyone sees it. And you know what? He's the only one of you lot I know will turn up on a Saturday for definite. He'd play anywhere on the park if I asked him to. And against any opponent. If I told him we were playing South Africa tomorrow he'd say "great, let's show them where Anghofiedig is on the map".'

Barry could feel the weight of people's stares on him now, but he also sensed their eyes were softening. A few even smiled at him. His heart was racing. He needed the toilet but he didn't want to miss a second of Uncle Derek going to war to fight for him.

'He's played for this club sick and he's played injured. I told him to stop coming and he refused and kept coming. McQueen shoved his head down a toilet – his own captain, the guy who should be protecting and helping him – and he shrugged it off and carried on. Why? Cos he loves this club and he wants it to mean something. He's worth ten of any of you lot. He's more of a club legend than me or you or even his old man. He's got more bollocks than all of us – and yes, I know he proved that to everyone today by getting 'em out on display for all to see. But after everything that happened earlier, look at him, still here, putting his money behind the bar, taking all your crap. Fronting up. He's tougher than you ever were, that's a fact.'

Uncle Derek's words cut through the boozy, defeated air and brought most people back to their senses. Those stood over Llewellyn's shoulders slowly moved away from him. Llewellyn felt the shift in the room's atmosphere and didn't know what to do or say.

Come on, Barry, let's go – let's leave them to their club,' said Derek.

'Wait, I'll drive you both home,' said James.

———

There wasn't much conversation in the car on the way home but Barry felt genuine love and respect for his uncle, for the things he had said and the way he had defended him.

'Don't lose heart about today,' said James to Barry, via the car mirror as Barry was sitting in the back.

'I won't.'

'See you for training Monday night?'

'Sure.'

When James stopped the car to drop him off, Barry leant forward to give his uncle a hug.

'Thanks, Uncle Derek, and if you do manage to get a game with the Boks tomorrow, I'll be there.'

'What position do you want to play?' said Derek.

'Don't care,' said Barry.

Derek chortled. 'As long as you put some kegs on.'

Barry walked through his own front door feeling much better about himself. He could hear the sound of water running in the kitchen and a saucepan boiling over. The telly was blaring, something weird and wacky on Channel 4. He shouted for Ma but there wasn't any answer. Normally, she'd come and greet him. He walked into the living room and saw her sitting in her usual chair. She looked like she was sleeping because her eyes were closed but she wasn't asleep. She was still warm to the touch but her skin was a purplish grey with red splotches on her cheeks. Her mouth had fallen open and wouldn't close. Her whole body looked floppy.

Barry felt the whoosh of emotion he'd suppressed for days, months, maybe even years rise to the surface and overcome him. He sat at his ma's feet, held her hand and bawled his eyes out until he could cry no more. She always squeezed back when he gripped her hand but not this time.

His world was changing fast.

He wished he could go back to the way things used to be.

THIRTY-ONE
NO JOKE FOR APRIL FOOLS

THE NIGHT PASSED in a surreal dream. People crept in and out through the small hours, doing what needed to be done with unusual courtesy. Professionals tasked with protecting the good folk of Anghofiedig from waking to breakfast with the Grim Reaper. Taking Ma's body away so it couldn't be seen by anyone, to shock and scare, souring thoughts and memories. Doctor Humphreys said it was important that Barry remembered Ma for who she really was – and who he believed she still is. A soul in a body, not the other way around. A kind soul too. Once trapped in old bones but now free to run again, not that Ma ever did much running. Reunited with Barry Senior. If she wanted to be. Barry Junior suspected it wouldn't be at the top of her heavenly wish list.

Barry had no idea what he was supposed to be doing. He sat on the stairs, two from the bottom, and stared vacantly at the front door, expecting Ma to burst through, weighed down with shopping bags and bits of gossip. For the first time ever, he wondered how she managed to carry it all. She was stronger than she looked. Barry had got things the wrong way round most of his life; it wasn't his father who was the tough one, it was her.

His old man was weak and controlled by fears, expectations and bodily urges. She was solid granite.

The kettle never stopped boiling and copious amounts of tea got drank between bouts of crying. Visitors willingly washed up and put away their own cups in the wrong cupboards, instead of leaving them by the sink. They came and went with military precision as if scheduled in advance, and the whole village seemingly wanted to take it in turns to pay their respects.

Barry picked up the phone to call Romeo.

'Whatsappp...'

'Romeo, I've some bad news. Ma's dead.'

'Ha! Good one, loser. You ain't catching me with no April Fool's prank.'

Barry wasn't sure he had the patience to cope with Romeo. 'I wouldn't joke about something like this, ever. Ma's dead. She went peacefully. In her sleep.'

The line went quiet; Romeo having no words.

'She's gone?'

'Yes.'

'Whoa, no... I gotta. Sorry...'

This time the line went dead for real. Romeo had run for the hills of Feelgood. Death was different there. Ma could live on and she'd put the despicable Mr Bronson back in his rightful place, that's for sure. For the first time, Barry felt a pang of envy for his friend's make-believe, imaginary haven and he wished he could go there too, just to speak to Ma one more time.

Barry felt ashamed that he had never told Ma he was a millionaire. Why would he hide such a thing from the person he was closest to in the world? All those pretences and lies – and pretending to work when he'd quit his job. Surely Ma would have been excited for him and it might have taken away some of the worries and anxieties she'd had about his future once she was gone? Or it could have created new anxieties. Ma was never impressed by wealth and she certainly didn't approve of his gambling. She thought he used to bet in pence and fivers, not hundreds and thousands. Ma viewed having lots of money as a handicap, a disability on a par with mild arthritis or nagging backache, a hindrance that overcomplicated life. Barry felt much the same way, which is probably why he never shared his good news – not just with Ma, but with anyone. He didn't want anything to change or for people to start looking at him differently. He had enough obstacles in all his paths, he didn't need more.

He couldn't help feeling that he'd been a terrible son all these years who took far more than he ever gave. Other grown-up sons took their mothers on holidays or bought them expensive gifts – cars, watches, spa days and the like – to pay them back for all their earlier sacrifices. He hadn't grown up though. He was still stuck in the adolescent phase that he'd been in for thirty years. It suited him. It suited Ma too. Living in a time warp to cover over all the cracks. And there were cracks aplenty. They both ignored them. Barry knew Ma had been struggling lately but put it down to age and let her carry on. He noticed her feet had become like two small blocks of Stilton. Her lips were tinged blue. She got more breathless walking and doing stuff.

Reverend Hill came around after church and filled in a lot of the blanks for Barry. He'd been her go-to person when she needed someone to drive her to hospital appointments. On the way there and back they would chat about life and death and God. Reverend Hill helped Ma make sense of things and get her beliefs in order. She did the same for him.

'You should have told me she was ill,' said Barry, crossly.

'It wasn't my story to tell,' said Reverend Hill.

'She didn't trust me?'

'She wanted to protect you.'

'I thought she just went to sleep in her favourite chair and that was it.'

'She wasn't ill for long. There was no cure.'

'Was she afraid?'

'Yes.'

'Did she say so?'

'Yes.'

'What was she afraid of most? Dying?'

'No, leaving you.'

'I wasn't there for her and I could have been.'

'You were always there. She didn't want things to change. You kept her going.'

Reverend Hill collected a cup of tea from a tray that Aunty Ruth was ferrying around. His tea was milkier than he liked and didn't have any sugar in it but he wasn't going to make a fuss.

'Your Ma was diagnosed with chronic pulmonary hypertension. It all happened really fast, from going to see Doc Humphreys to getting a terminal diagnosis. She knew she didn't have long.' Reverend Hill sipped his disgusting tea and pulled a face.

Suddenly, things made much more sense to Barry. Those episodes of tightness in her throat which forced her to black out twice. He'd ignored them and put it down to age. On both occasions, she went out like a light and came too on her own – though Barry had been in the house, upstairs, 'working hard'. Ma told herself she couldn't disturb him. The people at LesCargo needed him. The companies using their services to move their freight, cargo, people and boxes from A to B relied on him more. If he didn't do his job, what then? Some hard-working warehouseman might not get paid. His family would feel the pinch and have to cut back. And all from her selfishness, her black-outs. Her secret was bigger than Barry's. He failed to tell Ma he was awash with cash. She failed to tell him she was dying, or rather, living, but on borrowed time.

'She'd started having kips in the afternoon,' said Barry, reflecting.

'I was aware,' said Reverend Hill.

'And when she went to bed at night she couldn't lie flat anymore. She had to have four pillows plus a fan in order to breathe.' Barry punched himself hard in the thigh and started to cry. Reverend Hill gently began to massage the spot where he had hit himself.

'She had good days and bad ones, but learnt how to hide the bad ones from you. As I'm sure you did for her.'

Barry's voice began to splutter. 'But she hid so much. All those hours spent hanging about in hospital waiting rooms with you. Where was I? Eh? Where was I? I should have been there with her, not you. And all those medical letters marked urgent.' He looked across towards the sideboard where they were neatly piled. 'What did you talk about most? When you were just sat waiting, doing nothing?'

Reverend Hill knew he had to get this right so he composed himself with a few deep breaths, like he did before an important preach.

'Did you know your Ma loved animals? She would tell me about your passion for gorillas in the wild. She said she always longed to see elephants close up, because she'd had a toy one as a child. She said her dream was to splash about in a waterhole with a real baby elephant. Somewhere hot. She said she never told anyone else about this because it was just a silly fantasy. Her being a poor miner's widow, she reckoned it would never be anything else.'

This was almost too much for Barry to take. He knew that years ago, just after Barry Senior died, she had bought herself an expensive ornamental elephant and put it on the mantelpiece so she could sit and dream a bit. She looked at it often. Barry had never cared for it much but now it was the most precious thing in the whole house. He could feel butterflies fluttering in his stomach as he glanced nervously over to make sure it was still there. It was.

The toughest time was when everyone disappeared and Barry found himself completely on his own, with no one to say goodnight to. It was now his responsibility to go round the house locking doors, turning off lights, drawing curtains and unplugging appliances. He'd have to learn to wash clothes and clean next. To fend and mend, and pay the bills too.

Going to bed knowing there was no one else in the house and no one in the room across the landing was unsettling, and Barry wept uncontrollably for his loss and his own guilt.

Unable to sleep, he got out of bed, walked across the landing and climbed into Ma's bed. He could smell her: fresh lavender soap and mint imperials. In the bottom of her bedside cabinet he found a stash of her pills and medications. Momentarily he thought about taking the lot, then cursed himself for being so pathetic.

'Time to grow up, Barry boy,' he said to himself.

Everything was too quiet so he turned on Ma's portable telly and watched *Dog the Bounty Hunter* whilst eating two packets of custard creams.

After that he went for a walk. He pounded all of the streets Ma knew and loved, the streets that bore her, shaped her, held her back and spat her out.

He walked until he had blisters on his feet and it was light again. He talked to Ma all night long and asked for a sign that she was okay. A silver star flashing in the sky gave him some comfort and led him down to the rugby club. Yesterday, he longed to escape this place and everyone in it but yesterday was several galaxies away now.

He fell asleep, curled up in a ball in the away team's dugout – not waking until a dog with sad eyes cocked its leg and pissed all over him.

'Foxy, bad boy, leave the tramp alone,' shouted a large, formidable woman in double denim and spotted wellies, swinging a bag of poo.

THIRTY-TWO
SHOTGUN OR COPS? YOUR CHOICE...

BARRY RECEIVED a text from Honest Pete the bookmaker.

I'll transfer the remaining £500k I owe you today. My house sale is going through quicker than expected so that's a bonus. Going to live with my son for a while. Have a good life and enjoy the money. I'd quit gambling if I were you. It's a mug's game.

Barry missed everything Ma did for him but he missed her a million times more. It felt strange rattling around in the house alone and he wished she was still there. He used to look at her favourite chair with fondness, whether she was sitting in it or not, but now he decided it had to go because it was the place where she died. He felt bad but he already wanted to move on, make Angharad's changes to the house and put his stamp on the place. He told her as much in an email.

Earlier, he'd felt bad for watching half an hour of Chico and laughing out loud at the sight of the gorilla playing peek-a-boo with his keeper. How long did people mourn for? What did they do with themselves during this time? His kitchen was full of food because everyone who visited brought him something to eat. He had more frozen meals than he could fit in the freezer; more cakes and sponges than even he could pig out on. He was still on a diet officially. Was he allowed to remain on a diet or would that be considered too self-indulgent in the circumstances? What kind of bereaved son turned down a pork pie or a beer at a wake because they were watching their weight? He didn't have much of an appetite, which was unusual. He told himself that was a good thing because at least it proved – to himself mainly – that he really was grieving and not completely heartless.

He was also sick of do-gooders feeding him clichés along with their apple pies and Battenbergs. He'd heard them all this past twenty-four hours.

'It's okay to cry.'

'Time heals all wounds, eventually.'

'You don't get over it, you just get used to it.'

'Things do get easier. Trust me, I've been there.'

'Guilt is normal.'

'Anger is normal.'

'Grief is different for everyone. There's no right or wrong way to grieve.'

Barry's own feelings confused him. He wanted to run away from people and their judgements, and the gloom of death that now enveloped him. He wanted to fill his mind with ridiculous stuff that made him forget all about what had just happened. He wanted to get out of the house because Ma was everywhere and nowhere and there were too many reminders and not enough. He wanted to laugh and meet people who didn't know that his mother had just died. People who didn't creep around with their heads slightly bowed, watching their P's and Q's, not knowing what to say. He wanted to run forwards in his life as fast as possible, as if setting off on another ill-fated decoy run designed to create space. He didn't want to look back because it scared him. So did standing still.

'Romeo, what you doing today?' said Barry down the phone.

'Nothing much. Watching *Avengers* at the mo. Can't really think straight.'

'Let's go somewhere. Where no one knows us.'

'Where?'

'Dunno.'

'Go drinking? Get pissed?' suggested Romeo in a loud voice.

'Don't drink Mondays no more,' replied Barry.

'Just as well cos The Dragon's shut.'

'Is it?'

'Yup, owners did a flit yesterday. Owed shedloads left, right and centre apparently. There's a big for sale sign right outside.'

'No Ma and no pub,' reflected Barry, mournfully

'Terrible losses for the village,' said Romeo.

'What about horse riding?' Barry was keen to do something that involved animals.

'Really? Can you ride?' asked Romeo.

'Don't think so,' came the reply.

Grenville Grayson's stables were only thirty miles or so away on the outskirts of Herefordshire. Grenville was a farmer-cum-racehorse trainer who had eight horses in training – running them over the flat in summer and the sticks in winter. Grenville was proper old-school: insensitive and straight-talking, the sort who worked his animals hard and his staff harder. The kind of guy who activated panic buttons whenever he started a sentence with 'I'm not sexist but...'

Through the pandemic it had been a struggle for him to stay afloat. The only thing stopping him going under was his own cussedness and the loyalty of one wealthy owner, an American widow called Delores Hamilton who had a strange fascination for Grenville's quirky nineteenth-century ways. Delores owned Brecon Beacon Boy, whose recent triumph at the Cheltenham Festival had made Barry a millionaire and turned around Grenville Grayson's fortunes almost as spectacularly.

The sight of Romeo's Citroën Dyane spluttering into the yard forced the cantankerous old trainer out of his warm office and away from sorting his race entries for the coming week.

'Get that heap of steaming French muck off my land pronto.'

'Ah, Mr Grayson, lovely to meet you,' said Romeo, offering a hand.

'Who the fuck are you?' said Grenville, ignoring Romeo's outstretched hand as if it was something that had plopped out of the back of one of his horses.

'I'm Romeo,' explained Romeo.

'And I suppose that lump of gristle in your passenger seat calls himself Juliet?'

'No, that's Barry,' said Romeo.

'Gibb or Manilow?'

'White,' said Romeo.

'Get yourself gone before I fetch my shotgun,' barked Grenville.

Barry got out of the car, sensing that this situation called for his superior diplomacy and negotiating skills. 'Mr Grayson, I'm Barry White.'

'You're the right size, I'll give you that.'

'I want to say hello to Brecon Beacon Boy. If I could ride him that would be amazing. I was there at Cheltenham for his Challenge Cup win and it was a life-changing moment for me.'

'And I thought you were going to serenade me.'

'His mother has just died,' said Romeo.

'So will my horse if he sits on it,' said Grenville.

'You don't understand, I'm a big fan of yours,' pleaded Barry.

'Shotgun or cops? Your choice,' said Grenville.

Barry wasn't finished. He told the trainer he'd pay him £1,000 in cash for an hour's riding lesson for both him and Romeo, with a tour of the stables, lunch and some photographs thrown in. The deal was that Barry would ride Brecon Beacon Boy, whilst Romeo would partner the stable's next best thing – Never Been Kissed.

'I want the full experience,' said Barry. 'I want to feel like I'm a proper jockey. I want to imagine I'm the horse's Cheltenham rider Dr Phillipson P. Montague.'

Grenville's jaw dropped open before he addressed Romeo. 'Your mate is fucking loopy juice.' Romeo nodded.

'Can we dress up? Like real jockeys?' asked Barry.

'How much do you weigh?'

'Dunno exactly.'

'What size waist are you?' Grenville eyed him up and down, wincing.

'Forty-four-ish... on a good day.'

'The only jockey outfit I got that big is one I wore to a fancy dress party about ten Christmases ago.'

'That'll do.'

Grenville whistled a sad-faced boy over from his Dickensian life of sweeping up horseshit.

''Ere, take these two clowns and get them kitted up.'

'Come again, gaffer?' said the boy.

'These two dickheads want to be pretend jockeys for the afternoon. The big one's got a fetish for Beacon. It's okay, they're paying me a grand. Suit 'em and boot 'em.'

'But they're too big, boss. Well he is, anyway,' said the boy, pointing at Barry.

'Just do it, no lip,' said Grenville.

The boy led Barry and Romeo away to a small room leading off the main office.

'What do we need?' said Romeo.

'Are you really gonna do this?' asked the boy.

'Think so.'

'Why us? Why here?'

'Brecon Beacon Boy changed my world,' said Barry.

The boy picked up the largest saddle he could find. 'Did you back it at Cheltenham?'

'Yes, I did.'

'How much did you win?'

Barry waited until Romeo was out of earshot and whispered into the boy's ear.

'Wow, you're weird,' said the boy, backing away whilst trying to recall the lesson he'd had at school just a couple of years ago about the perils of stranger danger.

After half an hour or so, Barry and Romeo emerged from the tack room looking like creatures from a faraway dwarf star. Romeo wore the colours of Brecon Beacon Boy – or rather, the colours of Delores Hamilton, a white cap with red stripes, plus blue and red silks with a white star in the centre. He wore a helmet and goggles. Beneath his silks he had on a mesh long-sleeved top and a padded vest, to stop him breaking any ribs should he fall off his horse. His waterproof breeches were grubby grey, skintight and very light. His shiny, long leather boots came up to his knees and had zips at the sides. He carried a whip and felt more like a dominatrix than a jockey.

Still, he looked better than Barry in his fancy dress garb. His colours were the green and gold of the legendary Irish owner JP McManus. His goggles were designed for swimming. His trousers were big and baggy, like the ones MC Hammer wore in the 1990s. The boots he had on were two sizes too big and packed with someone's dirty football socks. He looked like a court jester. Grenville Grayson burst out laughing when he saw the pair of them waddle towards the gallop where two big brown placid horses stood waiting. The horses were held by a couple of teenage girls, who were trying not to laugh – for fear of losing their jobs – but failing miserably.

'Oh, boys, I'm a miserable bastard at the best of times but you've made my Monday,' said Grenville.

Grayson refused to let the duo ride the horses unsupervised. Getting them in their saddles was a mission in itself and Barry slid right over the back of his horse on first attempt, splitting his breeches in the process.

'Why do you always have to get your John Thomas out wherever you go?' said Romeo.

'Better than flashing Dennis Waterman at the world with my ring piece for his gob,' snapped Barry.

The girls led the horses on a slow walk, never rising to a canter. Grayson told them their job, first and foremost, was to make sure the animals got back into their boxes unscathed in time for their feed. Their next priority was to ensure no serious harm came to Del Boy and Rodney.

The jockeys got their lunch, their photographs and the experience they paid for. Barry fell off three times and Romeo twice. They both suffered bruises but broke nothing bar part of a plastic rail and one of the saddles. Grayson got his £1,000 and a few quid extra on top for costs. The horses survived an adventure that carried more risk to them and their well-being than the Grand National. Everyone was happy, relatively. Barry was as happy as he could be, less than two days after finding the most important person in his world dead in the armchair.

Before departing, Barry got to briefly meet and speak to Brecon Beacon Boy's regular jockey Phillipson Montague.

'You'll never appreciate just how much inspiration I got

from watching you succeed at Cheltenham,' said Barry, sounding like a grovelling, starstruck fan.

'I heard you made a few quid out of us.' Montague's tone was stand-offish and unfriendly.

'I did, but watching you perform in the saddle gave me something else, something far more precious.'

'What's that?' said Montague, half-expecting to be asked for a selfie or an autograph.

'Hope,' said Barry.

THIRTY-THREE
DO IT YOURSELF: AN SOS

BARRY HAD NOTIFIED loads of people about Ma's death via countless email exchanges and hours on the telephone – but there was one glaring omission. Nurse Diana Fenwick.

Barry wasn't actually sure if Diana was his girlfriend or not. They'd had one date, got on well and agreed to see each other again, but at what point do you decide a girl is more than a friend and actually a girlfriend? Diana had never met Ma so Barry's insecurity left him fearing he'd get a shrug of the shoulders and a 'so what?' And what would that tell him about her? Plenty that he didn't want to know.

Alternatively, what if he broke down in tears in front of her – would she consider him weak, emotional and needy? Dating and all these unwritten, unspoken rules that went with it were a foreign language to him so he reverted to what he was good at – putting things out of his mind, doing little and saying nothing. It was straight from the ditherer's handbook on decision-making, which he could easily have authored in his LesCargo downtime had he not procrastinated so much.

Lying on the sofa, Barry immersed himself in Dean Martin's greatest hits. Ma did love a bit of the King of Cool. 'Volare',

'That's Amore', 'Sway', 'Everybody Loves Somebody'. Every track brought back a memory of Ma and made her seem closer. He hadn't heard Diana knock on any doors but somehow he recognised her hand tapping at his own front door. He opened it and she threw her arms around him immediately, almost knocking him off his feet.

'Why didn't you call me? I'm so, so sorry for you.'

Diana was inwardly miffed at being shut out but she was determined not to show it. She'd read about Ma's death in the obituary section of *The Bugle*, whilst sitting in the staff canteen drinking hot chocolate on a rare break. A friend agreed to cover the rest of her shift so she could clock off early to deal with 'a family matter'.

Barry held on to Diana tightly. 'I hoped you'd come round.'

Diana stayed for three hours. They talked for spells and sat in silence at other times but it was never awkward. They listened to the whole of the Dean Martin album and another by Matt Monro. Diana had never heard of the latter but liked some of his songs, particularly 'Born Free' and 'On Days Like These'. She cuddled up to Barry on the sofa and they even slept in each other's arms for an hour or so.

When they were talking, Barry felt like he was introducing Diana to his mother for the first time to win her approval. He showed Diana old photos and told her old stories. He regretted the fact that Diana and Ma would never get to know each other for real. He'd never experience the joy of being important to two women simultaneously. An overlap would have been nice instead of this precise and clear cut-off with one chapter ending and another beginning. Still, he was glad, at least, to have a new chapter, rather than feel his whole story was ending. That was the worst sort of loss. When the person left behind realises they have died too because they have nothing left to go on for. He was a mummy's boy but the apron strings had been loosening for a while and maybe that was what finished Ma off in the end.

'Do you think Ma's watching us now?' said Barry.

'I think she'll be looking in from time to time.' Diana balanced the Matt Monro album cover on the arm of the sofa.

'Does that bother you? Her looking in on us?'

'No. What about you?'

'Nope.'

'I think she'd want you to live your life. Your way. Not hers.' Diana picked the album cover back up and used it to fan herself.

Barry watched her. 'Don't know what that is.'

Diana's eyes sought out his. 'I think you do.'

They came in three vans like a mini army, carrying saws, trowels, paint pots, Stanley knives and power tools. *DIY SOS* on the march, led by their very own Nick Knowles – Angharad. Barry watched them approach the front door and waited for Angharad's press of the doorbell.

'I've recruited some extra help,' she said.

There were around fifteen people from the village in old clothes and overalls, including Uncle Derek and Aunty Ruth, James, Pricer, Romeo, Jonah and Reverend Hill. Doctor Humphreys was there with a cordless drill, cracking jokes.

'Frontal lobotomy, anyone?' he said, giving his drill a whirl.

'Bad taste, doc, remember who you are, where you are and why you're here,' said Uncle Derek.

The doctor dropped his bottom lip like a chastised teenager.

Even McQueen was on hand to do what he was told and muck in.

'Listen, Barry, I know me and you don't always see eye to eye but I'm sorry about your mum.'

'Thank you, Stevie, means a lot.'

'It's Stephen. Never Stevie.' McQueen's face hardened so lines appeared across the whole length of his forehead.

'Sorry, Stephen.' Barry sat upright, remembering who he was talking to and hoping he wouldn't find himself suspended upside down from his own repainted ceiling.

'Never call me Stevie again, okay?'

'I won't.'

'Cup of tea?'

'Yeah, milk and two sugars, please,' said Barry, offering his mug.

'No, cup of tea. For me. You're making it.'

Barry kept all the workers going with an endless river of tea and several packets of chocolate Hobnobs. It was humbling to see so many people giving their time and skills for nothing and he had to go outside into the garden several times to stop himself from blubbing in front of them. He reasoned that they probably weren't there for him, they were there for Ma, but it didn't matter. It was still touching that they held her in such high regard. That they were willing to give to her, even though she was gone. They respected her and missed her; her simple politeness and courtesy, her genuine 'pleased to see you' hellos and the kindly way she stuck up for the underdog when they were the butt of someone else's joke. Now, they wanted to say thank you to her in their own little way, the Anghofiedig way. Showing not telling.

Seeing the house being stripped back to the bare bones was unsettling for Barry. It felt so final, like another death happening right in front of him. He momentarily mourned the loss of old wallpaper that carried the marks and memories of past laughs and fights. Carpets full of his and Ma's DNA were lifted out on shoulders as if they were coffins, bearing the skins that had been shed over decades of unnoticed reinvention and renewal. Over a lifetime these tiny flakes of who they were and who they used to be would have made up half of their bodyweights. Barry wiped his finger across the back of a dusty wardrobe heading for the skip and talked to it like he was talking to Ma. Her skin. Her dust. Her ashes. On his fingertips.

Since Ma's passing, he'd spoken to most of the people currently in his house but had never gone beneath the surface with any of them. Now, more meaningful words came to each of them as the honest sweat of work – and not having to look anyone directly in the eye – introduced a fresh sincerity to their conversations.

'I'm a bit overwhelmed by all this,' confessed Barry to Angharad.

Angharad smiled a toothy smile. 'You don't always have to be the one who gives.'

'I'm not. I took from Ma for way too long. Always did.'

Angharad shook her head in disagreement. 'No, that's not true. You gave her what she wanted, even when it held you back.'

Instantly, and surprisingly, Barry realised that Angharad was right. She'd flipped his thinking upside down with a single throwaway sentence that carried an incredible revelation. Deep within himself he had always felt bad for taking so much from Ma: her money, her energy, her time, her focus. But the reality was, he wasn't the one doing the taking. Every dream he'd ever let go of in his life had been given up for her. He'd stayed cocooned in his room all these years because it was safe, comfortable and easy – but also because he didn't want to be responsible for crushing Ma's daily routines and robbing her of her purpose. It wasn't just him sheltering from the world at large. It was her too.

It wasn't his fear of failure or of being alone that kept him hidden in his bedroom, it was hers. As he sat on a box of old birthday cards and photo albums, drinking his mug of tea from a LesCargo Logistics mug, Barry was approached by Aunty Ruth who sat down beside him.

'Don't you think it's a bit soon to be doing all this?' said Aunty Ruth, concerned.

'Nah, it needs to be done now.'

'As long as you don't regret it when everything's new, shiny and different.'

'I won't,' said Barry, appreciating his aunt's ability to read people and situations without judgement.

'Well, if you change your mind, just say. We'll all understand.'

'Ma's gone,' said Barry.

'I know,' said Aunty Ruth.

Barry pinched himself on the underside of his arm in a way no one could see. 'And I'm still here.'

Aunty Ruth sipped tea, from a china cup, not a mug. 'And so are we.'

THIRTY-FOUR

FLESH AND BLOOD

'OH HELLO, love, come on in, you've been on my mind all day,' said Dotty when she opened the door. She had just returned home from a rendezvous with a new gentleman friend she'd been chatting to online for three weeks called Maximilius Percival, when Barry called at her house unannounced.

'I'm an old tart aren't I for going out on a date and wanting to enjoy myself? Pearl would understand though. I cried all day Sunday and Monday. This morning too. But when you get to my age you don't have time to grieve the way the young do. He was a dead loss anyway, Mr Pepsi Max. I won't be seeing him again. Deaf as a post and proper stingy. Wouldn't even buy me a drink. Only thing he talked about was fishing. I didn't hang around for any afters. I didn't want to hear no more about him getting nibbles on his dangling bait.'

Barry had gone round to Dotty's to make sure she was all right, but he also longed for some old stories from Ma's past, preferably yarns from her youth that he had never heard before. Dotty seemed distracted, however, flitting from one subject to the next and struggling to make anything connect. She spoke faster than usual and her body language was restless. She went off to the kitchen to fetch coffee and biscuits for them both but came back with nothing. She scolded herself and her aging memory, went back to the kitchen, only to return with tea – and no biscuits.

'Don't worry, sit down, tea's fine,' said Barry.

Dotty continued to stand, twitching, puffing up cushions. 'It's not fine.'

'Just sit down, will you?'

'I can't.'

'Why can't you?'

'Cos there's something I have to do.'

'What you on about?' Barry was starting to think something was wrong.

Dotty finally perched herself down on the edge of a chair but she was far from relaxed. 'Your mum. She made me promise to do something. To tell you something. If she died first.'

'What?' said Barry.

'I don't want to tell you because I know it's going to hurt you. But I must. Cos I promised I would.'

'So just tell me.'

'But you'll hate me,' said Dotty, slapping her hand up and down on the side of her chair.

'I won't.'

'You will. And you'll hate your mother more.'

'Hate my mother? You're scaring me now.' Barry stood up and walked to a different chair to put more distance between himself and Dotty.

Dotty got up and went to the top drawer of a bureau in the cluttered living room, neatly sidestepping a purple pouf and a pile of *Take a Break* magazines.

She rifled through the drawer and pulled out several sheets of yellowy blue Basildon Bond paper folded together. She stopped and stared at the sheets of paper, looked up at Barry and wiped a tear from the corner of her eye. She slowly walked over to Barry, like a condemned woman going to the gallows, and handed him the letter. She sat on a chair further away from Barry than before, deliberately giving him more space. He looked at her warily then back at the letter, which he started to read. It was dated 5 November 1979. Bonfire Night.

> *Dear Dotty,*
> *I don't know how to say this and I'm a bit scared of putting it down on paper in case you leave it lying around for any prying eyes to read. But you know me better than anyone else in the world and understand what I've been through because you've been through a lot of it too with your Lionel. I am ashamed of what I'm about to tell you. And frightened of what might happen to me if people find out. Especially Barry. Or Derek. Or your Lionel.*
> *You remember the rugby club dinner when I got a bit giddy on gin and Schweppes? I left early and said I was walking home because I needed the fresh air – and you had a right go at Barry for not going with me? And your Lionel wouldn't let you go with me cos he took Barry's side, as usual?*
> *Well, I didn't walk home alone. Outside, I ran into John, who saw me all wobbly on my feet and offered me a lift home. I invited him in because I was lonely. He was nice to me. He was always nice to me. And before either of us knew what was happening, it had happened.*
> *No one must ever know. But I have to tell someone because this baby I'm carrying isn't Barry's. We've not slept together in ages. More than four months. The dates just don't add up, so either it's an immaculate conception or it's John's. John doesn't have any idea. He can't ever know the truth, you understand? But one day, if anything happens to*

me – you might have to tell my son or daughter who they really are and where they come from. They have a right to know that much. One day.

It's a mess, I know, and nothing you say will make me feel worse than I already do. I don't believe it's right for a married woman to ever sleep with another man. It's a sin before God. But I will love this baby, and me and Barry will raise it as ours. Barry will be pleased, I hope, because we didn't think we could have children. He didn't think he could have them. He got really down about it because he felt less of a man than other men. In the end we gave up trying. Maybe it's just what we need, to bring us back together. To bring him back to me and make him less angry about life. Who knows, it might be a boy with broad shoulders, a good right hook and a thick neck who's a natural at rugby? Why not?

Please don't think bad of me. I am determined to be a good wife and a good mother, to make things right and put my mistake behind me. I hope and pray that some good will come of all this. But I have to keep it a secret, or rather we do. I thought long and hard about telling you because it means you're involved now. It puts you at risk, but I'm not sure I can cope on my own. I need you.

No one can ever find out, Dotty, you understand? For John's sake, cos Barry would kill him. For the child too. And for Barry – because he would most certainly end up hurting himself, one way or another.

I'm so very sorry.
Your best friend always,
Pearl

Barry dropped the letter on the floor and looked at Dotty. 'Who's John?'

'John John,' said Dotty.

'From the mart?'

'Yes.'

'And he doesn't know?'

'No.'

'And my dad never knew, I mean Barry Senior?'

'No.'

'Nor Uncle Derek or Aunty Ruth or anyone else?'

'No, it's just me now your Ma's passed.'

'And me.' Barry picked the letter up off the floor and held it like it was kryptonite.

'Yes, and you,' said Dotty, tapping her foot on the floor without realising she was doing it.

Barry walked towards the kitchen. Dotty followed at a distance. Barry lit the gas hob and put the letter in the flame. He watched it smoulder down and threw it in the metal sink. He turned on the tap and flushed the ashes away.

'When you die, it'll just be me,' said Barry.

He walked out of the door without saying goodbye, his head in a mighty spin. Pieces of jigsaws that never quite fitted were now slotting into place, things that never made sense were now climbing out of secret closets to justify and explain themselves.

All his life he had felt like a failure for not being a proper chip off the old block. For being weak and unathletic and semi-studious and oversensitive. All those years he'd spent trying to make his dad proud by playing rugby, whilst he lay oblivious in the cold ground. All those cheap hammerings and hidings he'd meekly accepted in thousands of painful scrums and rucks and mauls. Many of them paybacks for his father's misdemeanours on a rugby field across previous generations. All those put-downs and snide comments. All for nothing.

Barry was never going to succeed at rugby because he didn't have it in him. He didn't have the right genes. He'd have been better off standing behind the counter of the mart from morning to night, making polite, pleasant chit-chat with anyone who came in and stocking his shelves with everything under the sun that a man – or woman – with limited means and even more limited ambition, was ever likely to need.

And yet he was now Barry John. He bore the name of one of Wales's all-time rugby greats, arguably the finest number ten his country has ever produced. A Llanelli legend. A British Lions legend. Oh the irony of it all. After a lifetime of taking abuse for carrying the name of an oversized American soul singer.

Ma always was a bit flirty around John John, acting like a silly schoolgirl. All that gushing stick-em-up water pistol rubbish. Barry never thought anything of it. Sure, he realised Ma probably had a soft spot for him, but she was old. And she wasn't Dotty either, she wasn't going to take things any further. It was all harmless fun. A bit of a game to make her feel alive. To make her remember what it was like to be a real woman. Barry didn't realise there was actually history between the pair of them. That he was conceived in a moment of unlikely passion on Ma's bedroom floor – her consumed by a longing to feel wanted, both physically and emotionally, and too much gin and Schweppes. Him overcome by what exactly? Her sweet nature and unusually coy outlook for a thirty-five-year-old housewife? Or was it his desire to throw off the shackles of wearing an apron and serving Polo mints, Golden Wonder crisps, boxes of Fairy Snow and packets of Embassy cigarettes to the wives and widows of gnarled old miners, who looked at him and saw an inferior man to the one they viewed in their own mirrors? A man who didn't know how to wield a pick or an axe. Who didn't do hard manual graft or hard drinking, who stayed clean and safe above ground with his pores free from clogging coal. Someone who had nicer fingernails than most of the wives.

As Barry walked out into the dusky night with nowhere in

particular to go, he thought of Barry Senior and the disappointment he must have been to him as a child. He couldn't remember much about him, but he knew how Uncle Derek sometimes looked at him now. With a puzzled sideways look. Outwardly smiling but inwardly thinking *how the heck can this be our Barry's flesh and blood?*

Now the truth was out.

Well, almost out...

THIRTY-FIVE
FOR THE GOOD TIMES

HE HADN'T SLEPT at all. He hadn't even been to bed. Instead, he paced around the house intensely – as if he was Romeo – searching for a kind of emotional peace that could not be found. This house was now part prison, part safe haven, part war zone, on account of all the renovation work, with bare stone walls poking through, grim floorboards exposed and all comforts and cosmetics packed away in boxes and containers, gathering a layer of dust. The secrets of this house were definitely out. Just waiting to be picked up and picked over. Realities laid bare for all to see.

With everything going on lately, Barry had almost forgotten that he was a millionaire. He'd made plans for the money though. He'd decided relatively quickly in the aftermath of Ma's death what to do with it and how best to invest it. The discovery that he still had a living father gave him palpitations and made him question some of his decisions, but by sunrise he was happy once more with what he planned to do. The wheels were already turning. Things were in motion. Soon, people would see...

Sitting amidst a pile of rubble, drinking blackcurrant squash from the beaker he usually kept his toothbrush in, Barry thought about hiring a load of proper workmen to come in and get the renovations done as quickly as possible. He resisted though, because he'd made Angharad project manager and didn't want to step on her toes. She thought she was doing him a massive favour by recruiting half the village as unpaid labour to save on expenditure. She'd make sure the work was carried out to a high spec and Barry trusted her. Maintaining the trust in their friendship meant more to him than restoring cleanliness and order to his home, though it was a close-run thing.

Uncle Derek came through the open front door and saw Barry sitting amongst the living-room debris.

'All right there, Stig of the Dump?' he said.

'We've got a date for Ma's funeral cos they've had a cancellation. It's next Monday. April 9th at 3pm. Reverend Hill's doing it.'

Derek pulled up a box next to Barry's and they started to thrash out funeral plans together. Ironically, he had brought with him an old Basildon Bond notepad to write things down on and the pad's pages were yellowy blue. Derek had already arranged for Matthews' Funeral Directors to sort out the bearers, four rather than six as Ma wasn't very heavy. And she already had her little plot next to Barry Senior, paid for years ago by her late husband.

'Do you think Ma would want to rest there forever?' said Barry.

'What do you mean?' said Derek, sternly.

'I'm only asking.'

'Well don't.'

Barry chose an old black-and-white photograph of Ma in her mid-twenties for the order of service cover sheet and fetched her favourite blue dress from upstairs, which Derek said he'd drop into the undertakers. She wore it to every important occasion so it seemed fitting that she should wear it to this one. They sorted out cars and seating plans easily enough. Ruth was put on flowers and bouquets and pencilled in to chase up long-lost uncles, nephews, nieces and cousins, seldom seen from year to year except for days such as these.

'Who do you want to read the eulogy?' said Derek.

'What about John John?' replied Barry, instinctively.

'Stop pissing about for once, this is serious.' Derek began doodling on his notepad.

'Dotty then?'

Derek tossed him another scowl. 'Okay, I'll do it.'

They chose Ma's two favourite hymns, 'Make Me a Channel of Your Peace' and 'How Great Thou Art'. And the poem 'Do Not Go Gentle into that Good Night' by Dylan Thomas. Derek put Aunty Ruth down to read it. Barry thought Derek was putting Aunty Ruth's name down for quite a lot of things.

'We gotta get Dean Martin in there somewhere. "Welcome to My World",' said Barry.

Derek scribbled. 'That can be the going-in tune. And "Bread of Heaven" coming out?'

'No, don't want a rugby song.' Barry scratched his brow. 'And it's not called that. It's called "Cwm Rhondda", or "Guide Me O Thou Great Redeemer".'

'Really? Your dad had that one.'

'I know, but Ma wasn't so keen on it. What about "For the Good Times" by Perry Como?'

'Not gonna fight you. How's about a bit of scripture? Shall we leave all that to the Reverend?' said Derek.

Barry shook his head, instructing his uncle to write. 'No, I want Matthew 5. "A burning light is not put under a vessel but on its table so that its rays may be shining on all who are in the house. Let your light be shining before men so that they may see your good works and give glory to your Father in heaven".'

'You never stop surprising me,' said Derek, writing nothing.

'More of that coming,' said Barry.

John John worked six or seven days a week, fifteen or sixteen hours per day, despite being well beyond retirement age. Barry certainly hadn't inherited his work ethic from his biological father.

He had known John John all his life and yet he didn't know him at all. They never chatted or took any personal interest in each other's lives, though on reflection John John would often ask him about Ma and how she was doing. Ma usually preferred to do her shopping in the mart on her own. Now that made sense.

Loitering up and down the aisles like a shifty shoplifter, Barry just wanted to stare at the stranger who gave him much of his DNA. He was looking for clues into his own past and his own future. John John didn't have a hair on his head – and hadn't for as long as Barry could remember. That was a concern. He also walked with a lopsided gait, as if carrying an extra leg everywhere he went. He whistled nonsense made-up tunes. And endlessly sucked on peppermints. He was amiable enough but what had Ma seen in him all those years ago? He had been married to Thelma for over thirty years but was now a widower. He liked cricket apparently. And Ma once mentioned he collected butterflies, whatever that entailed.

Strangest of all was his name. Why did his parents – effectively Barry's grandparents – think it was a good idea to give their only offspring the same Christian name as his surname? Not only did it reveal a shocking lack of imagination, ambition and good judgement but it probably erred on the side of madness. Perhaps they were both psychopaths? Or sociopaths? It would certainly explain where John John's only recognised son, Sidney, who helped out in the shop sometimes, got his weirdness from.

There was a time when Barry would have regarded calling a child John John a criminal offence, on a par with pissing against lamp-posts or speeding in a fifty miles per hour zone. It was certainly worse than stealing chocolate bars or underage drinking. Not quite as bad as burglary but marginally more acceptable than sheep rustling.

Of course, Wales was full of people with double names – Barry knew a Dai Davies, a William Williams, a David Davies and a Pete Peters. Yet somehow, John John seemed worse. And everyone called him John John all the time. Not John. John John.

Romeo reckoned John John was the dullest man he had ever met in his entire life, and that included some proper boring bastards from his years of working at LesCargo, including Meryl Dandy, who said 'another day, another dollar' every time she left work – five days a week, forty-eight weeks a year, for eleven years. Romeo told John John what he thought of him to his face once and reckoned he took it with good grace. Romeo's family – the Davies clan – were close to the John family and related somewhere down the lines. For every birthday and Christmas, from the age of seven to seventeen, John John gave Romeo a Terry's Chocolate Orange. At every family gathering they attended – of which there were plenty – John John also never called him by his correct name, always referring to him as Roman. The only other thing he ever said to him was 'lovely cake', usually with his mouth half full of the stuff.

John John's son, Sidney – scarily, now Barry's biological half-brother – was eccentric, to say the least. He had transitioned from childhood oddity, someone to be humoured and tolerated, to what Sergeant Sargent (who also had the strange double name combo going on) would call downright dangerous. He'd recently got fined £500 in court for gross indecency. Whilst out cycling he stopped on a grassy bank at the side of a busy A-road to drink a bottle of lemonade and pleasure himself. In that order apparently. At least five passing motorists reported him, whilst two senior citizens had minor collisions and another suffered a giddy turn.

Peeping at John John from behind a pyramid of tinned fish on special offer, Barry could not accept that this man was his actual father. This man sticking price labels on bananas – and loving every minute of it – had rolled around with Ma on her bedroom floor in unbridled and unscripted lust and passion over four decades ago, when his limbs were supple and his bones didn't creak. This man who lived by the clock and who used to have bunk-ups with his wife every second Friday from 10pm to 10.25pm precisely. Romeo said he knew this because he'd seen 'conjugals' marked up on the John family calendar in the kitchen above the bread bin. Always the day before the bedding got changed.

Barry approached the counter to buy a packet of ginger nuts. John John saw him coming and straightened out the creases in his white coat. 'So sorry to hear about your loss.'

'Thank you,' said Barry, staring at John John's bald head and noticing a tiny mole.

'When's the funeral?'

'Monday, three o'clock. Will you be there?'

'Most definitely. Me and your mother went back a long way.'

Barry looked for knowing clues in everything John John said. 'She told me.'

ROB HARRIS

'She was a lovely lady, a real Pearl. You know, there was a time when–'

The bell on the shop door chimed as another customer entered and approached the counter. John John would never get to finish his sentence.

'Have the ginger nuts on me,' he said.

Barry smiled. 'Ta very much.'

In that moment Barry knew nothing was going to change. He wasn't going to tell John John he was his son. What could he possibly gain? And what could John John give him apart from the occasional free packet of ginger nuts and the complications of an older half-brother in his fifties, who was sure to end up on the sex offenders register if he wasn't there already?

Ma's secret could go to the grave with her.

'I'm Barry White,' said Barry to John John as he departed his shop.

'Go steady, Barry White,' said John John, adjusting his newly priced-up bananas into bunches, so they could sit on a shelf next to boxes of cherries and overripe plums, reduced to clear and unlikely to see the day out.

THIRTY-SIX
RE-ENTER THE DRAGON

BARRY HAD SHAVED, showered and put on a suit, all before 8am. The day was packed with scheduled meetings; with solicitors and accountants and advisers and friends. By the end of it all he would no longer be rich. Not in cash terms, at least. It would be a massive relief to him to look at his bank account app and see only two or three zeros at the end of totals rather than six. He was not cut out to be wealthy. The money did not make him feel powerful, it paralysed him and left him racked with guilt. Making decisions had become harder, not easier. He felt he didn't deserve this good fortune and that it was wrong for him to have so much money at his disposal when those around him were struggling to pay bills and feed their families. He wasn't at all political, his feelings weren't driven by any ideologies whatsoever, just an inner voice goading him. That squatter in his head again – that rogue angel within, urging him on to self-destruction.

He had protected the secret of his monster-winning Cheltenham bet as if the world would end if the truth ever got out, but lying to himself and everyone around him had made him feel like a fraud. He lived in a permanent state of shock, disbelief and fear. As if he was suffering from some kind of trauma. Had he won the National Lottery, he would have been assigned counsellors and therapists to help him transition to his new instant wealth. Not so with Honest Pete the bookmaker, or former bookmaker, of Pontefract, who probably had even greater need for a therapist of his own these days, considering his journey from the rings of Epsom, Royal Ascot and Cheltenham to the checkout tills of Homebase.

Barry still woke each morning as if nothing in his life had changed, but a few minutes after coming to he would remember his new reality and sink into a trough of despair. Ma's death affected him the same way. Every morning he'd rediscover the fact she had gone forever as if it was the first time – and the grief would slap him in the face anew. Today was the start of his fightback, however. From here on in he would begin to get a grip and regain some control.

In amongst the meetings lined up with various suits, Barry had asked Romeo to pop round at 11am for a 'work review'.

'Morning, boss, need me to drive you somewhere? More horse riding?'

'No, sit down. I've got something important to tell you.'

He told Romeo he would be laying him off because he no longer needed a PA. However, he handed him a set of keys and a box file full of paperwork.

'What's all this?'

'Your new start.'

'What do you mean?'

'You are now a fifty per cent shareholder in your own business.'

Romeo recognised Barry's expression and knew it was safe. 'Doing what?'

'Important work. Making the men of Anghofiedig feel good about themselves.'

'How so?'

'Mostly short back and sides.'

From today, Romeo was the joint owner of Kenneth Wick's barbershop on King Henry Street. Barry had struck a deal that would see Kenneth train Romeo up, with a view to the younger man taking over the day-to-day running of the shop once he was proficient with scissors and a pair of clippers. Kenneth would continue to help out behind the scenes, mainly with administration and advice. His grandson, Olly, had been sent home to Somerset and wouldn't be part of the new venture. He'd already lined himself up a more appropriate and lucrative apprenticeship in a slaughterhouse.

'The men of Anghofiedig deserve this,' said Barry.

'For too long we have put up with mullets and skullets, bowl cuts and rat tails, unblended fades and unbalanced pompadours. Poor Pricer got landed with a mohawk. Mostly we've been given buzz cuts that we have not asked for or deserved, haircuts which have made us feel less like men, highlighting the imperfections in our scalps and making our heads look much smaller than they really are. We have been shorn like scruffy, bedraggled free-roaming Forest of Dean sheep without proper thought, care or attention. As if we are Siberian prisoners.

'But today, through you, we will start to retaliate. We will reclaim our masculinity and pride in our own locks. You will learn how to provide a neat slick-back and drop fade, a temple fade with a side-swept long quiff, or a tapered business cut. You will understand the power of textured stranding and side partings. You will look after our domes and not cut them to ribbons. You will reduce the shine for the follicly challenged and spare them from painful Bobby Charlton comb-overs, God rest his soul. And best of all, you will learn to talk to us like we are the most handsome men in the world, about things that really matter – rugby, music, church, love, food, family and beer.'

'I won't let you down,' said Romeo, responding to the rally call.

Later, Barry met with Reverend Hill in the church.

'Reverend, I'm going to make your day,' said Barry.

'Are you going to start attending organ practice more regularly?' said Reverend Hill, sarcastically.

'Heck no, but I am going to give you one hundred grand.'

At first, Reverend Hill didn't understand what Barry was saying. Then he didn't believe him. Then he fainted. When he came around, thanks to a dose of smelling salts, he thanked Barry, then the Lord. In that order.

'Why are you giving me so much?' said Reverend Hill.

'Because you looked after Ma when she needed someone the most,' said Barry. 'For driving her about. Making time for her. Listening to her. Doing the things I should have done. Being the person I should have been.'

Barry told the reverend he wanted him to use the money to set up a raft of new schemes in – and for – the community, including the food bank he wanted to launch and the Teddy Boys Music Club for the over seventies. He also wanted him to sort out the necessary fixes for the church building. Plus any urgent fixes needed on his own motorbike.

'Where did you get so much cash?' asked Reverend Hill.

Barry crossed his fingers behind his back for one more gigantic lie. He felt especially bad because he was in God's house. 'From Ma.'

'Inheritance money?' said Reverend Hill.

'Exactly.'

Reverend Hill had to sit down. 'I never knew she was so well off.'

'Neither did she.'

'She lived very modestly for someone so wealthy,' said Reverend Hill.

Barry clasped his hands like a good Christian. 'Within her means. As the good Lord instructed.'

Reverend Hill put up two hands to the skies. 'God will reward her for that. He is good. He is faithful.'

'That he is – unlike Ma as it turns out,' said Barry.

'Come again?' said Reverend Hill.

'Oh, umm… ignore me, reverend. It's the grief.'

'Would you like me to pray for you?'

Barry shrugged. 'Okey-dokey.'

'Cup of tea first?' asked Reverend Hill.

Barry gasped. 'Amen to that.'

On and on it went, throughout the day. Many good, and not so good people of Anghofiedig received surprise visits and unexpected anonymous gifts delivered to their doors by vans belonging to Amazon, LesCargo, the Post Office and other assorted distributors.

Dotty got a brand-new collection of fancy dresses. There were some new work tools for Pricer. An all-expenses paid week on a residential anger management therapy course for both McQueen and Psycho Daniels. A prize heifer for Jonah.

John John was surprised to receive a season ticket to watch Glamorgan County Cricket Club, plus a series of extremely rare, framed butterflies – including a black, red and white *Bhutanitis lidderdalii* and a Vietnamese female *Teinopalpus aureus*. He'd never had a birthday card, let alone a present, from his son Sidney in his entire life. Now his wife was no longer around he never really got gifts from anyone. He scratched his head and tried to work out who might have given him such wonderful treats.

Few people even knew about his butterfly collection.

He knew Ma knew.

He would think of her and remember her every time he looked at those beautiful creatures with their wings like kisses.

───────

Most of the village turned out for the reopening of The Dragon under mysterious new owners. What really pulled them in were the posters splashed around the place throughout the day promising a 'free bar for all' at tonight's grand opening.

They packed tightly into the public unmanned bar, waiting restlessly for their unknown host and the promise of free booze on tap to materialise. With nothing much happening, a few started to grow restless, thinking they'd been taken in by a grand hoax. Several were spoiling for a fight. The mood was edgy. Then a suited Barry appeared from a back room to call them all to attention.

'Friends, Romans, countrymen... lend me your ears,' he said.

Barry told them the same lie he had told Reverend Hill earlier in the day. That Ma had left him a small fortune, as opposed to the reality of a trail of debts which he was paying off as he encountered them. He announced that she'd left clear instructions for him to use the money to empower Anghofiedig and reward its loyal servants. With that in mind he had bought the pub – not for himself, but for the community.

He would be recruiting volunteers to help him run it but it would be much more than a pub. There would be Space Invaders machines just like they had in The Buck and a mini library. A big-screen TV would enable the village to come together as one for important national events like royal weddings and funerals, Wales rugby matches and the final of *Strictly Come Dancing*. There would be quiz nights, music nights, theatre nights, and couples nights – all with reasonably priced, top quality menus showcasing local produce and the finest ales. Barry assured a perplexed Uncle Derek that The Dragon was not looking to put the rugby club bar out of business and it would close on Saturdays from 2pm to 7.30pm.

The vision – now 'Ma's vision' – was to develop something more akin to a community centre, offering tea and biscuits, yoga and keep-fit sessions alongside the beer and burgers. Something for everyone. The Dragon would become the go-to place for people to meet and chat and keep warm, and for clubs to hold their weekly gatherings, including the Brownies, the WI and the pigeon fanciers.

'It all sounds very nice but it's going to cost a bloody bomb,' said farmer Dirk Shingles.

'The building is yours, the first year is costed. Then it's up to us,' replied Barry.

'Can the fishing club meet here on Tuesdays?' asked Rex Blunkett.

'Yes,' said Barry.

Amy Sharples stood on a chair, supported by her sister Ena. 'Can I hold my fiftieth birthday party here on July 17th?'

Barry climbed upon a chair too. 'Don't see why not.'

'What about a skittles team?' said Clever Trevor Peacock, earnestly.

Barry was still on the chair. 'Look, none of this is up to me. This place is yours now. We'll get a committee together to run stuff but The Dragon belongs to everyone, so nothing's off the table from here on in.'

'It'll be shut again in six months cos this is all dreamy

Socialist bullshit.' Village curmudgeon Harold J. Jones loved nothing more than a good piss on a good bonfire.

'Not six months, Harold, my little ray of summer sunshine. Everything in the first year is paid for,' said Barry.

'It's up to us to make this work,' bellowed Benny Hawkins, local town crier and part-time Brian Blessed impersonator.

Carrie Taylor thumped her large bosoms. 'Yeah, Ma's giving us a chance.'

'Sounds like we've nothing to lose by giving it a go,' said Lizzie Saunders, half-cut on Pinot Grigio.

'And it won't cost us nowt?' Pricer's mohican appeared to speak for everyone.

'Nope – not for a year. Then we'll review things and see where we are and where we want to go.' Barry toppled off his chair but styled it out nicely with a steady pose.

Rocky Blewitt didn't usually say a lot, preferring to settle disputes with his fists. 'Worth a try, I suppose. I fancy a bit of Space Invaders if nothing else.'

'All those in favour say aye,' said Barry, raising an arm high.

There was a chorus of approval from the floor.

'Right then, who fancies getting behind the bar and serving for the first hour? The drinks are on Ma!'

'Three cheers for Ma,' said Romeo.

'Hip hip hooray, hip hip hooray, hip hip hooray,' roared an entire village.

A village used to being mocked, ridiculed and forced to do without now had something worth shouting about. A bit like Barry himself.

Meanwhile, a handful of miles away over the Forest border at The Buck pub, a troop of travelling French entertainers were hanging around the car park with the star of their show, a performing brown bear called Napoleon, locked in a cage and growing restless in the back of a van.

'Who are you lot?' said the pub landlord.

The troop leader spoke the best English. 'We are the Parisian Prancers. We have been booked to perform here this very night – we've already been paid.'

'Listen, pal, if I were you I'd do one quickly, before people spot you and things turn ugly,' said the landlord, aggressively.

'But we've travelled a long way to get here and we are all hungry, including Napoleon. He dances like a young Anton Du Beke, you know.'

The pub landlord shoved the troop leader in the chest. 'I won't say this again but bugger off pronto, else I'm calling the law on you.'

'I don't understand. We were promised a warm reception.' The troop leader muttered several expletives in French under his breath.

'Oh you'll get that all right if you hang around here much longer,' said the landlord. 'Don't you know where you are?'

And with that he slammed the door hard and bolted it shut from the inside. Napoleon let out an almighty growl. And old Foresters stirred uncomfortably in their terraced homes as the ghosts of bears long gone joined in Napoleon's chorus.

THIRTY-SEVEN
AND SO THE SEASON ENDS...

THINGS WERE CHANGING QUICKLY. Some doors were shutting and others opening. Nothing would be the same as it was.

It was the final rugby game of the season and Anghofiedig were playing Warriors at home with not much at stake.

Barry went down to the ground around 10am to help Uncle Derek mark the pitch.

Derek looked like he had things on his mind and didn't see Barry coming until he tapped him on the shoulder close to the twenty-two metre line.

'Need a hand, Uncle?'

'No it's all right, almost done.' Derek carried on pushing his pitch marker, taking pride in his perfectly parallel white limestone lines.

Barry shoved his hands in his pockets. 'Got a full team?'

'Waiting on a few. Think we'll just about scrape fifteen.'

'In that case I might give it a miss today.'

Derek paused to look at his nephew. 'Understand, son.'

There was a long, uncomfortable silence before Derek finally blurted out what was really on his mind.

'There's something bothering me, Barry. I can't stop thinking about it. But I know Ma didn't leave you all that money.'

Barry stared at Derek's white lines and pulled a face which implied they weren't straight. 'Dunno what you're talking about.'

Derek pulled off his bobble hat and threw it on the pitch marker. 'I'm not bloody stupid. You... buying the pub. And splashing the cash elsewhere. Reverend Hill and Kenny Wick are looking pretty pleased with themselves, aren't they? Your mate Romeo too.'

'News travels fast,' said Barry.

'That's Anghofiedig for you. No secrets.'

Barry didn't like lying, even though it felt like he'd done it all the time lately. He especially disliked lying to people he respected, like Uncle Derek. 'You don't have to worry.'

'Is it legal?' said Derek.

'Yes.'

'And no one will get hurt?'

'No – apart from one unfortunate, actually quite nice bookie.'

'I see.' The penny was starting to drop in Derek's mind. 'That's some monster bet you must have had up. Did you stake the house?'

'No. And I don't gamble no more,' said Barry.

'Glad to hear it.' Derek scooped up his bobble hat and put it back on his head.

Barry adjusted it so it looked better. 'I never thought I would ever win.'

'Nor did I.'

Barry took over on the pitch marker and started walking. 'I haven't forgotten you and Aunty Ruth. I haven't forgotten everything you've done for me.'

'It's nothing,' said Derek, walking alongside his nephew.

'It's not nothing.'

'You're family.'

'I'm a White,' said Barry, proudly.

Derek cackled, a dirty laugh. 'Yes, you bloody well are.'

Barry told his uncle that there was a special thank-you present on the way to him. A brand-new Land Rover Defender would arrive at their door on Wednesday.

'You're going to be skint again pretty soon at this rate,' said Derek, holding back a tear or two.

'That's the idea.'

Walking away, Barry stopped, turned around and looked back at his uncle and saw him for who he really was and who he had always been. Someone solid, whose bark was a lot worse than his bite. A big softie, who vented his rage at the world on a rugby field for all those years just so he could cope with the rest of life and everything it threw at him. He was an old man now. Not much rage left within.

'Good luck today,' shouted Barry.

'Thanks,' said Derek.

'Is James playing?' said Barry.

Derek nodded.

'You'll be fine then. And don't think I've retired either because I haven't. I'll be back for pre-season training in August. I want one good season, in the centre though, not the front row. I reckon my best year is just around the corner.'

'See you Monday. We'll give Ma a proper send-off, eh?' said Derek.

'Yes we will,' said Barry.

When he got home Barry found Angharad hard at work in his lounge. She was ferociously scraping wallpaper off the wall with a rare venom.

'Glad I'm not him,' said Barry.

'Who?' said Angharad.

'Whoever it is your stabbing with that knife.'

'It's Greg. He's back from Barry's Island.'

'I see.'

Angharad sat herself down on a box and sipped from a bottle of water. 'She's left him. His floozy. He's potless and has got nowhere to live. He says he wants me back, which means he wants me to take him back. He says he's sorry and he knows he was an idiot. Says he loves me and it won't happen again.'

'You believe him?'

'Course not.'

'What yer gonna do?'

'Don't know. I don't really want him back. I don't want to live like this anymore, but I don't want to be the one who presses delete on our shared history either.' Angharad tossed her empty water bottle into a plastic bin.

'Long shots come in occasionally,' said Barry.

'He won't change,' answered Angharad.

Barry said nothing.

Angharad returned to her wall and started scraping hard at the paper, which wouldn't budge. 'I won't trust him again.'

'I don't want to see you get hurt,' said Barry.

Angharad kissed Barry on the cheek. 'Thank you. You've done so much for me.'

Barry blushed. 'It's nothing.'

'It's not nothing. It was never nothing,' said Angharad.

A&E was packed with life's unfortunates but Barry spotted a familiar face waiting patiently amongst them.

'All right, Pricer. Bollock not infected again?' he said.

'Bollocks are fine and dandy. Piles are like a bunch of cherry tomatoes.'

Barry spied Diana in the distance, trying to calm down a woman in her late twenties who had her arm around a small child of about five. He wore a metal baking tray around his neck. Diana whipped off the tray like she was performing a magic trick and sauntered over to speak to Barry with the tray still in her hand. 'Nice surprise seeing you, hope it's personal, not professional. Everything okay?'

'Yes, though there's something important I need to talk to you about,' said Barry.

'Sounds ominous. Shall we sit?'

Barry told Diana that he'd never met anyone quite like her before. That in a short space of time she'd become the most important woman in his life. He asked her if she would accompany him to the funeral on Monday – travel to the church with him in the family car, be at his side through the service, hold his hand, listen to his outpourings. She said she would. That she had wanted to do all those things but was too scared to offer in case he said no.

'Afterwards will you come away with me?' said Barry.

'Where to?'

'Rwanda for two weeks. Then a tour of Europe. See where we end up.'

Diana squirmed on the spot. 'Oh, love, I can't.'

Barry tried to reassure her. 'I've squared it with your bosses – six weeks' unpaid leave. You won't need any money. I've got enough for both of us.'

'But there's Eddie,' said Diana.

Barry smiled. 'I know. Bring him.'

'What about school?'

'Life's too short. The trip will be educational. You need to make memories with him now, while you still can.'

Diana paused in thought, weighing up pros and cons, pursing her bottom lip as she did so. Behind her, she could see her friend Sarah urging her to say yes.

'Okay, let's do it,' she squealed, squeezing Barry tightly, like an excited schoolgirl.

'We fly early hours on Tuesday,' said Barry.

Sarah was now clapping. Diana had never looked so happy. 'Why Rwanda?' she asked.

'A good friend of mine lives there,' said Barry.

'Who's that?'

'His name's Chico. He's the coolest guy you'll ever meet. In fact, I should probably be worried that you'll fall in love with him instead of me. He's quite hairy but he's got these beautiful eyes and a rare sense of power about him. He's got a brilliant sense of humour too. You'll love him. I just know you will.'

THE END

ABOUT THE AUTHOR

Rob Harris grew up in the Forest of Dean but now lives in Oxfordshire with his wife and daughter.

For more than 15 years he worked as a regional newspaper journalist, sports editor and editor.

The Absurd Life of Barry White is Rob's first novel, but he is also the author of a memoir about the rare highs and frequent lows of being a committed but frustrated village cricketer, called 'Won't You Dance for Virat Kohli?' (published 2021).

For more about the author go to www.robharrisauthor.com

A NOTE FROM THE PUBLISHER

Thank you for reading this book. If you enjoyed it please do consider leaving a review on Amazon to help others find it too.

We hate typos. All of our books have been rigorously edited and proofread, but sometimes mistakes do slip through. If you have spotted a typo, please do let us know and we can get it amended within hours.

info@bloodhoundbooks.com

Printed in Great Britain
by Amazon